For the gardener

.

Note for Librarians: A cataloguing record for this book is available from Library and Archives Canada at www.collectionscanada.ca/amicus/index-e.html
ISBN 1-4120-9284-1

Printed in Victoria, BC, Canada. Printed on paper with minimum 30% recycled fibre. Trafford's print shop runs on "green energy" from solar, wind and other environmentally-friendly power sources.

Offices in Canada, USA, Ireland and UK

Book sales for North America and international:
Trafford Publishing, 6E–2333 Government St.,
Victoria, BC V8T 4P4 CANADA
phone 250 383 6864 (toll-free 1 888 232 4444)
fax 250 383 6804; email to orders@trafford.com
Book sales in Europe:
Trafford Publishing (UK) Limited, 9 Park End Street, 2nd Floor
Oxford, UK OX1 1HH UNITED KINGDOM
phone 44 (0)1865 722 113 (local rate 0845 230 9601)
facsimile 44 (0)1865 722 868; info.uk@trafford.com
Order online at:
trafford.com/06-1038

10 9 8 7 6 5 4 3 2

Cover design by Castledine & Castledine

Acknowledgements

My thanks go to Dr. Rosemary van den Berg (Murri Murri) for her initial review and encouragement; Robyn Mathison for copy editing and her support; Janice Bird for the final editing; and Steve Castledine for the cover design.

Graham McDonald was born in 1948 in a coastal suburb of Perth, Western Australia. Much travelled and with many varying occupations behind him, *Footprints In The Wind* is the product of his time spent prospecting the West Australian goldfields. He now lives with his wife, Coral in the small town of Denmark on the south coast of his home state.

Footprints
in the Wind

A NOVEL BY
G.A. McDonald

TRAFFORD
PUBLISHING

One

Charlie leaned forward in his seat, stared towards the east for a moment then slowly leaned back again. He had been listening to the vehicle's approach for the last couple of minutes and, though not surprised to see the familiar red Land Rover utility that finally emerged from the grey-green horizon, he was curious about its speed.

"Johnno must be thirsty," he said, his words drifting through the late afternoon like the languid, faraway call of a crow.

Roused out of a half-dozing state, his mate Reg lifted a battered old hat above his eyes and watched as the former fire-brigade ute came rattling in from the flat landscape, bucked wildly over the railway line then sped up an avenue of red-brick ruins. It finally skidded to a halt in front of the hotel, engulfing the veranda in a cloud of dust.

Charlie coughed in a weak, theatrical way. "An' I just vacuumed, too," he drawled.

Reg gave a brief snort then pulled his hat back down over his eyes.

A man in his early forties climbed out of the vehicle and rushed up the three steps and across the wooden floor of the veranda, striding past the two figures as if they weren't there.

"Come ta put out the fire, eh Johnno?" Charlie sang out, waving his hand slowly across his face as he squinted through the dust.

Kevin Johnson didn't reply. He wasn't talkative at the best of times and now he looked thoroughly distracted, strangely wild-eyed. In his left hand he was carrying a small cloth bag held in a guarded way against his side.

Charlie's attention quickly shifted to the bag and the way it hung heavily in the man's hand. He nudged his mate and Reg's hat lifted again, his head turning slowly in the direction that Charlie's jabbing finger was pointing. Then, with reflexes belying their age, the two men jumped to their feet and turned to stare through the open window of the front bar.

Jim Donnelly, the hotel owner, looked up from his newspaper as his third customer for the day strode into the room.

"G'day Johnno... time fer a break?"

Johnno halted at the sound of the voice. His body began to rock in a strange, nervous manner as he stood two paces from the bar, eyes staring wildly at the floor. Suddenly he yelled out, "Carton o' cans!"

Jim glanced at the two men staring through the window, their eyebrows raised in puzzlement. He raised his own and shrugged his shoulders before tentatively asking the question they all wanted answered.

"What's in the bag, mate?" he enquired in a feigned casual way, as he turned to take the beer out of the fridge behind.

There was no reply to his question, but what confronted him when he turned around instantly set him back on his heels. He dropped the carton on the bar then drew back. "*Jesus*, Johnno!" he cried out, both hands raised in defence.

Johnno was breasting the bar now, his mad, reddened eyes staring straight at the barman, one hand hiding the bag behind him, the other raised and fisted as if about to deliver a roundhouse right. Suddenly he let out an eerie, anguished kind of cry then grabbed the carton from the bar and began to storm out.

About to see a large part of the day's takings disappear through the door, Jim put his shock on hold and shouted out to his departing customer. "'Ang on! 'Aven't ya forgotten somethin'?"

Johnno stopped in his tracks, turned around and fixed Jim with a look of deep concentration, as though confused about where he was.

His gaze shifted to the barman's open palm and the request for payment seemed to momentarily snap him out of his manic state. He placed the carton under one arm and put the bag on top of it before reaching for his wallet, but as he did so the carton tilted and the bag slid off. A heavy thump came as it hit the floor and several objects tumbled out of it.

The onlookers stared with astonishment at what lay on the floor. Next to a few smooth, dull, flat nuggets was a piece of gold nearly as big as a man's fist, a sharp-edged, bright and jagged specimen that had obviously been hacked out of something much bigger.

Johnno's mania returned with a rush. He leant down, grabbed the gold and stuffed it frantically back in the bag. Hands shaking and eyes flashing with panic he ripped some banknotes from his wallet, hurled them towards the bar then wheeled around and rushed out of the room, almost knocking down the men on the veranda as he hurried to his vehicle. He started the ute with a roar and reversed on spinning wheels before speeding off in a cloud of dust, heading west towards the highway.

Jim had quickly followed Johnno out of the bar and now stood with the two men on the veranda, staring gob-smacked at the vehicle rumbling towards the horizon.

Several seconds of stunned silence passed before Charlie spoke.

"Told ya 'e was thirsty."

The comment brought only a fleeting sniff of amusement from the others and soon after the Land Rover disappeared over a small hill the puzzled trio ambled inside to the bar.

"Medicine anyone?" Jim asked, as he picked up the banknotes from the floor then walked to the other side of the bar and drew three beers. "These are on Johnno... it looks like 'e can afford it now," he muttered, as he placed some of the money in the register and the rest in his pocket.

But the prescription didn't go down well at all, and for a few minutes the drinkers remained suspended in their stunned state, sipping their beer without tasting it, each locked in their thoughts, before Charlie finally gave voice to his.

"Aaar, Jeeesus… mate! 'Ow c'n we go out ta the patch this arvo and sweat our guts out fer a measly few grams after seein' *that*! Makes a man wanna spew!"

Reg sat in mute agreement, but he was thinking about something else too, wondering why an experienced prospector would bring the gold into the pub and take the risk of others seeing it; wondering what that look in the eyes of the usually quiet and controlled man was all about.

Jim broke into Reg's thoughts as if reading them.

"D'ya see 'is eyes? Looked as though 'e was crook or somethin'!"

"Yeah… it's called gold sickness, mate, and pretty soon now they're gunna find a large lump in 'is bank account." Charlie chimed in.

The comment brought a brief, thin smile to Reg's face before he quietly said, "It was fear. Somethin' out there frightened 'im."

"Aaar… don't go startin' with all that spirit-in-the-land shit!" Charlie cried. "There's nuthin' out there t'frighten ya… unless the rabbits 'ave grown fangs and the roos are carry'n' shotguns now. More 'n likely 'e's frightened o' droppin' some o' that gold on 'is foot… the bastard!"

Reg's face straightened. There was a time when he would have smiled at such a comment, maybe even extended it into a joke, but this one had been delivered with a sharp edge and he just swirled the last of the beer in his glass before swallowing it, placing the empty container down in a way that sent an unspoken message to his mate.

Jim broke the uncomfortable silence. "Smiler wasn't 'is usual self either. Didn't even come in for 'is drink."

Smiler was a six-year-old Blue Heeler-Labrador cross, considered by all the locals to be half crazy. He had the knowing, responsive eyes of the cattle dog and a distinctive kick up at the corners of his mouth that made him look as though he was constantly amused by a private joke. A garrulous hound, he was always barking, growling and whining his opinions to people, although they were regularly ignored, dismissed or laughed at, bringing a certain frustrated edge to his voice. He was also very fond of a drop. Whenever they called into the pub he hardly waited for the Rover to stop before racing inside and jumping up onto his stool at the end of the room. There he would sit whimpering until his bowl and a can of beer was produced, the pouring of the foaming liquid greeted with an ear-piercing bark, followed by the sound of a furious lapping tongue, a burp or two then a slow measured walk out to the veranda to sleep it off. And one can was all that he was allowed now, having disgraced himself the only time he had been given two and like the classic two-pot screamer had barked and howled all night long until he was finally kicked out for biting another patron.

"Yeah, yer right... 'e was a bit quiet wasn't 'e?" Charlie responded half-heartedly, glancing towards his mate as he spoke.

It was just another question to add to the mystery and it brought a further pondering silence, before Reg eventually got up and walked outside to the veranda. He sat down on the bench and gazed for a while at the gravel road that ran towards the setting sun. No matter what Charlie said, he had seen more than gold sickness in the eyes of the man who had just sped away. He had spent enough time in the desert to understand how it could affect the isolated mind. He had experiences out there he couldn't explain; he had felt things, heard things. Recently he was woken in the night by what he thought was the faint sound of clapsticks and a woman's voice singing in the nasal monotone of the Aborigine. Both had quickly faded into the sound of the wind whispering and sighing through the leaves of the mulga and desert oaks, but the fleeting experience continued to nag.

Like a shadow of Reg's thoughts, a warm gust of wind suddenly blew up the hill and along the veranda, swirling around him briefly before the dust of its progress whisked out along the road, as if following the path of the red Land Rover. For a moment he pondered the strange sensation that had come with the breeze, before a voice interrupted his thoughts.

"The ol' witchdoctor's kicked in a bit early tonight," Charlie observed. His nickname for the east wind was an apt one. Usually it arrived later in the night, giving only belated relief from the heat of the day before chilling them to the bone in the early morning. He sat down next to Reg and held out a glass of beer.

"Yeah," Reg replied, nodding slowly as he took the beer, still distracted by what he had just experienced.

"Beer up," Charlie toasted.

"Beer down," Reg replied.

They both took a long draught and, after a moment's contemplation, Charlie said, "Ya know what that lump o' gold reminded me of?"

Reg responded with another slow nod. He had been in the same gang as Charlie one day twenty years ago when, as they were jackhammering the rock face of a mine in Kalgoorlie, the rock fell away to expose a seam of gold three centimetres thick and about a metre long. They had all been shocked by the slash of bright colour, a glorious sight to those who rarely saw any free gold down in the mines, just the occasional faint trace in the ore that they dug out for ten backbreaking hours a day. They wouldn't see it for long, however. Soon after, their supervisor hacked into the seam with a geologist's pick, gouging out a sample for the mine bosses and then heavy steel plates were fixed across it and a guard placed there around the clock. This 'jewel shop' was then only visited by the chosen few, when they would withdraw part of the rich concentrate and add it to low grade ore, gilding the overall grades for shareholder and stock market reports. The supervisor, however, had allowed the men who had exposed it to hold that heavy, twisted and sharp-edged piece of gold in their hands for a few seconds, and it had been just long enough to give Reg and Charlie the first dose of an incurable disease.

"The bastard's found a reef," Charlie needlessly concluded.

Reg nodded again. For now, nothing more needed to be said about Johnno's gold. He appeared to have found his fortune somewhere out in the desert wilderness that he roamed in search of the heavy metal, while all they had was a dryblower waiting for dirt to be shovelled onto it. Nothing needed to be said about that prospect, either. Instead of doing their usual dusk shift on the end of a shovel, the two men remained on the veranda of the Grand Hotel silently watching the sun going down on what was left of the old gold-mining town of Jimblebar.

As the tumbledown remains gradually melted into the darkness a much stronger gust of wind rattled a piece of corrugated iron on the veranda roof, snapping the two men out of their reflection. A light went on in the front bar and Jim called out.

"It's nearly seven o'clock. Are you old buggers gunna eat 'ere or not?"

"Yeah, steak sandwich, mate… an' not from that roo I saw bein' bled out the back yesterday," Charlie replied.

"Don't worry, I wouldn' waste that on you. I'm savin' that for the terrorists."

Jim's words were delivered jokingly, but he wasn't kidding. The pub owner had to take every advantage to keep his business running. He always kept the hotel freezer well stocked with the main ingredient for the 'beef' stews, pies and sandwiches he served up as specials to the tourists. The cost to him was as low as a few accurate bullets and the first stage of meal preparation was to ensure his customers had enough to drink before eating. But his special kind of beef would be in the freezer for a while yet. It was still high summer and the metal-detecting fossickers from the city who provided a major part of his living wouldn't be venturing out to Jimblebar until the autumn. The heat and the pub's location made sure of that, set as it was almost on the edge of the Great Victoria Desert, a hundred and fifty kilometres from the Kalgoorlie-Leonora main road and a good four-hour drive from either of those centres.

The corrugated iron rattled once more before the wind suddenly stopped, the strangeness of its unusually early arrival matched by the abruptness of its departure.

Charlie stood up, took both glasses and went inside to the bar. He leaned over and filled them from the beer tap then put two strokes in a little notebook resting on the counter.

"Two more on the tab," he yelled out to Jim in the kitchen. "An' 'urry up with that food, will ya, its gettin' close to me bedtime."

Ten minutes later Jim leaned through the open window and passed the two men their steak sandwiches. "Eat 'em quick before they 'op away," he said, before chuckling his way back to the kitchen.

Charlie lifted the toasted bread and checked the colour of the grilled meat, confirming it wasn't a tourist special before biting into it. Not that he was bothered about eating kangaroo, it was a regular part of his and Reg's diet, but he wasn't about to pay for anything he could pot from the door of their hut.

The two men ate quickly, yelled out some friendly abuse about the quality of the meal and then did what the cook told them to do, climbed into their old Holden ute and 'pissed off' back to their camp ten kilometres away. They arrived there twenty minutes later, where they each had their rationed half-bucket wash standing in a basin by the fire and then the regulation cup of tea, before retiring to their summer residence located under the narrow veranda of their hut.

As usual, Charlie fell asleep almost as his back hit the bunk, having a last quick moan about Johnno's gold before his ritual snoring began. But Reg would remain awake for a while. He had been quieter than usual since leaving the pub; thinking not of gold but of what he had experienced on the veranda, where for one fleeting moment it felt as if the wind had embraced him. It had brought a faint but familiar voice whispering through his mind and, as he lay staring up at the stars and beyond, it spoke to him once more, a young boy calling an old man back to the search again.

*

Born in 1918, Reg Arnold knew little of his beginnings. All that he had been told as a boy was that he was the proverbial abandoned baby left as a newborn on the steps of Kalgoorlie hospital, his natural parents unknown. It was a vague explanation that he struggled to accept, but what he did know was that one of his birth parents was Aboriginal, a fact consistently and colourfully pointed out to him as he grew up on the tough streets of Kalgoorlie; streets that would quickly toughen him, too. Raised well enough by the white and childless Jack and Madge Arnold, but with total exclusion of his Aboriginality, he soon learned to deal with the confusion of being treated as a sun-tanned white boy at home and something else outside by using his fists. He also developed a sly sense of humour that made light of his in-between status whilst effectively mocking those who mocked him, and the man who became his lifelong friend was one who felt the deft touch of both survival skills at a very young age.

Like many of the white children in Kalgoorlie at that time, Charlie Anderson had been fed on a steady diet of yarns about Aboriginal savagery spun by people who could still recall some of the spearing incidents of the gold-rush days. The knowledge that his grandfather had been one of the victims added a razor-sharp edge to the young boy's conditioned disdain of Aborigines and it would eventually find a target in Reg. For the better part of a year after first meeting at school, the two six-year-olds virtually scrapped on sight, until Charlie's bull-headed nature finally capitulated to Reg's innate calmness and sense of humour, and the knuckles that won every fight Charlie started.

An unlikely friendship was born and Reg gained wider respect as he and his reputation for being tough but fair-minded grew. As a teenager he developed into a fine all-round sportsman and an exceptional Aussie Rules footballer, his regular top performances furthering his acceptance by white society and guaranteeing him a job down the mines. In his early twenties he was drafted into the Second World War, starting as an army private and ending his service as a sergeant after two years in the Middle East and one on the New Guinea front. A year after the war ended he married the white and pretty Gloria, a girl from Melbourne who had stopped over in Kalgoorlie for a day and ended up staying for the rest of her life. Reg's honorary status in the town overrode most of the difficulties that such a union would usually face in mid-twentieth century Australia and, with two daughters, they lived contentedly in the community. For most of his life, Reg remained comfortable with his identity. He had accepted reality early, travelling a path he knew he had to take if he wanted a life, but as he approached his sixtieth year it was his wife's death that eventually put the hounds of the blood back onto the trail.

When Gloria finally succumbed after a year of suffering from ovarian cancer, Reg was left exhausted and alone. His two daughters had stayed with him in shifts as Gloria's illness moved into its terminal stage, but after she died they went back to their lives in Perth and he felt nothing was holding him to Kalgoorlie. Weary of everything, he quit his job at the mine, sold his house, packed his ute with prospecting gear and went bush. Although he found little gold of the physical kind his months of solitude eventually eased the pain of losing the woman with whom he had happily spent over half of his life. But it also had an unsettling effect. A part of him felt at home out in the wilderness, but as he emerged from his grief he also began to feel the desire to be back amongst people. So he compromised, settling in at his bush camp near Jimblebar, close enough to hear the call of the desert and just near enough to civilisation to enjoy some of its pleasures without its stress. He had been there now for nearly nine years, finding some contentment in the free and independent lifestyle, but the searching of the spirit continued and of late it had begun to create a conflict of another kind.

Charlie had joined Reg about seven years earlier. He left the mines a year after Reg when he broke his back in a rock fall. The injury laid him up in hospital for several months and then nearly a year at home, his long period of rehabilitation eventually taking its toll on a marriage that had begun to sour years before. When he was literally on his feet again, his wife left and the chronic dull ache of their dying relationship was replaced with the one in his permanently straight back, where a steel plate locked his middle vertebras to enable him to walk. He was grateful, however, to be alive and still moving around, but after nearly eighteen months of recovery he had grown very weary of his unemployed and unemployable state. When Reg invited him to go out prospecting, he instantly accepted. Gradually the occasional weekend trips turned into one-week trips then one month and longer, until he finally decided to join his mate permanently.

Fortunate to be there at the beginning of the metal-detecting gold rush of the late 'seventies and early 'eighties, the two men initially found enough gold to provide a good living. As with any gold rush, however, the number of prospectors quickly grew into a flood and the number of nuggets recovered slowed to a trickle. When the decent pieces became harder to find, Reg and Charlie had a customised dryblower built onto the back of a large trailer and moved it around the old alluvial patches, re-treating the heaps of dirt dug out nearly a hundred years before. The work was dirty and hard, with less reward than detecting. The gold price had dropped three hundred dollars an ounce over the six years since its peak of 1980, when the oil shortage fear inspired by the Iranian hostage crisis pushed it to eight hundred US. Yet they found enough to pay for their food, fuel and booze, allowing them to save most of their pensions, and for a long time the two men had been content with that, but recently a subtle shift had come into the relationship. Their lack of a greater financial success was beginning to bother the more ambitious Charlie and so, too, was something else.

There was an unspoken rule in camp, instinct born of friendship telling them when it was time to give each other breathing space. Either Charlie would head off to Perth or Esperance to visit his son and daughter, or Reg would pack up his ute and take off into the desert for a week or more. But it was his mate's increasing need to seek the solitude of the wilderness that had started to irritate Charlie. He had once asked Reg why he went out there, but the only explanation he got was 'Dunno, can't really explain it. It's somethin' in the land. Its spirit, if ya like. It seems ta have a voice, an' I jes' 'afta go and listen to it sometimes.' Charlie didn't understand or like the answer. He figured gold was the only thing worth finding in the land and he had grown resentful of the voice that called his mate away from helping him dig it out. He was always happy to see Reg upon his return, but lately he had begun to feel as if some sort of clock were ticking down on their friendship.

*

Reg lay awake until the first whisper of the east wind began to sigh through the camp, listening to its song for a while until, just as earlier on the veranda of the pub, a rougher voice interrupted his reflection.

Charlie's night chorus had shifted into full roar and Reg reached down for his 'snorin' stick', a two-metre piece of mulga he kept by his bed for occasions such as this. He raised it into prodding mode, but then a sly smile formed on his face and he lowered it to the ground again. Recalling his mate's outburst in the pub he began to moan spookily in tune with the wind. "Chaaarlieee... Chaaaarlieeee," he sang out, and then stopped abruptly when the snoring ceased.

A shifting sound came from Charlie's bed and an uncertain voice drifted out of the night. "Reg?"

Reg remained silent, his smile widening into a grin, his body beginning to tremble with mirth as he heard the restless movement in the other bed and then saw his mate lean up on an elbow and look around. But he kept control, and when the snoring began to idle again a couple of minutes later he moaned softly once more, but in a reflective way this time, the smile gone from his face.

"There's nuthin' out there ta frighten yaaaaaa."

Two

The next morning, lethargy clung to Reg and Charlie like the bush flies to their backs. The insects reflected the general mood, only occasionally lifting off to buzz briefly around before heading back to their hosts. One of them missed its landing strip and crashed into the cup of tea Charlie was drinking. He scooped it out on a finger and casually flicked it away.

"We workin' this mornin'?" he enquired disinterestedly.

"Gettin' a bit late for it," Reg replied, even though the sun had not yet risen.

With those words consensus had been reached. Instead of going out to re-treat an old alluvial patch about five kilometres away, they would remain where they spent most of their time in the summer, lazing the hottest hours away in the relatively cool shade under the veranda of what they called their mansion in the bush. It was a kind of log cabin built out of railway sleepers, perched on a hill with a view that stretched nearly all the way to the edge of the Great Victoria Desert. Although the pub was always an option on a lazy summer's day, this was where they most preferred to be.

The partners' mansion was built in a single day three years before, when their former home of a canvas lean-to strapped to a couple of trees could no longer offer their aging bodies enough protection against the harsh elements. They had gathered the building materials from old spur lines and the long-abandoned mine sites in the district, finding the construction crew in similar locations, their pasts abandoned too.

That gathering of refugees from society included characters like 'Birdman', an ex-British merchant seaman and bachelor in his sixties, who always had sick or injured birds convalescing around his small mine and was constantly shadowed by a foul-mouthed pink and grey galah called Bosun; and 'Claude Contradiction', a fifty-two-year-old failed farmer with a broken marriage, who had shrunk his existence down to living in a two-man tent fixed to the roof rack of the Landcruiser. Like Reg and Charlie, he too dragged a trailer dryblower around the district, but his main occupation was disagreeing on virtually everything with anybody he came across. He had a shadow too, a Fox Terrier called Rabbit, who spent most of his time chasing his namesakes but hardly ever barked, prompting Charlie to observe that it was probably because the dog was afraid of being contradicted. Then there was 'Professor', an ex-banker and widower in his seventies who spent more time reading the books he kept in a metal locker in his hut than detecting the gold he only found in dribs and drabs around the district. Like the others he spent a lot of time at the pub, where he loved baiting Claude and was the only one who could play the decrepit piano that stood in one corner of the front bar next to the long-handled shovel marked 'snakes'.

The final member of the crew was 'Klaus the Kraut', a thirty-nine-year-old former East German border guard who had simply dropped his rifle one day and walked to the west. He had been drawn to the goldfield six years before, during the peak of the 1980 metal-detecting boom, and had made a big living detecting for a couple of years but, like the others, he'd had to adapt to leaner times. Now he spent his days digging out a small and barely profitable alluvial mine, but constantly raved about the freedom he had found, although something from his past continued to haunt him. Most of his nights at the pub ended with him singing slow, sombre Germanic ballads, before collapsing in a blubbering heap, babbling to anyone within earshot about the virtues of a female called Anna. It was suspected that in his desperation to escape his former country, Klaus had left his woman behind, but not even the ever-inquisitive Professor pressed the likeable German on the obviously painful subject.

When their hut was completed, Charlie nailed a plank of wood above the entrance with the words 'Pentous Sweet' scrawled across it. Then he placed an old goat's skull above that. But no penthouse could be complete without a proper toilet, so they erected a fully functional long-drop over a mineshaft about thirty metres away from the hut, using lengths of drilling pipe to straddle the top of the shaft and crisscrossing that with whatever floorboard material they could find, tying it all together with rusty fence wire. In the middle of this they placed an old studded ore bucket rusted through at the bottom, and on top of that they placed a genuine toilet seat. For privacy they used more drilling pipe to form the frame for a tepee-like structure and covered it with the canvas from their old lean-to. They weren't sure how deep the shaft of their toilet went, but the springy, creaking base that moved disconcertingly under the user made a visit to the loo a whole new experience in uncertainty. Sitting there listening to the rocks and soil crumbling from the edges and rattling into the darkness below, the occupant could never be sure that he too wasn't destined for the long drop, and wondered what would be worse: the broken bones, or being covered in what waited at the bottom. In consideration of either prospect, Charlie had named their toilet 'the Laxative', guaranteed to 'scare the shit out of ya'.

Charlie was walking back from one of those laxative experiences, still moping over Johnno's gold, when he suddenly halted and cocked an ear. After a few seconds he continued on down the hill, then stopped to wash his hands in a basin that sat on top of a large quartz boulder. After wiping them dry he listened intently again.

Reg was sitting on a chair having a shave in the shade of a large desert willow that grew next to the hut. Without raising his head he casually stated, "Someone's comin'."

"Mmmm," Charlie concurred, now clearly picking up the sound of the vehicle making its way along the track that led to their camp. He walked back up to the top of the hill and looked to the west. There was one point about half a kilometre from the camp where the dull green foliage of the stunted mulgas broke open into a clearing and he waited for the approaching vehicle to enter this spot. When he saw it was Jim's he began to walk back towards the hut, puzzled. It was rare that the bachelor hotel owner ventured out their way, simply because he had no one to mind the pub until the tourist season – when he hired temporary help, and then he was usually too busy to make social calls.

"It's Jim… wonder what 'e wants?"

"Maybe our bar tab's gettin' a bit serious," Reg said, bringing a snort of a chuckle from his mate.

About two minutes later Jim's Ford utility pulled up in front of the hut and he climbed out.

"Jimbo!" Charlie called out. "It's a bit early, mate, but I'll 'ave a middy, thanks."

"Ya might need one after ya 'ear what I've got to say," Jim replied, serious-faced as he slumped down in an old kitchen chair.

"What's up?" Reg asked.

"Johnno's dead!"

The two men flinched and stared at Jim in disbelief.

"Gary rang me early this mornin', to ask me if Johnno'd been drinkin' at the pub yesterday. Apparently 'e's gone and run the Land Rover into Frog Rock. Elliot came across him last night."

"Bloody 'ell!" Reg finally exclaimed.

"Jesus!" Charlie responded. A short silence followed before he added, "Christ… 'e must 'ave bin aimin' at it! That rock is the only bloody object fer miles on that stretch!"

Frog Rock was located in a hollow, much like a dried-up water hole, about twenty-metres off the road in a five-kilometre section of plains country that ran unbroken for a kilometre either side of the roadway. Several years earlier, hearing a story that the Wongai believed it was a bullfrog stranded there from the Dreamtime, a couple of drunken mineworkers had painted it green, adding some yellow eyes and a red tongue, turning it into a comical landmark, for some.

"Did Gary mention anythin' 'bout the gold?" Charlie quickly enquired.

"No, and I didn't ask. But I wanted to, especially considerin' it was the Bush Pig who came across Johnno."

Bill Elliot, the man of whom Jim so sourly spoke, was the owner of the Full Stop Roadhouse, situated halfway between Menzies and Leonora. He had earned his nickname because of the career he had made out of putting people offside with the miserly and dishonest way he ran his business and his life. Twice married, twice divorced, he was devoid of all social etiquette; a friendless soul: even his three children eventually grew to hate his mean-spirited nature. He had come from Perth a couple of years before and made no secret of the fact that he was in the goldfields for the short term, to make a big buck quickly and then get out of what he considered the arse-end of the earth. He was achieving that goal simply by cheating people, mostly the Wongai, who came in to his roadhouse to buy car parts and fuel, and from whom he preferred to take gold nuggets as payment, the value of which was often up to four times the cost of the purchase. The tourists were soft targets too, one-offs whom he figured he would never see again, and his policy of savage overcharging guaranteed that he never would. But the locals didn't take long to recognise the man's porcine qualities and treated him with the contempt he inspired. None would work for him, leaving Elliot with only drifters and backpackers as employees, of whom few remained very long. And rather than give him any business, anyone in the vicinity would drive the extra fifty kilometres to Leonora or Menzies whenever they needed anything from a service station. But they would always greet him as they went past, two fingers raised in salutation.

But abuse was like fuel to Bill Elliot, a man who enjoyed the stress he could cause and returned contempt with interest. It was that characteristic which had brought a smile to his face when, returning from a business trip to Kalgoorlie, he saw Johnno's Land Rover wrapped around Frog Rock.

*

Elliot's eyes settled on the wreck like a vulture's, dollar signs ringing up at the prospect of what he could salvage. But when he parked his car and shone a torch towards the crumpled vehicle he saw the form slumped over the steering wheel and cursed his luck. Then a tiny spark of decency glimmered. He got out of his vehicle and headed towards the Rover, but after reaching it and shining the torch in the cab he could see that there was no need for any assistance. He studied the macabre sight of the dead man for a few moments, wondering what could have brought the look of horror to his smashed face: his wild, staring eyes seemed to convey something more than the shock of a car crash.

A glutinous gob of blood slid from the steering wheel and Elliot's torch beam followed it down to a puddle on the floor. He shivered a little at the gory sight and was about to turn and go when, amidst the jumble of beer cans on the floor, the torchlight picked up a different kind of glint near the dead man's foot. Suddenly the glimmering spark of decency went out. He wrenched open the door and grabbed greedily at the large sharp-edged piece of gold, studied it for a moment then picked up the bloodstained bag that had lain near it. His pulse quickened once more when he felt the weight and saw what was inside. He placed the larger piece in the bag and quickly searched the rest of the cab for more. Finding nothing, he ripped a small bluebush from the ground nearby and walked quickly backwards to his vehicle, scrabbling his footprints as he went. He shoved the bag behind the driver's seat and was about to get in and drive away when, like a conscience, a dog barked at him from somewhere in the darkness. He picked up a rock and hurled it in the general direction of the sound, sending a volley of abuse after it. He then got into his car, but before he could drive off the headlights of another vehicle came sweeping along the highway.

"Fuck it!" he cried out. With a scowl on his face he stepped out of his ute and slowly walked back to the Land Rover.

*

The information that Elliot gave to the police about blood still flowing from the body when he first saw it would allow the coroner to eventually set the time of the accident at about seven o'clock that night – very soon after Johnno was draining the last mouthful from his fifth can of beer and just before his attention had been drawn to Smiler's deeply troubled voice.

Johnno had ripped the first can from the carton only seconds after he had sped away from the pub, emptying the contents down his throat without taking a breath. The second, third and fourth ones quickly followed as he tried to drown the confusion and fear that spun crazily around his head. Yet the same panic-stricken state that had sent him into the pub with the bag of gold still controlled him as the Land Rover careered off down the gravel road. The vehicle was almost running on automatic pilot now, his frantic thoughts blocking out nearly all attention to the journey. He didn't know where he was going, he just wanted to go, and hardly registered when the vehicle turned left at the bitumen and headed south towards Kalgoorlie.

Smiler stared worriedly at his owner. He had seen plenty too. His instincts had picked up on the presence well before his human partner could do so. He had tried to warn him – several times – but his owner had the fever and it still appeared to be holding him in its grip even after all that had happened out there in the desert.

Johnno ripped a fifth can from the carton and guzzled it down. But just as he was taking it from his lips, the Land Rover rocked with a sudden gust of wind, followed by a growl of deep fear in Smiler's voice. He turned around and then saw it too, his eyes widening in horror as its malevolent form rose up to hover before him; the nightmare from the desert upon him once more. He screamed, let go of the steering wheel and raised both arms to his face, no longer caring where the vehicle was going as it veered off the bitumen and bounced madly across the undulating dirt surface.

A pair of yellow, cartoon-like eyes was the last thing Johnno saw as the Land Rover ploughed into the large boulder. Death came quickly from his head's cannonball-like collision with the steering wheel. But Smiler survived the impact with the help of some uncontrolled acrobatics. As the vehicle careered its way towards the rock he was violently bucked off the seat into mid-air, and as the Land Rover hit he was catapulted from the back of the seat and straight through the shattering windscreen. Barely missing the rock, he landed heavily a few metres in front of the car, rolled over a couple of times but then instantly scrambled to his feet and began to hobble away, fear overriding his pain. When he was a little distance away, he stopped briefly and looked back to survey the scene, sniffing the air for the scent of the terrifying thing that had followed them from the desert. Soon after, the headlights of another vehicle appeared in the distance, slowed down and came to a halt near the Land Rover. He stood and watched as a figure got out, moved to his partner's vehicle and, not long after, headed quickly back to the other car.

Smiler limped tentatively forward, but after a few painful steps he heard that terrible sound again. He barked a warning, but the figure picked up a rock and threw it at him.

"Piss off, ya bloody mongrel!"

Once more the angry sound hissed through the darkness and Smiler's canine instinct finally issued the command to flee. He headed off as fast as his damaged body would allow and didn't stop until he was into the scrub country well away from the highway, where he crawled under a bush to hide and literally lick his wounds. He was on his own now. He knew his partner was gone; it had been like a light going out the moment the car had hit and he could no longer find a sense of Johnno anywhere in his field of instincts. Now there was only one place to go, and the next morning, driven by the quest to reach Jimblebar, he wandered further into the scrub where he wouldn't hear the vehicle searching for him nor the voices that called out his name.

*

Their day of rest now disrupted, not long after Jim drove back to the pub, Reg and Charlie decided to have a look around Frog Rock to see if they could find Smiler. Jim said he had asked the police about the dog, but was told there was no sign of the animal at the scene. If he was injured maybe he was holed up somewhere nearby. They also wanted to go into Leonora and speak to Gary Armstrong about the accident, to try and find out if the gold had turned up, although Reg was already privately wondering about another connection to it. He had never mentioned it to anyone, but he knew that Johnno was in the habit of keeping careful records of his travels out in the desert, mapping the threatening landscape as much for his own safety as for any pegging locations. The lone prospector had spoken to Reg about it once, when they came across each other out on the fringes of the desert. Usually the younger man kept to himself, even when he dropped into the pub between his prospecting trips, but out there he had opened up a little more.

The two of them had spent most of that late winter afternoon drinking coffee next to Reg's campfire and reaching into each other's lives. Reg learnt that the younger man had been orphaned too. Born in Wellington, New Zealand, Kevin Johnson had lost his parents in a road accident when he was six years old and, along with his twin sister, Cassie, had been sent across the sea to Sydney to be brought up by an uncle and aunt. Cassie settled in reasonably well with them and had lived around Sydney ever since, but it would never be a happy arrangement for Johnno and at the age of sixteen he hit the road, where he had remained. It was also during that afternoon he told Reg of his fear of getting lost in the desert. He didn't have the prospectors' instinct for place and direction, and explained his method of finding his way back from some of the areas that even Reg was reluctant to go into – the salt-lake country deep in the desert. Johnno even showed him the diary with which he kept track of his movements, matching the words with marks on a map folded up in the back of the book.

So, somewhere in Johnno's Land Rover should be the records he kept, maybe even showing the exact location where he had found the gold, and that thought lingered in Reg's mind as he and Charlie drove off down the gravel track towards the highway. But it was closely attended by another, of a man with fear and panic in his eyes, speeding off in a cloud of dust and leaving a trail of questions behind; not only about where he had been but what he had seen.

Three

Johnno had ventured much further east this time, travelling almost two hundred kilometres from Jimblebar before calling a halt in the salt-lake country well out in the Great Victoria Desert. He knew they all thought he was mad trying to find gold out here, but he had the stubborn determination of a prospector with faith in a theory. In the history of the Eastern Goldfields several good mines had been discovered on the fringes of salt-lakes, much further to the west of where he was now looking, but common enough to encourage him to spend his time searching the more isolated and desolate parts of the country. His faith had kept him at it for nearly two years now with nothing to show from the wearying effort, but no longer for him the sniffing around old areas, picking up just enough leftovers to pay for his fuel and food. If he were going to break his back it would be over a decent find, a new patch in virgin country. Then he could retire; do some travelling and see the world in comfort; buy a property on the ocean somewhere and feel the cool sea breeze blowing the desert heat out of him.

For now, however, he had to live with the evil intent of that heat, as he stood on a small rocky hill scanning the surrounding area with his binoculars, the sun pounding at him like a hammer, his head heavy with its effect even protected as it was under the wide brim of his bush hat. It was only mid-morning, but soon he would have to set up the canvas lean-to beside his Land Rover and rest in its shade until late afternoon, conserving energy and sipping water constantly to replace the moisture that the desert air sucked out of him by the minute. And during his rest, as always, he would update the course of that morning, meticulously writing down notes in his diary and marking the map with directions and distances travelled. He would also try to sleep, just as his dog was now attempting to do, where he lay under the shade of the vehicle, eyes closed, head resting on his paws and body rocking in time with a rhythmic panting.

Johnno decided to scan the horizon one more time before setting up his temporary camp, but halfway through the sweep he suddenly stopped, his forefinger rapidly adjusting the focus on his binoculars. He had seen something moving through the blurring, distorting waves of heat about two hundred metres away and now he strained his eyes through the lenses trying to distinguish the shape. His first thoughts were that maybe it was a kangaroo or a dingo, but as his sight adjusted, even allowing for the distortion shimmering across the landscape, it told him that the shape was human. He stared with disbelief at the naked, dark-skinned figure shuffling slowly across the pale, pink-white surface of the dried-up salt-lake. He or she appeared to be carrying something under an arm and seemed to be heading towards another rocky outcrop, which floated like a dark beacon on the horizon about a kilometre away.

Johnno followed the figure through his binoculars until it slowly began to melt into the heat waves like a swimmer wading into deep water. Confusion and curiosity danced through his mind. From what he knew there hadn't been Aborigines living in this part of the desert for many decades, and the only ones he ever saw remotely near the area were driving cars and waving metal detectors instead of boomerangs. He scrambled quickly down the small hill, anxious now to find an explanation for what he had seen.

"C'mon mate, we're goin' fer a drive," he called out, as he climbed into the cab and started the vehicle.

Smiler raised himself up from the ground and gave a low moan as he slowly walked around to the passenger side, tiredly pulling himself up onto the seat, to sit there, panting heavily and staring imploringly at his owner.

"Don't worry, mate. Ya c'n 'ave a drink shortly," came Johnno's response to the sad look.

"Just make it bloody soon, will ya? A dog's dyin' o' thirst 'ere!" Smiler whined, as he slumped down on the seat

Johnno drove the Land Rover down the side of the hill, making his way slowly and carefully over the rocky ground before passing through the stunted growth of the maroon-coloured samphire on the edge of the lake. Once on the lake's firm, smooth surface he was able to get the Rover's speed up to about sixty kilometres an hour and quickly began to close on the rocky island that the mysterious figure seemed to be heading towards. But about three-quarters of the way across he felt the sinking sensation of soft ground dragging back the speed of the Rover. Using all of his experience to prevent the vehicle from losing its momentum, he tried to manoeuvre it carefully through the trouble spot without allowing it to come to a halt, yet against his best efforts it gradually dug in. He tried once to reverse and then run forward but the wheels only spun deeper.

Although he was well practised in the art of extracting a bogged vehicle, out here on the lake bed where the furnace-like heat reflected savagely from the salt-encrusted surface he was dreading the effort it was going to take.

"Fuck it all!" he yelled.

Smiler jumped up with fright and peered out of the window to see what had annoyed his owner. Then he saw the rocky island up ahead and a faint sense of foreboding came with its dark, boulder-strewn appearance. He gave a brief, muted bark of concern, before lowering himself again.

Johnno got out of the vehicle, dragged down one of the two spare wheels from the tray-back and rolled it up to a point about fifteen metres in front of the vehicle. Then he went back to get the winch hook and a shovel that was strapped to the front bumper.

By now, Smiler had left the oven-like interior of the cab and crawled under the chassis in the vain hope that it might be cooler there. Johnno looked at the dog and spoke as if in answer to an accusation. "Yeah, yeah. I know. I've got us in the shit."

"You said it, mate", Smiler snorted, and then got up again as his owner grabbed a tin bowl and half-filled it with water from one of the tanks fixed under the tray. The liquid was warm, running to hot, but he lapped it up quickly.

After taking several gulps from his own water bottle, Johnno dragged the winch cable up to where the spare wheel lay, then started to dig the hole. He was encouraged by the firmness of the surface as he walked over it and hoped it would remain so until he reached the island of rock a few hundred metres away. But for now the firmness was a hindrance and it took him a debilitating ten minutes to dig through the first thirty centimetres of compacted dirt, emptying two litres of water down his throat in the process. Finally, he had the wheel buried to the required depth, its full diameter below the surface and slanting at an angle away from the vehicle. He connected the wire cable and walked back, exhausted now and growing nauseous as the stifling atmosphere tightened its grip. He engaged the winch, and slowly the vehicle moved forward, the wire cable pulling it out of its trap centimetre by centimetre until it finally rested on firm ground. He sighed with relief as he tramped up to retrieve the cable and the wheel, dearly hoping that the process would not have to be repeated out here in the inferno. Five minutes later they were on their way again, fingers and claws crossed for the stretch ahead.

The combined wills seemed to work and the vehicle covered the remaining few hundred metres to the island with ease. But now Johnno had to find somewhere to rest away from the white-hot atmosphere of the lake's surface, a thumping headache now joining his nausea.

He drove around the base of the hill that rose some thirty metres above the lake, and scanned its dark edges for somewhere to run the vehicle up, quickly realising that the rocky island was much bigger than it first appeared. It ran back in a long oval shape tumbling down in a shallower incline towards the other end about half a kilometre away, where it disappeared under the surface of the lake again. To his delighted surprise he saw that there was a healthy grove of marble gums on the higher end of the island and he found a suitable entry point and drove halfway up the slope, coming to a halt amongst the shade of the unusually large trees. They were almost double the size generally found in the area and growing out of rocky ground rather than the deep sand that they preferred, obviously having found some extra source of moisture in their unlikely location.

There was no movement of air now, not even the slightest wisp of the desert's hot breath, and a deathly silence reigned as all forms of life took refuge from the crucible of noon.

Johnno quickly joined them. There was no need to set up the lean-to amidst the shade of the trees. He just pulled his swag down from the back of the Land Rover, kicked a few rocks away and rolled it out on the ground. He would be taking a long rest before exploring the place. It had not escaped his notice that there was a scattering of quartz gravel amongst the rusty, dark-coloured ironstone rubble, which eons of a severe climate had broken down from the top of the hill and sent fanning out all around. When the temperature dropped in the late afternoon he would check out the source of that, but before settling down to take his rest he scanned the surrounding countryside with his binoculars, searching once more for the person he thought he had seen. There was nothing, and he began to accept that the sighting must have been a mirage. After all, he had seen plenty of those in his time out here, and if there were anyone about, surely they would be resting in the protective shade of where he now stood.

He put the binoculars away and opened the dog's pantry, a giant bag of dog biscuits which constituted most of Smiler's diet when out in the bush, only occasionally supplemented by the odd kangaroo that he brought down with his old .303 rifle. He grabbed a handful and tossed them to the mouth that had been cocked and waiting the moment the familiar rustle of the bag was heard.

Smiler ate his snack hungrily, and then walked over to lap up the water his owner was pouring into his bowl.

Johnno looked with concern at the red blotches on the back of his hands, a sure sign that he had pushed himself too far. Out here the sun didn't need any help to boil the blood and his effort on the lake bed had just provided it. He took a long satisfying drink from the canvas water bag he kept permanently on the roo bar of the vehicle, its simple method of evaporative water-cooling still working even in the worst of conditions. He thought about getting himself something to eat and rifled through his larder to find a can of tuna, looked at it for a few seconds then threw it back into the box. He still felt crook, and instead of nourishment he took a couple of headache pills from his first-aid kit and washed them down with another long draft of water. Then he grabbed his diary and a partly finished paperback novel from the glove box, before settling himself down on his swag, the end of which had already been taken up by Smiler.

As tired and as unwell as he felt, Johnno still paid the usual close attention to the task of updating his records, adding a little more of the black biro to his lifeline. After doing so, he studied the worm-like markings on the map, reflecting again on just how far he had pushed the boundary on this trip. He had realised earlier in the day that he had been stretching it a bit and had virtually decided to head back to Jimblebar and enjoy some relatively civilised comforts for a while. Then he had seen the figure, and the memory of that sighting entered his mind once more. He wrote in his diary, '*Strange experience today. Thought I saw someone on foot out here crossing a dry lake bed. Got bloody bogged chasing whoever or whatever it was. Obviously a mirage, or an animal. Feeling crook at the moment. Bit of heat stroke. Stupid. Camped on an island in middle of lake. Nice grove of trees here. Saw some quartz and ironstone. Will check that out later. Buggered for now.*' He put his pen down and closed the diary, re-confirming his decision to head back in the morning.

He attempted to read some of the novel, a mystery-thriller set in the misty greenness of Ireland, the type of book he always looked for whenever he flicked through the racks of the second-hand bookstore in Kalgoorlie. They were mostly pedestrian paperbacks, but they provided air conditioning of the mind, set in cool or freezing locations far away from the harsh environment through which he moved. They gave him somewhere else to go when he was out in the scrub with no one to talk to but his dog, and he vowed, that if he ever made the big find, he would visit some of the places he read about. Right at this moment, however, he was not up to any sort of travelling and after reading a couple of pages he began to nod off to sleep.

The rest of the day followed a pattern of dozing for a while, waking, sipping water, reading a few pages of the book then dozing again, until the heat started to relent in the late afternoon and he began to stir out of his lethargy. He sat up, scratched his head and rubbed his face. He felt a little better. The headache had receded and the nausea had almost gone.

Smiler moved at his feet, raising himself with some effort before he yawned and stretched. Then he sat on his haunches and looked at Johnno, his trademark smile defying the discomfort in his mind.

Johnno smiled back at him. "Never mind, mate. Soon we can have a *beer!*"

Smiler cocked his head to the side and barked his approval, the sharp sound echoing back from the hill behind.

Johnno stood up and looked around him now with fresher eyes. The shadow from the peak above had moved across their temporary camp and, combined with the dark colour of the ironstone surface, it gave the place an eerie atmosphere. Then, suddenly, the whirring sound of a large flock of finches passed just above his head. The tiny birds flew on and rapidly disappeared over a ridge about fifty metres away.

The sudden break in the silence startled Johnno at first, but then he smiled. Finches flocking around in late afternoon usually meant only one thing: there had to be water nearby. He was energised now, eager to find out where the birds had gone, thinking only of the luxuries that went with the discovery of an unexpected water source; a decent wash not the least of them.

"C'mon mate," he called, as he set off at a brisk pace towards the ridge.

Smiler followed, but not enthusiastically. He didn't appear to be his usual self. By now he would normally be off investigating, sniffing out the wildlife in his restless way, satisfying the part of his breeding that had to round something up. But now he kept close to his owner's legs, almost clinging to him as he moved up the slope, and causing him to trip at one stage.

"Jesus, Smiler! What's the matter with you?" Johnno cried out as he stumbled. "Get out from under me feet, will ya?"

Smiler moved a few millimetres away.

It took only about a minute or so to reach the top of the ridge and, when Johnno looked down into the small amphitheatre-like basin before him, he smiled again. The birds were all tweeting happily away, drinking, washing and fluttering around a small rock pool located at the bottom of a few boulders of quartz, glaring stark white against the background of rusty-coloured ironstone. Lush vegetation grew all around the water hole and pushed thickly up against the cliff, the lime-green coloured moss around its edge bearing witness to the freshness of the water.

Johnno strode quickly down to the pool. It was only about two paces in diameter but when he got to its edge he could see that it had some depth, maybe an arm's length or more in the middle. The water was obviously coming from a permanent source; but it was an unlikely place for it, stuck out here in the middle of salt flats.

The finches weren't concerned with the sudden appearance of the two large creatures and created a constant stream of traffic as they flitted back and forth from the bushes around, drinking and washing then preening their feathers.

Johnno quickly joined them, leaning down and filling his hat with water then upending it over his head. The cool liquid splashed down onto his shoulders, soaking into his shirt and washing over his salt-encrusted skin, slowly pushing the heat down through his body. He repeated the process several times, luxuriating in his good fortune. Then he quickly grabbed Smiler as he attempted to wade into the pool.

"No... it's not fer swimmin' in!" he commanded.

He pulled Smiler away by the collar then filled his hat again and gave him the treatment, upending it all along his body, until four hatfuls later the dog appeared to have had enough and shook his body, spraying water everywhere and causing the birds to flutter away momentarily.

Johnno scooped up a double handful of water to taste it. It was sweet. A slight earthy flavour about it, but as good as any he had found in the bush. He stood up again and looked around, his prospector's eyes surveying the tumbledown conglomerate of quartz boulders before following their course down the slope to where they and the ironstone had eroded away to a salt-and-pepper-coloured gravel wash. He strolled off down the slope, eyes to the ground, occasionally picking up a piece of rock to examine it, but after a couple of minutes he was brought to a sudden halt.

He stared at the object on the ground, hardly believing what he could see. Oh, he knew what a gold nugget looked like; just a few years back in the early 'eighties there were times that he almost became offhanded about the many he dug up. But not often did he see them sitting on top of the ground.

He leaned down quickly and picked up the small nugget. It was clean and weatherworn. He threw it up and down in his hand, estimating its weight at about five grams. His heart started to race as his eyes darted around, scanning the surface like a metal detector. A few steps further on he found another piece, a little smaller than the first but no less significant, and as he glanced up again he saw another about two paces away, as big as the first two combined. His mind struggled to comprehend what he may have stumbled onto here. He dared not hope that this could be the big one. He knew how fickle the yellow metal could be, how cruel it was at getting those hopes up and smashing them again. Dusk was falling now and he cursed the fact there would be no moonlight to work by tonight. But he could still get half an hour or so in with the metal detector before the daylight faded.

Johnno walked quickly back to the vehicle and pulled out his detector, moving just as quickly back to the slope, closely followed all the way by the clinging Smiler. He clipped the hip-mounted Garrett to his belt and quickly tuned it in. Then he started to methodically sweep the ground below the area he had picked up the nuggets, eagerly waiting for the telltale sound; that concentrated but mellow beep that only non-ferrous metal produced. He didn't have long to wait. After one false alarm from an ironstone pebble, he stepped only another few short paces before he heard the sound that made all metal-detecting prospectors' hearts sing. He knelt down and, with his small geologists pick, quickly scraped a hole in the red dirt. He checked the dirt handful by handful over the back of the disc, but nothing showed up. He smiled with satisfaction: the deeper the hole, the larger the nugget. This time he dug much deeper and dragged the dirt out, then waved the detector over the hole. Back came a solid whack of a sound. He dug deeper still, his hands beginning to shake with the excitement, but he didn't have to test the hole again with the detector, he could feel the solid weight of the one-ounce nugget as he pulled the fine dirt away with his hands.

Johnno sat back on his heels, staring almost in disbelief at the piece of gold in his hand. This was not happening, he kept telling himself, although he had often dreamed of stumbling across a find in the middle of nowhere, digging up nuggets like potatoes in a field. He stood up and worked on, stopping to dig up two smaller pieces of about a third of an ounce apiece, before the onset of darkness would allow him to work no more. He begrudgingly made his way back to the Land Rover, but was full of excited anticipation for what tomorrow might bring.

After starting a fire he heated up a can of sausages and vegetables, at least that's what the label said, but he had never really believed it and he ate the bland, unappetising mess with his usual disinterest before retiring to his swag.

Smiler, having also finished his evening ration of dog biscuits, once again settled down at Johnno's feet. Something was still bothering the dog, but Johnno was oblivious to its abnormal behaviour. All he was thinking about before finally closing his eyes was what he had written as a postscript to the day's diary notes '*Found gold today. Looking forward to tomorrow.*' Then his gold-fevered mind was off and running, eagerly galloping through the realms of fantasy, where, by the time he fell asleep, he had managed to excavate a huge open-pit mine out of the hill and the salt flats around.

*

Late in the night the east wind set in, its cool, whispering voice gradually turning to one of harsh and chilling abuse, forcing Johnno to get inside the canvas protection of his sleeping gear and pull a blanket up around his head.

Smiler just curled his body against the cold, still unable to sleep, his eyes remaining wide open after his master had drifted off again, still scanning the darkness for whatever his radar told him was out there.

It was about midnight when the howling woke Johnno up, although at first he had to fight his way out of the canvas cover where Smiler's body now lay almost wrapped around his head, shivering uncontrollably.

"What the hell, Smiler! Piss off will ya! You've 'eard dingoes before!" he protested, as he emerged unhappily from a deep sleep, where trucks full of gold-bearing ore had been heading off to the treatment plant and coming back as crates full of gold ingots.

"Not like these ones... mate!" came the whining reply.

Now a shiver went down Johnno's spine as he listened more closely to the blood-chilling tone of the late-night chorus. It sounded like the animals were very near. He got up and threw some large pieces of wood on the fire then sat on his haunches, warming his hands over it, appreciating the heat which fought against the cold wind moaning through the trees around. He listened to the eerie howling for a little longer and then he walked to the cab, pulled down the .303 from behind the seat, fed in a round and fired it off into the night. The howling stopped. He stood there for a minute and listened. Satisfied that the job was done he leant into the cab to put the rifle back, only to find Smiler curled up on the passenger seat.

"You bloody chicken!" he accused the dog, which dared not look up at its master for fear of being ordered out of the cab. Johnno shook his head. "Okay, ya can stay there," then, before closing the door he asked, "Would ya like me to leave the light on for ya?"

"If ya wouldn't mind," came the snort, as the door was slammed shut.

After crawling back into his swag, Johnno stared at the blazing fire for a while, a little disconcerted now about Smiler's behaviour. His dog was not normally the timid type. The occasional scraps he had with other dogs whenever they went to town could testify to that, always sending his opponents yelping away no matter how big they were. Still, he reminded himself of the time about a year ago, when they had been intimidated by a pack of wild dogs not far from an old gold find called Eucalyptus. They were dingoes bred with domestic dogs lost or dumped out in the scrub, mostly during the metal detector boom. Some of them were big animals, and with the combination of dingo cunning and a lack of fear of humans they had become a real menace to prospectors and station-hands alike.

Johnno had been woken that night by Smiler's growling, which soon turned into a vicious dogfight, sending him scrambling out of his swag to the Land Rover, where he turned on the headlights to see several brutes surrounding his dog. Smiler gave back as good as he got in the savage encounter, as dust and animals whirled around in a ferocious dance, but Johnno had to shoot two of them dead and wound another before they would give up the fight and slink off into the darkness. Smiler was limping for several days after, and by his behaviour now it seemed he hadn't forgotten the experience either.

Thoughts of the encounter with the wild dogs made Johnno get up again to throw more wood on the fire. Then he went back to the cab to get his double-barrelled shotgun.

As the driver's door opened, Smiler's eyes glanced furtively up at Johnno. An audible sigh came as the door was closed again.

Johnno climbed back into his bedroll and with the security of the gun beside him he fell quickly asleep, only to be woken again about two hours later by what felt and sounded like something thumping the ground. At first he dismissed it as a kangaroo hopping by, but it persisted, in a rhythmic, constant way. There was another sound also, faint and far away, coming from somewhere over the ridge. He strained his ears to listen. He was sure he could hear the sound of chanting drifting in and out of the moaning wind. Leaning up on one elbow he peered out into the darkness towards the ridge. For a moment he thought he could see a reflection of light on the underneath of the branches of trees that grew on the other side. But it soon disappeared and he dismissed it as an illusion caused by the light of his own fire, the flames of the wood he had placed there two hours before still being fanned by the bellows of the icy wind. The singing sound had also quickly faded away and he shrugged his mind and closed his eyes once more.

Four

Johnno crawled out of his swag and shivered in the cold of pre-dawn before getting up and walking quickly over to the fire and scraping its coals. He added a few twigs, blew the flames into life and placed a partly filled billy on them. Then he went to the vehicle, opened the food box and put two teaspoons of instant coffee into a large mug. He banged on the side of the passenger door. "Rise and shine, mate! We've got a fortune to make!"

Smiler looked up sleepily from his bed as Johnno opened the door and gave him a friendly whack on the rump "C'mon… out!" he quietly commanded, and the dog stiffly clambered down from the seat.

The water in the billy was soon boiling and Johnno poured the steaming liquid into his cup, sipping the bitter-tasting fluid with relish, while Smiler chomped on his breakfast of the same old biscuits in the same old bowl. He still appeared to be enjoying them even after two weeks without a break from the monotonous diet, wolfing them down quickly but, whilst his owner dreamt of gold, he was dreaming about a three-course meal: meat followed by meat followed by meat.

The sun made its appearance just as they finished breakfast, rising swiftly over the east horizon and bringing an instant promise of another furnace-like day. Johnno strapped on his detector and surveyors pick then quickly made his way up and over the ridge, Smiler once again following like a shadow. Soon he was at work marking out the ground where he had found the nuggets, scraping the surface with his boot occasionally to define an area about thirty metres square, before scuffing parallel lines about two paces apart within. Then he set to his task, swinging the detector with enthusiasm and meticulous care as he slowly walked between the lines, methodically and expertly passing the disc over the ground, sweeping it only millimetres over the top of sharp-edged pieces of quartz, his hearing acutely tuned for any sound.

Two hours later Johnno's hard work had yielded nothing. As so many times before, gold appeared to be playing its cruel trick on him and his body and mind began to buckle under the heat of the day and the tiredness that came with disappointment. His headache too came back with a vengeance and he began to wander off his marked-out area, his earlier discipline seeping away with the hopes and dreams.

With his reluctant partner following, he strolled casually down the slope, now swinging the detector lethargically in a wide, disinterested manner, occasionally banging the disc on a rock and cursing his carelessness. Then, as he reached a point where the ground flattened out, he stopped suddenly and stared with surprise at an area that appeared to have been meticulously cleared of all rock and gravel. It was a large circle of about fifteen metres diameter, marked around its edge by the charcoal of old fires equally spaced a few metres apart.

Johnno looked at the ground with puzzlement. It seemed to him to be man-made, the formation of the circle and the old fires too precise to be otherwise. He remembered the light he thought he had seen last night and crouched down to wave his hand over one of the blackened patches, instantly feeling silly about doing so: the weathered condition of the coals made it obvious that the fire-makers were long gone. He sauntered towards the middle of the circle, only to be brought to a sudden halt again by what he saw there. In the very centre was an area of soft, dusty ground, conspicuous against the compacted soil around. On that soft patch were dozens of what appeared to be blurred human footprints, overlaid on each other as if someone, or several people, had been stamping on the dirt and, in the middle, one more clearly defined print remained. Johnno stared incredulously at it. In reflex, he quickly looked up and around, the image of the figure moving across the lake bed once again walking through his mind. Yet he could see nothing; hear nothing, as the dead silence of midday descended with the dying of the wind.

But Smiler had detected something, as he sat on his haunches outside the circle, ears pointed sharply, eyes fixed on the centre.

Johnno's gaze returned to the metre-wide circle of stamped ground, struggling to understand what it meant. He crouched down to look more closely at the footprint. It appeared to be smaller than a man's. A young boy's or a female's perhaps. He blew on the soft powdery soil and the footprint disappeared. He straightened up again and studied the ground around him. Apart from his own, there were no signs of footprints leading in or out. He shivered in the heat, stranded in confusion as he tried to make some sense of it, until the sun finally began to re-assert its authority, demanding attention even over a mind totally distracted by what it was struggling with. He turned and walked away, heading back up the hill to the pool. Maybe it was the heat stroke causing him to hallucinate. They couldn't possibly be human footprints. There must be a logical explanation; there always had to be for a mind to survive out in the desert.

He called Smiler to follow, but the dog remained in his place outside the circle, eyes still locked on its centre, something buzzing along the circuits of his instinct holding him transfixed. Then the wind gusted briefly, before it suddenly stopped, accentuating the silence that followed and amplifying the faint sound that reached only Smiler's ears. The dog jumped back with a yelp when he heard a light thump on the ground and saw the puff of red dust. He raced off after Johnno, quickly passing him and barking with alarm as he went.

Johnno watched him gallop by and shook his head. "What's up with you, ya crazy bugger?" he called after the speeding form.

Smiler stopped a little way ahead, turned and barked more harshly.

"If ya know what's good fer ya, mate, you'll get us outta 'ere!"

"Shut up, will ya!" Johnno yelled, sorry now that he had asked a question as the sharp response hammered into his aching head. He stopped and turned around to see what could have upset the dog, but was too far away from the circle to see the footprint that had re-formed in its centre. He walked on again, delivering another command to his garrulous companion, "Just shut it, will ya, I've got a fuckin' 'eadache!"

"Yer gunna 'ave more than a fuckin' 'eadache if we don't piss off outta 'ere!"

"Get!" Johnno yelled out angrily.

"Get? Get? What the bloody 'ell does that mean anyway? Get what? Get where? Get the fuck outta 'ere is all I want!"

Johnno had had enough and picked up a small stone as if to throw it.

"Yeah… that'd be right! Typical bloody 'uman! When ya don't understand somethin', ignore it, or 'url a rock at it!"

As if to confirm Smiler's comments, Johnno put his hands over his ears. With his head banging away the last thing he wanted was to get involved in one of their end-of-trip domestics, when they both became fed up with the heat, the dust and the flies, the canned food and the dog biscuits, both of them going off at the slightest thing, shouting and barking at each other.

But for Smiler the reason was anything but slight, and he kept his side of the argument going all the way up the slope, while his partner kept his hands to his ears, firmly in denial. And Smiler knew where it would go from here. Unless he wagged his tail again, and soon, he was going to get the silent treatment. But this time his owner could go and get buggered and, just to tell him so, when they reached the pool, he jumped in and splashed about.

"Get outta there! I told ya it's not fer swimmin' in!"

Smiler slowly walked out and stood before Johnno, and then, fixing him with his defiant look, he shook his coat.

"Take that, ya bastard!"

But he didn't get the usual response from the shock treatment; the exclamation and the sudden jump back that he enjoyed seeing whenever he performed the trick. As a matter of fact his owner seemed to positively enjoy it. He walked off with a disappointed growl and sat down in the shade of a bush.

"Jus' stop ya bloody whingin'!" Johnno said, as he unhooked the control box of the detector from his belt and knelt down to splash water over himself. Then he fanned the now slightly murky water, trying to clear it enough to take a drink but, as he did so, he saw something suddenly flash at the bottom of the pool. He fanned the water again, and the flash came once more. His hand dived towards it and closed around the gleaming object.

Johnno sat back on his heels, stunned, his headache instantly relegated. He figured the nugget to be around five ounces, and it was Smiler's little petulant display that had shifted the silt and uncovered it. He turned around and called out excitedly to the sulking form.

"You bloody little ripper, mate! Look what you've just found!" He got up and walked over to the dog then leant down and gave him a big kiss on the head.

Smiler looked at the object in his owner's hand. What was the big deal? From where he sat it just looked like another one of those rocks, but he understood the excitement in the voice and it didn't please him.

"I suppose this means that we're not bloody leavin'! Well... be it on your 'ead, mate!" He then slumped to the ground and rested his own head on his paws, a last snort of disapproval raising the fine dust in front of his nose.

Even if it was possible for Johnno to decipher the message, he wasn't listening. He had walked quickly back to the pool and was kneeling down again, intent on seeing if the nugget had any relations in there. The silt wasn't heavy and had begun to settle quickly again, but he couldn't quite see to the bottom, so he plunged his head in, causing the tiny fish that lived there to dart for cover at the sight of the monster from the other world. He held his breath for as long as he could, fanning the silt at the bottom, but could find nothing. He pulled his head out, gasping for air as the cool water ran over his body, refreshing him and clearing his mind.

He sat back and examined the nugget again then stood up and turned on the detector, waving the disc over the shallow edges of the pool and plunging it below the water in the deeper part. There was no response. His eyes then drifted to the tumbledown quartz that led up to the base of the cliff and disappeared behind a group of healthy acacia bushes. It had been the first thing he intended checking before he had stumbled over the nuggets yesterday. It was the obvious source; they had to have weathered out of that location, where the water also appeared to come from, seeping down along a moss-covered trail that led through the boulders to the pool below. He headed towards the cliff and Smiler quickly rose to his feet and followed.

Johnno waved the detector's head hopefully over the quartz rubble as he went, until he reached the heavy vegetation below the cliff, where he unhooked the machine and laid it on the ground. Taking the geologist's pick from his belt, he began making a path through the bushes that extended some five metres away from the cliff-face, intending to knap some of the rock at its base in the hope of finding some colour where the ironstone met the quartz.

By now the mystery of the footprint in the sand had all but disappeared from Johnno's mind, but Smiler was still carrying it for him, the sense of foreboding growing stronger and stronger as he followed his owner to the dark rock face towering above them. He constantly relayed messages from his radar, but his whining and whimpering transmission once again went unheeded.

Johnno smashed at the branches, fighting his way slowly through the thick foliage and the heat bouncing off the blinding white of the quartz, his efforts twice forcing him to go back to the pool and cool himself down.

It wasn't until he was nearly half-way through the vegetation that he saw the opening to the cave, its dark, gaping entrance as wide as a double garage and reaching just above a man's height at its centre. He quickened his pace upon seeing the opening and was soon standing before it. He cleared away the heavy golden web of an orb spider and peered into the cave's shadowy interior, shivering slightly as an almost cold breath of air wafted out of the darkness, carrying the sound of dripping water to his ears. With it came a faint sense of something else and he hesitated at the entrance for a moment.

Smiler whimpered urgently at the heels of his now hesitant master, trying once more to tell him that there was something seriously wrong here, trying to formulate his dog sense into the human message, *"Don't go in there, ya stupid two-legged bastard!"*

But Johnno's strong curiosity eventually overruled all. Dismissing the uneasiness nipping at him, he went to work clearing more of the vegetation away to allow extra light to filter into the cave. When satisfied he had done enough he tentatively ventured into the shadowy interior, Smiler's constant nagging bringing a terse "Shut up, Smiler!" as he passed from the bright world of sunlight into the darkened one within.

Once inside, his eyes slowly adjusted to the half-light. The cave was about twice as deep and wide as the entrance, and to the left of him was the source of the dripping water. Leading from a small tunnel in the back wall was a rock pool, about half the width of the one down the slope, running the full length of the cave before trickling into a couple of smaller pools then seeping into the pebble-covered ground outside.

The permanent presence of water had made the interior of the cave very cool, and Johnno stood for a few moments appreciating the natural air conditioning. He called Smiler to join him, but the dog remained at the entrance, sniffing the air, trying to qualify what lurked inside. Whatever it was he didn't want any part of it, and told his owner so with another bout of whimpering.

Johnno once again ignored the complaining, his attention now drawn to what he could see on the back wall. As his eyes adapted to the shadowy interior they detected a rock face liberally covered with Aboriginal art. He walked up closer to examine it. There were the usual ochre outlines of animal life and human hand marks sprayed there by the mouths of people long departed from this world. He studied them for a while, before his eyes finally rested on two handprints right next to each other at the bottom of the gallery. Both were small, one obviously a very young child, the other maybe an older child or woman, and they appeared much fresher than the others, the white chalk standing out clearly against the dark background. Then his gaze was drawn to the right of him, his peripheral vision detecting something lying there. He strained his eyes to see what it was, then suddenly drew back. Lying curled up on the ground was a skeleton, positioned as if its owner had gone to sleep in the soft sand and hadn't woken up.

Although Johnno was no expert on the human skeleton he could see that it was not big enough to be a man's, and as he stepped forward again to look more closely he saw an object on the far side. It was a wooden dish, and inside it were the remains of a small child, its tiny frame laid out in the same manner as the bigger one, but with a skull split and misshapen. For a few moments he stared at the grisly sight before his gaze shifted to scan around the rest of the cave. He discovered more remains, skulls staring hollow-eyed at him from the middle of rough bundles of bones placed around the bottom of the wall on two sides of the cave and leading all the way up to near the entrance.

A strong desire to leave the burial place sent Johnno stepping quickly back towards the entrance, but as he did so he kicked a small rock that splashed into the pool of water and sent ripples of light running across the roof of the cave. Something caught his eye from the ceiling and he suddenly stopped and looked up.

Above the pool was a faded painting of a serpent, the yellow-ochre of its body outlined in dulling white and snaking back over half the length of the cave roof towards the small tunnel, its tail narrowing out to appear as though it was coming out of the hole in the wall. The roof of the cave was lower here, just under an arm's length above his head and Johnno stepped into the edge of the pool to look more closely for what had initially caught his eye. As he did so, the movement of his feet sent more ripples across the surface of the water and sharp reflections of light ran across the length of the painting, again bringing the glint.

Johnno stared almost in disbelief at the spot halfway along the body of the serpent. He took off his hat and plunged it into the water then used it to frantically scrub at the painting, removing enough of the ochre to expose more of the glistening surface beneath. "Jesus Christ!" he shouted.

There was no need now for Johnno to do any knapping of rocks. What he had been searching for was staring at him, in the form of a vein of gold as wide as a man's wrist, running right through the middle of the serpent painting and, as his mad scrubbing eventually revealed, along the entire length of its body.

"You bloodeeee beauteeee!" His voice echoed once more through the cavern and drowned out the sound that came like a rush of air from somewhere back beyond the cave wall.

The sound, however, had caught the ears of the ever-vigilant Smiler, and he was no longer able to contain himself as he whimpered and barked, "*Get out ya stupid bastard! Get out!*"

"You said it mate! We're bloody rich!" With an almost maniacal laugh Johnno took the geologist pick and drove it into the vein of soft metal. A sudden gush of ice-cold air blew across the surface of the water, followed by the sound again, much louder and angrier than before. Yet Johnno still didn't hear or feel anything above the noise and exertion of his frantic chopping job on the serpent. After several blows, he eventually gouged out a fist-sized lump and stuffed it into his pocket. He instantly drove the pick in again, but as he pulled it out to repeat the action, this time he finally caught the sound resonating above the dying echo of the pick's previous blow.

'*Hhhhhhhhhhhhhhhh!*' came the chilling sibilance.

For a moment, Johnno remained frozen in place, pick still held above his head and expecting any second to feel the fangs of an angered snake sink into his ankles. But when it didn't immediately come he slowly lowered his eyes to scan the ground next to the pool. There was nothing. His gaze now flashed around the cave until it settled on the distressed animal standing at the entrance, shaking uncontrollably and growling strangely, like the low interrupted idling of a car engine.

"Smiler!" he called out, fearful that his partner had been snake-bitten.

Smiler suddenly lost control of himself, spraying the ground all around him as he stared fixedly at something in the corner of the cave, his ears on full alarm.

"Jesus, Smiler!" Johnno cried out with greater concern, quickly stepping out of the pool to go and see to him, but as he did so he was immediately halted by something else. There was more than just a snake in the cave; he could feel it now; the overwhelming sense of another's presence. His eyes turned towards the shadowy corner where Smiler's gaze was fixed and, as he peered into the darkness, out of it came the materialisation of both their fears.

"Jeeeeesuuuus!" Johnno screamed as he backed away, stepping into the pool again to halt transfixed by the image before him.

The naked Aboriginal woman moved slowly towards Johnno, staring straight at him – into him. Blood dripped from her head and her dark brown eyes conveyed a deep sadness, a grieved and accusing look that held him hypnotised. She was holding out her arms as though offering him the grotesque form that lay there, its small arms and legs hanging limply down, crushed skull oozing with blood and brain matter. The child then squirmed and cried, a deep, painful sound that flooded through the cave, followed immediately by a loud swirling movement in the pool.

When Smiler saw what had made the movement in the water he turned and ran. "*Fuck this fer a game o' soldiers!*" he howled as he departed the scene in mad haste.

But Johnno couldn't leave. With the swirl in the water there came a gust of freezing air, as if the pool were exhaling, its breath slowly winding up his body, coiling around him, pinning his arms to his side and crushing the air out of him. And all the while the apparition of the woman kept coming, closer and closer, holding out the shocking form in her hands. She drew to within an arm's length and held the mutilated child up to his face. He shut his eyes, trying to will the image away. The child screamed, he screamed, and suddenly the coils fell from him. He opened his eyes. The apparition was no longer there, but now he could feel and smell a presence behind him, the icy stench of air breathing like death upon his neck. Slowly, very slowly, he turned around: what he saw exceeded all expectations of his dread.

Rising up before Johnno was a vision of terrible beauty: a giant golden serpent with a head as big as a large dog, its eyes blazing luminous blood-red; its evil smile revealing a pair of long gleaming fangs dripping with golden venom. It swayed from side to side as if studying his face, or measuring him, before its lower jaw began to contort, freeing itself and widening its mouth into a gaping black hole. Out of its depths came a hissing roar as the reptile arched back and flew at him.

Johnno went down in a screaming heap, forearm across his face, waiting for the fangs to sink into his head, but the hissing suddenly ceased and he was not delivered up to the beast. Slowly, he lowered his arm and looked upwards. Nothing. Now he followed Smiler's example, scrambling to his feet and exiting the cave with matching panic, his brain racing ahead of his body, his faltering legs stumbling over rocks and crashing crazily out through the entrance, only to stagger into the spider's web he had earlier cleared away. He fought to free himself of what now felt like strong, sticky fishing line, but as he did so his struggles stirred something in the dark centre of the bush next to him. He looked up to see the terrifying sight of an orb spider the size of a feral cat, scuttling out of the bush and bouncing swiftly across the gossamer trap towards him. As it came closer he could see its beady eyes glowing with the prospect of a feed, its fangs dripping with paralysing poison, its gnashing mechanism salivating. Soon it would be upon him, injecting the liquidising acid and sucking out his insides. Johnno screamed and madly kicked and struggled to get free. Then came the sounds of several dogs barking, snarling and yelping. The spider and its web suddenly disappeared and he rushed wildly on, coming across a dogfight on the ridge just above their camp, where Smiler was surrounded by a pack of wild dogs but bravely repelling each run they made at him. The attackers were a mixture of dingoes and mongrels, and a large mottled, black-brown dog stood to one side. It had a heavy-boned face that gave it all the appearance of a beast from the underworld, calmly surveying the savage scene like a general.

Johnno picked up some rocks and began hurling them at the dogs. He hit a couple but there was no yelp of pain, his actions just triggered a more frenzied attack. The larger animal then joined in, picking up Smiler by the neck and throwing him into the air. He landed in a dazed heap on the ground and the other animals moved in for the kill, biting and tearing at their victim's defenceless form.

The sight of his mate being savaged sent Johnno racing to the Land Rover for a gun. Three of the animals broke away from the dogfight and were soon onto him, snapping viciously at his kicking legs, until one sunk its teeth deeply into his calf and hung on. He yelled out from the pain and swung his pick at the animal, bashing it repeatedly on the head. But it had no effect. He dragged it painfully over the last few metres, until he finally managed to clamber into the cab and grab his shotgun. As he did so the pain in his leg suddenly disappeared. He looked behind him. The dogs that had chased him were gone. He looked up to the ridge where he had seen the dogfight, but there was no sound or sign of any animals there either. All he could hear was a whimpering from inside the cab and he turned to see Smiler where he hadn't been a few seconds before, curled up on the seat, just as he had been first thing that morning.

Johnno slumped down in the driver's seat, trying to pull his sanity together, fearful now that the sun had done a permanent job on his brain. The headache and nausea had returned stronger than ever and he suddenly leaned out of the door and threw up. Then he felt a twinge of pain and dampness on his upper leg. He looked at his trousers and saw a small red stain that had formed below his pocket, the blood seeping through from where the sharp-edged object within had sliced into his flesh. He pulled it out and stared at it, the bright yellow glint of the butchered metal telling him that at least one part of the nightmarish experience appeared to be true. He grabbed the cloth bag and put it and the nugget in with the pieces he had found yesterday, and then gazed back up towards the ridge. A tug of war now began; logic versus the inexplicable; justifying, explaining. It had to be the heatstroke. He still had the symptoms. Yes… that was it. Have another chunder. Swallow a couple of pills. That would fix it.

"Don't even think about it, ya stupid bastard!" came the sharp comment from the seat.

Once again the doggie advice fell upon deaf ears, all Johnno's reasoning fighting against what he now concluded was the work of a fevered mind, another fever now working its timeless power over him, hypnotising, overruling. Besides, he had left an expensive detector lying up there. He finally summoned the courage to go back but, just as he was about to get out of the car, he heard the sound of singing; the same nasal chanting he thought he had heard last night, rapidly increasing in volume until he was forced to place his hands over his ears. And above the singing came the whirring roar of a willy-willy as it raced over the ridge and down towards him. Dust flew everywhere as it closed on the car, and in its centre, dancing madly about and around as though it were alive, came his metal detector, flying into the side of the vehicle as the wind violently slammed the driver's door shut.

Dust filled the cab, blinding and choking Johnno, before the noise and the wind suddenly dropped away. He rubbed his eyes, and through his grainy vision he saw a shadow fall across the side of the car. He turned to see the woman standing only an arm's length away, wounds still glistening with blood, still holding the mutilated body of the child and still apparently pleading for something.

The lust for gold now lost the battle and Johnno reached for the ignition just as an ear-piercing command came from next to him.

"Whatever ya do, don't flood the fucking motor!!"

For once, man obeyed dog. The motor of the Land Rover roared into life, Johnno's foot almost going through the floor in the panic to get away, sending the vehicle careering madly along the shortest route out, rattling through bushes and over large rocks until it hit the smoothness of the lake's surface and rapidly picked up speed. He stared wildly ahead as he approached the spot where he had bogged the vehicle the day before and, with his foot still flat to the boards, he sent the Rover bucking and flying through the soft patch, hardly losing momentum.

Smiler banged into the dashboard and fell to the floor then pulled himself back up onto the seat. His ears swiftly rose to twin spearheads of concern as the vehicle rapidly accelerated towards the edge of the lake, his worried growl quickly followed by a sharp bark that came out almost like a scream.

Graham McDonald

The bark and the faint voice of his own survival instinct slowed Johnno down as he reached the rough terrain at the lake's edge, but only marginally so before he sent the Rover charging into the low dune country. Like an off-road slot-racing car it then followed its own wheel tracks west, churning through the sand and bouncing across the rocky tracts between.

Smiler spent the next half hour alternatively doing a rumba on the seat and a cha-cha-cha on the floor, until the vehicle began to slow down and he tentatively regained his sitting position next to the driver. But he placed himself well away from the bag that sat next to his partner's leg, watching it with cattle-dog eyes as he pushed his body against the passenger door. He had been wary of the object placed in it the moment his owner had taken it from his pocket and not long into their journey his instinct again proved to be correct.

Johnno didn't hear the loud warning bark. He was staring almost catatonically ahead, oblivious to all but the basic requirements of driving.

Smiler continued to whimper, growl and whine as he watched the thing inside the bag worming around, before the rough piece of gold suddenly spilled out to land on the floor, rolling annoyingly back and forth beneath the brake and clutch pedals.

Aware only of the inconvenience to his driving, Johnno leant down and picked up the object, but when he looked up from placing it back in the bag the assault on his mind began again. A large kangaroo suddenly appeared in front of the vehicle, not bounding across his path but just sitting staring at him. In reflex he swerved away, but like a projection of the vehicle the kangaroo followed the front of it, still in that same statue-like manner. He swerved away again. It followed. He slammed on the brakes, and suddenly the animal transformed into an eagle, flying towards the windscreen to land on the bonnet, wings outstretched and glaring at him with mean, dark eyes.

Johnno closed his eyes tightly and yelled, "Noooooooo!" When he opened them again it seemed the denial had worked, but it wouldn't be for long. As he drove warily on, he began to enter a timeless zone where the bush in all its forms would continue to grab and claw at

50

him from his feverish imagination. Not long after the eagle had disappeared a thick blue-black cloud of blowflies suddenly swarmed inside his vehicle, crawling all over him as though they had found a carcass to feed and breed upon. He screamed them away, only to be assailed by the sight and sounds of lizards, goannas and snakes banging onto the roof and sliding down the windscreen, scratching and striking at him as they went. Then came the bull ants, streaming into the cab through the gaps in the door seals, climbing up his legs and across his arms, sinking their pincers into any bare flesh they could find. He screamed their acid pain away too, but the visions kept coming. Rabbits, emus and kangaroos leapt madly at his vehicle. A swollen black-bodied spider with a vivid red stripe down its back scurried along his arm and up his neck, tickling his skin before it stung, the frantic slap to despatch it bringing more pain than the bite and killing nothing.

Smiler laid low, remaining on the floor where the last braking had thrown him, ears flattened and body flinching with each anguished cry of his partner, suffering with him as he had always done. Man's best friend, mates through thick and thin – that was his lot. Never mind boring bloody dog biscuits for weeks at a time, or freezing your arse off outside the sleeping bag at night, *and* not to mention the loyalty of remaining by his side until you piss yourself with fear, now he had the distinct feeling they were both for the chop.

By the time Johnno had left the virgin country and hit the road that led to Jimblebar some fifty kilometres away, his mind was nearing meltdown. His eyes had been constantly darting from one side of the vehicle to the other; to the sky, then back to the bush again; glancing in the rear-vision mirror and frantically looking over each shoulder, his head nearly doing a full rotation in his fear. Now, on the relatively flat surface, he stared straight ahead, trying to speed away from the hallucinations. He passed through Nangaturra homestead as if it didn't exist, totally oblivious to the jackaroo waving to him from a workshop and nearly wiping out a gatepost as the vehicle slid and drifted across the rutted gravel road. But the hallucinations kept up with him and then passed him, the sky suddenly coming over black with clouds, lightning flashing and thunder roaring as the dry storm sped like a battleship towards the horizon. The sun followed, soaring across the sky and carrying a day in what seemed a few seconds, dragging the night behind it and then quickly reverting to day again.

Finally, Jimblebar appeared up ahead and with nine-tenths of his reasoning gone and the last part rapidly heading that way, Johnno approached it with only one thought in his mind – maybe alcohol would drown whatever was slithering through it. He skidded the Rover to a halt in front of the pub, but as he began to climb out he suddenly became aware of the bag that had been pressing against his leg and the thoughts that had been suppressed by his wild ride rushed back. Of course! The gold! He still had the gold! He glanced up at the two men sitting on the veranda, grabbed the bag and held it furtively against his side. You bastards aren't gunna get my gold!

"Stay!" he hissed at the form lying on the floor of the cab.

After the door slammed, Smiler climbed back up on the seat and watched his demented friend go inside the pub. Then he moaned, *"Yeah...that'd be bloody right! After all that I'm not even gunna get me beer!"*

Five

It was mid-afternoon when Charlie and Reg finally made it to
Leonora. They had stopped over at Frog Rock to look for Smiler and
spent over an hour searching for him in the scrub, but apart from the
tracks they spotted leading into the bush then fading away on harder
ground, there was no further sign of him. They were puzzled that he
had wandered away from the vehicle but there was another matter
they were debating on the drive into town. As they pulled up in front
of the police station and stepped out of the vehicle, Charlie offered
his emphatic conclusion.

"I'll bet ya they didn't find it. Elliot's a lyin', thievin' prick. If 'e
saw the gold... 'e took it!"

Before going inside the building the two men walked over to the
yard for impounded vehicles and peered through the chain wire fence
at Johnno's crumpled Land Rover. The impact had left the driver's
door bent ajar and they could clearly see the dried bloodstains inside
the cab, spattered against the dashboard and puddled on the floor
and seat.

"Jesus... what a mess! You'd think they'd wash the bloody thing
out," Charlie moaned.

"Must've been quick," Reg observed. "C'mon, let's go inside."

The air-conditioned interior of the police station opened up like a
refrigerator as they walked through the front entrance and stepped up
to the service counter.

"Jesus… I should've brought me overcoat!" Charlie yelled out. "What a bunch o' wimps!"

The lass who handled all the counter inquiries just smiled, and Sergeant Gary Armstrong spoke without looking up from his paperwork.

"Just when you think the day is improvin', you two old bastards walk in."

"C'n we see ya fer a few minutes, Gary?" Reg asked.

"Yeah, hang on a second."

The policeman scribbled a few more words, then got up from his desk and walked to the counter.

"What can I do ya for, fellas?"

"Oh, we just wanted to get some info' on what 'appened to Johnno," Reg replied. "Jim came out to see us this mornin'. Bit of a shock."

"Yeah… not nice," Gary agreed. "But there's not a lot I can tell you. I can only guess that he was either drunk or went to sleep, or both. There were five empties out of the carton Jim sold him and I calculate he knocked them off in less than an hour. That's a fair old chug."

"He was actin' pretty strange at the pub," Reg offered. "We've never seen 'im like that before."

Gary nodded "Mmmmm. Jim told me… said he looked as though he was off his brain. Maybe he finally snapped bein' out there on his own all the time. It wouldn't surprise me. He always seemed to be a bit of a funny one anyway."

"Aaah, 'e was okay. Just a bit of a loner. 'Is dog was enough company fer 'im," Reg defended "An' speakin' of Smiler, we 'ad a good look 'round Frog Rock before we came in. It looks like 'e's run off, which is a bit of a worry. Don't like ta think 'e's out there sufferin'."

"Yeah… it was a bit strange that he didn't hang 'round. A dog will usually stay with its owner… no matter what. I've spread the word around town to keep a look out for him," Gary said, then after a brief silence he added, "Well, if that's all fellas, I've got heaps of work to do on this. I've gotta get back to it."

"Yeah, thanks mate… but there's just one more thing. Ya didn't happen ta find anythin' else besides booze in the cab, did ya… somethin' a little more interestin'?" Reg tentatively asked.

"Just a few diaries, maps… some personal stuff. Why do you ask?"

"Bloody told ya! Slimy, thievin' bastard!" Charlie chimed in.

"Aar, fer Chrissake, shut it fer a minute will ya!" Reg responded.

"Whaddaya gettin' at Reg?" Gary asked, more interested now.

"Johnno had some gold with 'im at the pub yesterday. It was in a cloth bag. We all saw it," Reg said, the experienced prospector deciding not to elaborate on its uniqueness. He didn't know for sure what was in those diaries and maps, but he wasn't going to alert anyone else to the possibility of there being a mother lode somewhere out in the desert. It was only at Charlie's earlier urging that he decided to raise the matter at all, arguing that it was pointless. Both of them knew that if Elliot took the gold he most certainly wouldn't admit to it or hide it where it could be found. So nothing would be proved either way. But Charlie had to know if it was missing.

Gary frowned. "Mmmmm. It looks like we'll have to speak some more to Mr Elliot then."

"I'll go out there and interview 'im for ya, if ya like!" Charlie contributed.

Gary smiled "Thanks, mate, but I think we'll be able to manage. Now, I've gotta get back to this bloody paperwork, so piss off."

The two men complied, singing out a casual farewell as they headed for the door but, just as they were about to open it, Gary called after them.

"Oh, and by the way, I hope you blokes have been in trainin' for the game next week, because we've got a secret weapon this year."

"Oh yeah… what's that?" Charlie asked "Ya gunna bring yer radar gun along and pinch me fer fast bowlin'?"

"You'll find out," Gary said with a sly smile. "We'll be bringin' the cup back here this time."

The annual cricket match was due to be held next to the Jimblebar pub on Sunday week. It was always played between a team from Leonora and the Jimblebar locals bolstered by half-a-dozen young jackeroos from the outlying stations. It was a big event in the social calendar of the district and, contrary to its frivolous name, the Hoogivsarats Cup was a prized trophy, and proudly held by Jimblebar for the past three years.

"In ya dreams, Gassa," was the last comment from Charlie as the two men left.

About an hour later they approached the Full Stop Roadhouse. As they drove past, they noticed Bill Elliot outside, standing near one of the bowsers with a spanner in his hand.

"Probably doctorin' it... the bloody mongrel!" Charlie remarked. He leant across from the passenger side and screamed out of the driver's window, "Ya thievin' bloody prick!"

"Jeeesus Christ, will you control yerself?" Reg cried out, his face screwed up with pain as he wrung a finger in his left ear.

Elliot glanced up briefly as the voice shrieked past. He didn't hear the words clearly, but when he saw whose car it was, he turned away. He waited till it had disappeared down the highway before he went back to what he was doing, quickly tightening something on one of the bowser casings. He had spotted the bolt sitting on top of the bowser when he was pouring fuel for a customer and cursed himself for not replacing it the night before.

"What an animal!" Charlie continued, as the car sped on. "Fer all we know, Johnno coulda still been alive when that bastard took 'is gold. Stealin' a dyin' man's gold... what a bloody animal!"

"We dunno fer sure what 'appened... someone else mighta come along before him," came Reg's quiet voice of reason. He agreed with Charlie's view of the man but he wasn't about to judge anyone without the proof. What he did know, however, was that, even if Elliot did take the gold, he didn't get the diaries. The coppers had them now, and that would appear to be the end of that. There was no way he was going to ask if he could have a peek at them. He'd feel like a vulture. And he was glad that he had never mentioned anything about their existence to Charlie. He knew his mate would have been all over Gary Armstrong if he had known about them; that he could probably justify being a vulture if he was to be a rich one.

"Well, it's back ta the dryblowin' 'eaps fer us mate," he said resignedly.

Charlie just stared glumly out the window.

It was nearing dusk when they reached camp. It was Charlie's turn to do the cooking so he began preparations for the evening meal. Reg left him to it and ambled off to a spot on the top of the hill, which gave a view to a line of breakaway cliffs that rose like a flat-topped island out of the ocean of treetops. He sat down on the ground and stared out to the far horizon, contemplating, still wondering what it was out there that could have so frightened Johnno. Maybe he had gone 'troppo'– finally snapped from the isolation. But somehow Reg just couldn't swallow that. Not from what he knew of the quiet man. What he did believe however, and increasingly so over the last few years, was that the desert was not a dead place; it had a soul and a voice that at times made him feel comfortable there and sometimes ill at ease. Maybe it had whispered something terrible to Johnno.

Reg's vision lowered from the horizon to the breakaways as the last rays of the sun washed across the cream and coffee-coloured cliffs. He could smell the aroma of Charlie's cooking drifting over the hill. It smelt distinctly like another one of his 'guess what it is dishes', but there was a hint of curry in the odour and Reg was pleased about that; a little camouflage for the palate to allow for the severe shortfall in the chef's culinary skills.

Soon the moment that Reg had been waiting for came, the parallel rays of the setting sun hitting the cliffs and making the breakaways glow like a vein of gold stretching out along the horizon. Just as they did so, he heard Charlie's footsteps behind him.

Reg nodded his head towards the horizon. "There ya are mate. There's yer real gold."

"Yeah… and I'm gunna get a gold plate fer me cookin'. C'mon, let's get it over with."

They retired early that evening. There had been little work done over the previous two days and they had made the decision to get back into it in the morning.

*

Later in the night, as the two men slept peacefully in the cool outside their hut, a familiar voice began to whisper softly from the east, its breath eventually picking up little wisps of dust on the driveway of the Full Stop Roadhouse and sending them scurrying across the concrete.

Bill Elliot looked up from his newspaper as the skeletal remains of a bluebush skipped and danced across the concourse and bounced off the front wall of the building. As it often did, the east wind was telling him it was near closing time. He looked at his watch. It was after eleven and there was not much chance of any more customers at that time of night. In just a few minutes he would lock up. He lit another cigarette and flicked through the last pages of the newspaper, then something made him suddenly stop and look up again. He thought he could hear a familiar sound coming from the driveway, something beyond the sighing of the wind. He walked to the doorway and paused there, took a drag on his cigarette and listened more intently. The hum of the bowser came to his ears again, and this time it was accompanied by a gurgling, gushing sound. Elliot hurried over to investigate. As he got closer to where the sound was coming from, the strong odour of petrol drifted into his nostrils.

"Jesus *Christ!*" he exclaimed, as he saw the small lake of fuel spreading across the concrete.

The hose of the bowser he had been fiddling with that afternoon was lying on the ground, petrol gushing from its nozzle. He rushed to turn the pump handle off, splashing through the pink puddle spreading out all around him, but as he neared the bowser he suddenly stopped and stared.

The hose had slowly begun to snake its way across the ground towards Elliot. When it was about a metre away, it halted, rising slowly up to hover before him, the nozzle pointing directly at his face, the flow of fuel now only a dribble. For a few seconds the hose swayed around in front of him, then the nozzle began to fade and blur, its dull-grey metal starting to shine with the lustre of gold. Gradually, the apparition formed, its blood-red eyes fixing its victim with a deathly gaze, a yellow glow spreading down along the hose like a mellow fuse burning. It arched its body as if about to strike, mouth wide open, golden fangs dripping.

'*Hhhhhhhhhhhhh!*' came the terrible sound.

Elliot put his arm across his face and screamed. But the serpent didn't strike: instead, out of its mouth fuel came gushing, splashing, drenching; the fumes suffocating as the liquid spread all over the terrified man, running into his eyes, blinding him, then finally igniting as it hit the red glow of the cigarette still dangling from his mouth.

At first Elliot didn't feel anything as the flames exploded about his cowering form. He just smelt the scorching of clothes; then of hair; then of skin – before the pain finally came; the acid pain, searing through the outer layers, burning into flesh; blood bubbling, boiling, charring, until the nerve-endings began to scream their agony to the brain and screech out of his mouth; then the brain began to cook, until, finally, it was unable to receive the cruel messages any more.

Elliot fell into the inferno, shrivelling up like a grub in a grass fire. Flames erupted all around, climbing up the bowsers, melting the hoses and chasing the fuel that still flowed from one, following it down into the underground tank where it detonated an explosion which lifted the ground with its force. That in turn fractured another tank, causing a secondary explosion, ballooning with the first and sending the bowsers spearing through the metal-roofed shelter above. And out of the side of one, spiralling through the black pall of smoke and flames, came several objects, catapulted from where Elliot had hidden them the night before, flying away in different directions, thudding into the red soil, returning to the land.

Soon the flames had engulfed the building, racing through until they reached the liquid gas tanks behind the roadhouse, which supplied the last explosive fuel to the conflagration, sending a ball of smoke and fire mushrooming up into the night sky and lighting up the country for kilometres around.

*

Two hours after ignition, the Full Stop Roadhouse had lived up to its name. All that was left now was a blackened, twisted mess of smoking remains, and a puzzled policeman standing before them wondering how it could have happened.

Given the alert by a truckie just before midnight, Gary Armstrong and the volunteer fire brigade had arrived at the roadhouse about an hour later. He had intended going out there to speak to Elliot later in the morning, but now he stood before the scene of devastation unable to find anything left to interview. He watched the firemen hosing down what remained of the flames and lifted the collar of his jacket as he shivered with the chill of the wind that sung innocently across the scene, carrying the smoke and the mystery away into the night.

Over a hundred and fifty kilometres away Reg Arnold shivered too, suddenly woken from a deep sleep by a voice. He had been having a wonderful dream, where he was out in the desert again, a tiny form lying naked on the sand, the red soil not harsh and scorching but soft, smooth and warm like the flesh of a woman's belly. He could feel a tender, comforting hand enveloping his and there was a sweet, milky scent exuding from the land, bringing a deep desire to press closer to it. Then the wind began to drift across his body, the earth and the hand grew cold and a woman's voice spoke the word that woke him.

Reg's hand had been dangling out over the edge of the bed and as the sound of the voice roused him he quickly pulled it back in under the blanket and looked around him. But he heard no strange voice now, just the wind gusting through the camp and Charlie's high-pitched snoring. He leaned down, picked up the 'snorin' stick, then reached over and jabbed his partner in the side.

"Wha... what's up?"

"Snorin'!"

Charlie grunted and turned over. Within a minute he was snoring again, but less noisily now.

Reg closed his eyes and listened to the muted sound, trying to convince himself that it was Charlie's voice that had woken him. Yet, that word *Mungatjarra* remained fixed in his mind and the memory of that soft, warm grip lingered, from a hand that felt much bigger than his. He pulled the blanket up around his ears and listened to the wind sighing through the sheoaks, until its sad moaning opera finally sent him drifting off to sleep once more, its voice picking him up and carrying him away, singing him along the ancient Dreaming trails, into the future, into the past…

Six

The band of Wongai warriors crouched low in the bush as they surveyed the camp. They had been doing a circuit of their territory's water holes in the semi-desert country well to the east of the new gold rush town of Menzies, on a mission to frighten away the white men who were entering their land and stealing the water. The levels were already very low for early summer and now the intruders were camping beside the *gnamma* holes as if they owned them, filling their strange beasts with the Wongais' lifeblood and frightening the people away with the loud booming of their invisible spears. Occasionally the Wongai had fought back, and sometimes their spears had found their mark in the invaders or the animals they rode, but they had kept coming in greater numbers and a greater stand had to be made.

The warriors crept into the camp, leaving two others resting in the bush nursing wounds received in an encounter with a booby-trap of dynamite, set by a sick and frightened prospector laid up in his bedroll near another water hole. Two of the Wongai had been killed when the ground erupted beneath them and, at first, the rest had fled in terror, but their anger soon returned. Approaching from a different direction, they speared the white man to death through his blankets. Their blood was still up and they were disappointed to find no white men in this camp, only a couple of their animals standing with front feet tied to stop them running. They took out their rage on the hobbled horses, spearing and beating until the helpless animals fell to the ground. They used an axe found beside a tent to hack off a couple of the animals' legs and then carted them away with other provisions and possessions of the intruders.

Later in the day, three prospectors returned to find their camp in ruins and the remains of their two horses being picked over by crows and eagles. They had left their excess pack animals there while they did a one-day prospecting stint through the country around the nearby gold find at Eucalyptus, hoping that the presence of other prospectors who regularly used the water source would keep the Aborigines at bay. But those men were also out looking for gold or digging it up and not even the terrified screams of the horses had reached their ears.

During that afternoon the three men had found some payable ground a little distance from Eucalyptus. They had pegged it and were anxious to shift to the location but, enraged by the scene at the camp, they resolved to first track down those responsible, intending to hand them a permanent lesson.

Mostly, the men that wandered this desolate region in search of gold were tough souls with adventurous spirits, but some were as savage as the land they entered. Jeremiah Hudd and his partners, Blunt and Morgan were three of the latter, Hudd the undisputed leader, a man as dark and brooding as the mist-covered moors of his native Yorkshire. He had left his homeland a few years before, after savagely beating his elderly father following an argument over his selling of some sheep from the family farm to pay for a gambling debt. Disinherited, disowned and banished from the farm by his pitchfork-wielding younger brother, he headed south and then worked his passage on a boat to Western Australia. Since arriving in the state he had followed one gold rush after another, always arriving a little late and having to work the marginal leftover ground, but making just enough money to finance his next move.

Hudd had eventually met up with his equally unsuccessful partners near Kalgoorlie and, soon after, they followed the rush to a place called Menzies, a fabulously rich find stumbled across in the latter part of 1894, when the discoverer's camel took fright at a kangaroo and bolted down a ridge. In his memoirs, L.R. Menzies would describe what he found as a quartz and ironstone paddock literally covered with gold nuggets and rich specimen stone, from which he, his partner and an Aboriginal tracker had picked up several thousand ounces of gold in just a few hours. But what Hudd and company found a few weeks later was just another overcrowded field and they spent only one night in the town before joining the others that had begun to filter eastwards in the hope of finding what Mr Menzies already had.

According to the quantity of footprints they saw around their camp, the trio figured they'd had about a dozen visitors. It was a little too many for their liking so they approached a prospector camped nearby, promising him a share in their find if he would go with them and help give the Aborigines a good 'fright'. Down on his luck and almost ready to head back to Menzies, Arthur Jennings agreed, and the next morning the foursome headed off, following the tracks that led east towards the Great Victoria Desert.

The band of warriors had moved eastward for a day, and in the late afternoon joined up with the rest of their people, the women, the children and the elderly, who numbered about another twenty in all. That evening they feasted on horsemeat and the women sang their songs of mourning for the two dead warriors late into the night. The next day they set off again, heading north this time to other hunting and gathering grounds, moving further away from the white intruders.

It was later that morning when a small family group of Aborigines, five in number, came across the empty night-camp of the larger group. They were Nangatadjara: people of the desert, unrelated to the Wongai, but who sometimes wandered into the outer fringes of the latter's territory where the red sand dunes and spinifex gave way to the rock-strewn mulga country of the semi-desert. They stood before the remains of the fires and stared at the large bones left over from the feast, quietly murmuring in puzzlement to each other before moving on again, following the tracks of the large mob for a short time before heading off east again, back towards their country.

Mungatjarra, the mature male of the family, walked on ahead, moving fluidly across the ground. Two small lizards hung by their necks from the thin cord of twisted human and animal hair which ran around the waist of his lithe and lean, naked body. He had a beard that grew down to his chest and the long hair on his head was tied with cord, pulling it tightly back off his forehead in the style of a bent beehive, making him look much taller than he was. In his left hand he held a spear-thrower and two long hunting spears, ever on the alert for an opportunity to use them. A pre-pubescent boy followed closely behind, watching every move his father made, learning the lessons of survival, of tracking and hunting. Occasionally the father would motion to his son, Burra, beckoning him to come forward. Then he would speak quietly to him, pointing to whatever had taken his attention, imparting his knowledge on the vegetation, the tracks on the ground, or birds and animals in the distance. The boy hoped that today he would get the thrill of watching his father hunting the kangaroo, stalking it with his graceful, silent movement and bringing it down with his expert spear-throwing skill. He was impatient for the day when he would be able to do it too, but for now he could only practise with the short sticks and spear-thrower his father had fashioned for him.

A woman followed further back, scouting out to the side, looking for the tracks of small lizards and animals, or signs of edible roots, berries and grubs. Yinindi was young and in her childbearing prime. She carried three-month-old baby son, Tjirrabin on her hip and balanced a wooden dish on her head, while Ngatji, her three-year-old daughter, walked by her side, belly sticking out and big brown eyes watching whenever her mother stopped to dig some morsel out of the ground. Ngatji hungrily gobbled up anything that wasn't immediately placed in the dish for the next meal, but had to be quick to devour the morsels before they were firmly taken from her hand. Sometimes a faint smile crossed Yinindi's face at her daughter's swift, snake-like attack upon the food, pleased that the infant too was learning something about survival.

The family were descendants of people who had roamed this desolate place for many thousands of years, surviving where only others of their race and the wildlife could, understanding all that was around them and having a name for everything that they surveyed. But they would not understand what happened that morning, nor be able to put a name to the demons that came down upon them from the west.

For more than a day the four prospectors followed the tracks of those who ransacked the camp, but hesitated when they came to where the two groups had joined together. They were unsettled by the numbers now and moved off uncertainly along the trail, wondering if they should turn back. A little further on they came across the footprints of Mungatjarrra's group leading into then moving away from the main bunch, and they decided that those numbers were more to their liking. They followed in haste and reinvigorated anger, eventually coming across the small group in the late afternoon.

When the family heard what sounded like a faraway sound of the sky making water they searched it to see which way they should proceed, but as they began to walk towards a dune for a better view of the horizon they all stopped and stared in confusion at what came over it.

The family knew of the white people. They had been told about their robbing of water holes and their strange desire for the soft stone, constantly searching for it in the rocks and sand. Some had been observed dancing about in a strange way after finding it, like crazy men. But Mungatjarrra's family had never seen them before and the sudden appearance of the ghostlike men sitting on top of strange beasts now caught them between wonder and fear, until the shouting and the booming sounds struck terror into their hearts and they ran as fast as they could to hide.

There was little chance of the family escaping. They had been caught on open ground with their only refuge a rocky outcrop some fifty metres away, and Hudd, Blunt and Morgan screamed with evil glee as they closed on their prey, while a now unenthusiastic Jennings brought up the rear.

Mungatjarrra sprinted away in the opposite direction from the outcrop, acting as a decoy in the hope that it would give his family a chance to hide. He could hear and feel the thunder quickly gain-ing on him but ran as far as he could before suddenly stopping and turning to face his pursuers. His body began to shake with fear at the sight of what was bearing down on him, but calm hands fitted the spear to his thrower. He took the ancient hunter's stance, feet firmly placed apart in line with where the weapon was to go, left hand balancing the shaft, right hand drawn back ready to catapult it. He could hear strange whistling sounds passing him but had no time to wonder as he aimed carefully at the terrifying image coming at him, waiting until it had closed to no more than twenty paces away. Then he threw the long, narrow-shafted spear, sending it with swift, unerring accuracy towards the upper body of the rider.

Hudd swung in the saddle and ducked to one side in an effort to avoid the missile hissing and whipping towards him then cried out with pain as it sliced across the top part of his shoulder, leaving a deep gash in the flesh. His cry quickly turned into a scream of fury, foully abusing the figure before him, outraged by the black savage's defiance. Halting his mount he holstered the pistol he had emptied unsuccessfully at his target and pulled a rifle from his saddlebag, carefully aiming it at the native who was now quickly refitting his other spear to the thrower.

Mungatjarrra was right on the verge of letting the spear fly when the booming sound knocked him flat on his back. He sat up and looked in confusion at his body. It had felt like the blow of a club, yet there was no real pain. But he could see the blood pouring from his shoulder and he knew what that meant. He looked up into the wild eyes of the giant animal now looming over him, snorting like a beast from a nightmare, and from the white devil's mouth he heard strange sounds.

"Damn thee t' hell, thou heathen nigger!" Hudd screamed, as he leant down from his saddle, placed the barrel of the Winchester .44 against his stunned victim's forehead, and then fired.

Trailing behind in the pursuit of Mungatjarra, Blunt and Morgan now turned away and raced back to where the rest of the family were frantically fleeing towards the rocks. Yinindi, making slower progress because of the baby she was carrying, had sent Ngatji and Burra on ahead, yelling out to them to run quickly and hide. And the two children had raced like rabbits across the rocky ground towards the outcrop, but just before they reached it Burra heard his mother cry out: he stopped and turned around. She was lying still on the ground. He ran back to her side and leant down to touch her. He could see the life pouring from her head and shoulder and hear the crying of his baby brother lying on the ground ahead of his mother's outstretched arms. Blind anger now gripped the young boy and, as the two riders approached, he fitted one of his spears and ran towards them, shouting out in defiance. He threw the shaft with as much strength as his underdeveloped body could muster, but the spear bounced harmlessly off the leather legging of one of his targets and they kept coming, loud laughter joining the terrible thundering sound of the beasts they sat upon.

Courage now deserted Burra and he fled in terror once more, but the riders caught up with him in seconds and one of them swung his rifle by the barrel and clubbed the boy across the back of the head. After pulling his mount around and slowly trotting it back to the fallen form, Blunt casually flipped the weapon back into a shooting position and calmly fired two bullets into the boy's head.

The four men then gathered together around Yinindi's body, where Hudd dismounted and, using his boot to lift the woman's body, checked for any sign of life. Finding none he muttered unhappily, "Shame that thee shot so well. We could've made use of 'er."

Hudd turned his attention to the bawling Tjirrabin and stood there for a few seconds staring at the stunned and distressed infant, a deep scowl on his face. He picked up the crying child by the ankles, strolled across to a large rock and swung the tiny body with great force, dashing his brains out on its surface, before hurling the small form away into a clump of bushes.

"Thee's one nigger who'll never grow up t' throw spear," he snarled, as he mounted his horse again. "There be another small one somewhere – spread out and search!"

Blunt and Morgan had shown no emotion when witnessing the brutal act, but Jennings had turned his head away in disgust. He had taken no part in any of the butchery, but his heart was now heavy with the guilt of acquiescence.

"Hasn't enough been done?" he asked weakly.

"Not by thee," came the quick reply.

Hudd had noted Jennings' lack of enthusiasm after the first day on the trail and was worried now that his squeamish attitude might lead him to speak out later about their little expedition.

"She ran up the hill there," Morgan said, pointing in the direction of the rock outcrop.

"Right, we shall find 'er, and then *thou* will join our brotherhood," Hudd said, his finger pointing with emphasis at Jennings.

Ngatji had quickly made it to the top of the small hill. Spotting the entrance of a bungarra lizard's hole on the other side, she quickly scrambled backwards down it. She lay there staring with bulging brown eyes at the broken-edged ring of brightness above her, terrified by the thought of what might soon appear.

The four riders mounted the rise, the sound of their horses' hooves resonating loudly on the rock-strewn ground as they scanned the location for the girl.

Ngatji began to shake with fear when she heard the clattering sound on the rocks and pushed further down into her cramped hiding place when she saw the strange hairy legs passing by the entrance. They were so close that their feet began to kick sand and pebbles into the hole, covering up the exit, and in the darkness Ngatji lost control of her bladder, whimpering as the warm liquid trickled down her legs.

Although there were no apparent footprints on the hard ground, Jennings could see where the girl had scuttled down the burrow. He was a better tracker than the others, finding the family's tracks where the others couldn't, but now he felt sick about leading his companions to them. It was clear to him from the first that they were not with the group that had ransacked the camp, but that meant nothing to those he was with, a bunch of killers that were intent on making him kill as well. When he first saw the child's tracks, he quickly moved his horse across them, erasing all sign, then reined the animal around, causing it to trample enough dirt to cover the entrance. It was all he could do. He knew he couldn't save himself or the girl from what was going to happen if her hiding place was discovered. Maybe she would find her way back to her people, although that improbability stabbed at him also. He moved a little further on, climbed off his horse and made a play of closely studying the ground and, after a few minutes, declared that he couldn't pick up anything on the hard surface. He then added that the girl was probably a mile away by now and maybe even heading for the bigger group they had followed earlier.

With the prospect of having to deal with dozens of angry Aborigines now planted in their minds, the others thought better of spending any more time on the pursuit. But Hudd was not quite finished yet. As he sat on his mount readjusting the rough bandage on his wounded shoulder, he told Jennings to go back to where the corpses lay and fire a bullet into one of them. If he couldn't incriminate him by forcing him to kill, he would make him commit the symbolic equivalent.

This suggestion was nearly as abhorrent to Jennings as the prospect of having to shoot a live person, but the threat was made clear. If he didn't do it they would simply shoot him. No one would be the wiser, or that concerned about another prospector going missing in a landscape that had provided a cemetery for many of his kind. Survival ruled over revulsion, and he did it, firing one single slug into Burra's body. The four then rode away, leaving the scene of evildoing quickly behind and the bodies to provide food for scavengers.

Ngatji lay in her hiding place for a long time after the voices and the thundering sound faded away, before warily digging her way out of the burrow. When she emerged from her hiding place everything seemed as it was before. The silence of the bush had returned, interrupted only by the occasional tweeting of birds, happily calling as if nothing had happened there. She walked to the top of the rise and looked down to see the still bodies of her mother and brother lying in the red dirt. She made her way down the hill; curious to see why they were sleeping so early. She went to Burra first and called out his name, urging him to wake up, staring at the holes in the back of his head then pushing his body with her hands when he didn't respond. She grew tired of trying to wake him and moved on to where her mother lay, calling out to her also as she touched the blood on her head, looking at it curiously. She wondered why her smaller brother wasn't there and then looked around for her father, unable to see where he lay beyond a small rise of sand some distance away. She called out his name several times before giving up. Maybe he was away getting food. That thought sent her back to the wooden dish that lay upturned on the ground. She glanced guiltily at her mother as she hunted out the grubs and roots from their scattered place and ate them quickly. Stomach full, she sat down and watched as the Sun Woman slowly pulled the darkness towards her sleeping place. But the fading light brought fear again, so she went back to where her mother lay and nestled against her body for security and shelter against the night and the cold desert wind. Then she slept.

In the morning, Ngatji could see that everyone was still asleep and, as she would always do in the cooler, early part of the day, she wandered off exploring the countryside, following the tracks of animals, lizards and insects. But there were no adults now to keep an eye on her and soon she had wandered far away from where they lay, heading slowly west on her innocent walkabout, not frightened now with the woman in the sky watching over her once more. She saw a kangaroo on the horizon and followed, calling out to her father several times once more, hoping he would be able to kill it and they could have a feast. But he didn't appear, so she kept walking, until thirsty, hungry and tired she decided to rest under a tree and wait for her family. She eventually fell asleep, only to be awoken soon after by a loud sound.

Ngatji looked up to the sky. Her friend had gone, and the blackened clouds of a thunderstorm were about to deliver a rare gift to the parched land. The thunder boomed again and soon the first heavy, fat drops of rain began to kick up the dust all around her, quickly turning into a roaring curtain of water that saturated her place of shelter. The storm moved as rapidly on, leaving her shivering with the sudden cold but surrounded by puddles of life-giving liquid.

The Sun Woman soon returned to the sky, reasserting her authority in an instant, pounding the earth with her relentless fire and drying the puddles by the minute. Ngatji walked over to the nearest one and drank deeply from the muddied water, knowing it would soon disappear, swallowing as much as her protruding little belly would allow before wandering on her way again. She was no longer thirsty, but craved food, constantly chewing the seeds of the spinifex as she moved along and sampling any insect she came across, including a couple of fat grasshoppers and a crawling thing that she spat out with disgust,

The afternoon gave way to dusk, and darkness soon followed again, once more sending Ngatji crawling in amongst some bushes to hide from the spirits of the night. The next day followed as before, with little to eat and her strength fast waning, but she managed to find some water in a small *gnamma* hole that had been partially filled by the brief thunderstorm the day before. Once again she drank as much as she could, then continued the search for something to eat. She spotted a small lizard scurrying into a patch of bluebush and it was while she had her head down, peering into the foliage that she heard the strange moaning sound and saw the giant shadow of the creature that loomed up over her.

*

The same brief thunderstorm that had washed over her daughter poured down on the badly wounded form of Yinindi. The heavy, chilling rain soaked in through her dull, comatose state and slowly brought her around. She groaned with pain as she rolled over and struggled to raise herself up to a sitting position, her head aching badly from the bullet graze on top of her skull and her left shoulder throbbing from the piece of lead that lay embedded in it. She sat dizzily in the torrential downpour, hardly able to see, her mind struggling to remember. She felt the top of her head to find out what was pressing down on her and then winced on contact with the furrow the bullet had cleaved across her skull, quickly withdrawing her fingers to stare with dull concern at the blood on them. Slowly, she reached her hand over her shoulder towards the deeper pain and cried out with shock as her fingers touched the raw flesh of a wound that crows had been pecking on as she slept. Then the rain suddenly stopped and, as the clouds began to roll away from the sky, the mist cleared from her mind.

With great effort, Yinindi rose to her feet, swaying giddily as she looked around for her family. She saw several crows and an eagle pecking and tearing away at something and staggered towards where Burra lay. As she approached him the birds flew away causing a cloud of flies to lift from the body. She sank to her knees beside the shredded form and rolled him over to see a face that was unrecognisable, torn apart by the bullets which had exited there after shattering the back of his skull.

A song of mourning now drifted from Yinindi's mouth, each intonation of grief increasing the aching in her head, until the noise of the crows flapping and arguing around something else drew her attention. She rose and stumbled towards the clump of bushes and, after a few paces, picked up a rock and threw it weakly at the birds. It sent them protesting away and as the flapping black curtain lifted it revealed the remains of her youngest child.

Yinindi groaned deeply as she dropped to her knees once more. She brushed the ants and flies away from his broken skull and pecked-apart body, the emotions kept suppressed by a lifetime of survival in this harshest of places now rising from the depths. Tears flooded down her cheeks as she picked him up and carried him to where her wooden dish lay. After laying his small body in it she covered him with the twigs and leaves of a mulga bush, placed her fire-making tools and her clapsticks next to him, then carried him in the direction she had seen her husband running. Another flapping curtain rose as she approached his body.

Kneeling beside Mungatjarra, Yinindi affectionately touched his beak-ravaged face, but she would no longer sing. She could not send his or Burra's spirit to sleep in this place. She rose, picked up her baby son and began to look for the last member of her family. Upon reaching the rocky outcrop where she had told Ngatji to run she was relieved to find no squabbling birds and, when she saw the recently disturbed mouth of the lizard burrow, her hopes began to rise. Wearily, she dug some of the loose soil away and called repeatedly into the dark hole. When no reply came she stood up and scanned the country around, weakly calling out her daughter's name, until the terrible thought slowly dawned that she had been taken by the devils.

Growing ever weaker, Yinindi finally gave up all hope of finding Ngatji and, in the late afternoon, left the place of sadness and headed east. She carried her dead son with her, back towards the desert, towards a place that held only good memories of her family, far from where their spirits had disappeared but where she would search for them again.

The sacred place of the Serpent was over a day's walk away, but there was water from the storm still sitting in shallow depressions in rock formations and this sustained Yinindi as she struggled along towards her destination. She travelled for most of the day and all of the night, shuffling through the harsh semi-desert country in an almost dream-like state, resting for brief periods, but only on her knees, constantly fighting the desire to sleep. Eventually she entered the harsher environment of the desert where, in the late morning, she finally crossed the edge of a large salt lake. Fever that had invaded her body through the festering wounds accompanied her as she staggered across the scorching, pink-white sand of the dry lake bed. She carried her boy-child with determination over this last painful part of her journey, knowing that soon they both at least would lie in a proper place.

She finally reached the island in the middle of the lake and made her way to the cave. Nearing the entrance she called out to the spirits inside, telling them of her approach and that soon she would be joining them. After entering the cave she knelt down by a rock pool and drank deeply of the cool water, but still she wouldn't rest. She looked around the interior until she found some chalk-like rock, broke off a small piece then crushed and mixed it with some water in her mouth. Taking the body of her child out of the cradle, she held one of his small death-swollen hands against the rock face at the back of the cave then sprayed the mixture in her mouth across it. She put his body back in the cradle and placed her hand on the wall next to the outline of his five small fingers, spraying her memorial beside his.

Yinindi stood back and looked at the ghosted images, seeing Tjirrabin there holding her hand for the journey beyond, his body laid out below the Serpent, a yellow snake that came out of the place of the water and made its way across the roof of the cave. Over the millennia, the people had outlined its form so that it could always be clearly seen, and now they would both lie under its protection along with the others that slept in the cave.

After briefly resting, Yinindi took her fire-making tools and the clapsticks from the cradle then made her way down to the place of the dancing. She gathered as many dry twigs and branches as her ebbing strength would allow and laboriously built up some of the fireplaces that surrounded it. Then exhaustion finally claimed her and she lay down on the red earth. Sleep came instantly and held her until the night, when, in her growing delirium, she rose in the light of a full moon and began the task of bringing the flames to life. The excruciating pain that shot down from her head and shoulder accompanied every part of the fire-making process, but she didn't stop until the first signs of smoke drifted up from the dry grass fragments she had placed against the whirring stick. Carefully and expertly she built the starting fire then carried its flame to the bundles of sticks, and when they were all alight she moved to the middle of the dancing place. Slowly her feet began to stamp the ground as she rhythmically tapped the sticks together, dancing the pain of her loss into the land, her voice singing her sorrow to the wind.

Yinindi danced to the edge of collapse then staggered back to the cave and lay down next to her son. And late in the night, as the flames of the fires died away, she joined hands with him again, her spirit flowing into the land, her voice joining the chorus of the desert wind, calling out for the lost ones.

Seven

Ngatji stood terror-struck at the sight of the great, furry monster stamping around above her, foaming at the mouth and with another of the white demons sitting upon it.

"What in God's name!" the man cried out, as he struggled to retain control of his startled camel. After a few curses and commands the animal settled and the rider returned his attention to the small girl, staring at the tiny figure for a moment before nervously scanning the countryside for any sign of her relatives.

For several seconds Ngatji stood frozen in place, staring back in wide-eyed fear, before she finally found the strength to run from the apparition. She screamed as she fled, her terrified voice startling the camel once more and causing the man to fight for control of the beast again.

"Jimmy!" he yelled.

A young Aborigine soon appeared next to the white man's mount. He had been walking a pack camel some thirty paces behind but had already begun to move quickly forward when he heard the high-pitched squeal.

"Boss?"

"Hand me the reins! Go an' fetch the child!" the man said, pointing in the direction of the fleeing Ngatji.

Jimmy took off when he saw the small brown figure weaving her way through the low mulga scrub. Although she had about a thirty-metre start it didn't take long for him to catch up with her, tuck her under his arm and carry her back kicking and screaming. He set her down as the other man lowered his complaining mount to the ground.

Ngatji screamed again at the sight of the monster's grotesque, foam-covered mouth. She was convinced that they were about to feed her into it and shook free to make another attempt at escape, but young Jimmy quickly gathered her in after a few strides and held her more tightly.

Dinny Fitzgerald lowered himself to sit on his haunches as he stared at the sorry little form, dusty from head to foot, sun-bleached hair sticking out in matted clumps and dried mucus trailing down from her nose.

"Well now... and just what would we be havin' here?" Dinny asked. He smiled as he spoke, but it didn't reassure Ngatji and she backed away at the sound of his voice.

"See if ye can get some sense out of her Jimmy. God knows what she can be doin' out here alone." He took a water bottle from his saddle and offered it to the dumbstruck girl. "Here, take a drink child, ye look as though ye might be needin' it."

Ngatji stared at the container without comprehension and Dinny had to demonstrate by pouring a little of the precious liquid into his hand, then gulping more from the canvas-covered flask. Ngatji got the message and tentatively opened her mouth as he offered it again, then, after the first small mouthful, began to drink greedily from it, holding the neck tightly until Dinny had to firmly take it away.

Jimmy began to speak to her, questioning her in all the dialects he knew, but the three-year-old stared back blankly, still without a full knowledge of her own language and too frightened to respond to this man who looked like one of her people but dressed like the strange ones.

"No luck, boss. She plenty scared. Maybe comin' from blackfella out dere," he said as he pointed toward the desert country.

"Well, we can't be leavin' her here. Seems to be that she is well and truly lost. If there were any others around they'd be down upon us by now. We'll have to take her back to Menzies... maybe Rosie'll look after her."

Dinny Fitzgerald had been out in the backblocks for over a month and was returning to the relative civilisation of the gold-rush town after doing a circuitous route north of there and to the east of Eucalyptus. It had been another long and fruitless search for the yellow metal and he'd finally had enough. No gold, nearly as little water and the ever-present enemy of the merciless sun had convinced him to pack up and leave this place of suffering. He had made the decision to head south, to somewhere cooler, maybe take up some land and become a farmer, at least then he might be able to eat regularly. The sporadic showers of spears that occasionally came sailing into his camp at night hadn't enhanced his enthusiasm for the prospecting life either, and the thought of that continued to make him feel nervous as he carried the small bundle he had found back to his friend Rosie.

*

Rosie Kilpatrick was a woman in her late thirties who ran a boarding house in Menzies, an establishment that consisted of a group of half-tents, weatherboarded on the bottom with a canvas roof over, all positioned in a square around a large dining tent. She was a boisterous, extroverted redhead, large in physical stature with a spirit larger than life, and her caring nature embraced all sorts of orphans. There was always some young member of the local fauna hopping or scratching around Rosie's place, scouting the ground for the leftover food scraps that were thrown out behind the dining tent. And inside, she had another orphan, a young Aboriginal girl, rescued from the hands of a rough type who had stolen her from a friendly tribe near Coolgardie. The trusting girl had been taken after accepting a ride on the man's horse and he had subsequently turned the pretty twelve-year-old into a concubine, whom he occasionally shared with two other equally rough companions.

Rosie had become acquainted with the three men after they had arrived in Menzies late one night to rest in the relative luxury of one of her tents. She had already retired to bed, speaking to them through the canvas wall of her quarters to tell them which tent to use and that she would sort out the money in the morning. She found out about their captive early the next day when making her way to the dining tent to organise breakfast, noticing a small black foot protruding out below the flaps of the tent's entrance as she walked past. When she pulled the canvas back to find the girl sleeping on the ground below a stretcher bed, one ankle tied to one of the men's by a leather thong, it didn't take long for her to assess what was going on. Enraged, she bustled back to her quarters and grabbed a double-barrelled shotgun then hurried back to the tent. She threw the flaps wide open, walked in and placed the twin barrels hard against the man's forehead, waking him and his companions with the bellowing words 'Cut that girl loose and git yer filthy, worthless bodies out o' my place! And don't ever let me see the rotten sight of ye again, or I'll introduce ye to what's in the other end of these barrels!'

The men left town in a hurry, with a stream of Rosie's colourful abuse following them all the way down the main street, the formidable sight of the angry woman waving a shotgun about quickly clearing a wide path through the boomtown activity. Some of the onlookers laughed, but all were grateful that they weren't the targets of the town's unofficial upholder of law and order, having learned very quickly not to mess with the tough woman from one of the toughest parts of the planet.

Brought up in the overcrowded slums of nineteenth-century Belfast, Rose Kilpatrick had survived in a tiny dwelling as one of four of an original seven children born to her poverty-stricken parents, the others having succumbed early to the ravages of childhood illnesses. She had escaped that dark, damp and depressing environment in 1881 when, in her early twenties, she sailed to a new life in Australia after responding to a marriage agency's advertisement in a Belfast newspaper. It was calling for young women to try their luck in the burgeoning colony where wealthy husbands-to-be were just waiting to be snared by the adventurous female. So Rosie took her lifetime's savings, scrimped and scraped from a succession of menial jobs, paid the agency's upfront fee for the promised introductions and

then bought her passage to Sydney. She arrived there in the swelter-
ing month of February, but initially found a place with a heart as cold
as the sleet-driven winters of Belfast.

Rosie never met her wealthy husband, or even a representative of
the agency that lured her there. All that her adventure brought her
was a succession of marginal human beings, mostly on the lookout for
a cook and a bedmate, and at first she had no choice other than to take
up with one of them. She was broke and had no means of support, but
after living in sin with the dockyard worker for a few months, suffering his drunkenness and foul habits, she left to take her chances on
her own. She found enough work scrubbing and cleaning to survive,
but was going nowhere at all until she met up with a prostitute. There
was quick money to be made on the streets, she was told, and after a
short period of reflection she decided to join the ladies of the night.
After all, a few months before, she had been used in that way for free.
From then on she decided they would all have to pay.

Rosie was not a stunning looker, but attractive in the buxom way
favoured by the males of the time, and that, combined with a win-
ning, sometimes overpowering personality, allowed her to turn over
more of the product than most of her better-looking rivals. Eventually
she had earned enough to get out of the field work and set up her own
premises, becoming the definitive 'Madam', her personality keeping the clients amused and happy, spending their money on drinks
while they waited to spend even more for the fleeting thrill of the
flesh. And the business thrived for several years, until thugs hired by
a rival enterprise began attacking her clients and scaring them away.
The intimidation of Rosie and her girls would prove too much in the
end, and one evening she shot a man in the arm after three of them
had broken in and started smashing up her premises. She pleaded
not guilty on the charge of wounding with malicious intent, although
the accusation was very close to the truth, her lack of skill with the
weapon the only reason that she had hit the arm instead of the head.
She was eventually acquitted on the grounds of self-defence, but the
police quietly suggested to her that she should leave Sydney, saying
they could not guarantee her safety, adding to her suspicion that

some of them were having their meagre wages fattened by her rival. This unofficial advice, allied with a growing desire to try something new, caused her to look for other opportunities. She had put aside a tidy sum from her enterprise, enough to set up elsewhere, and the new goldfields of Western Australia beckoned.

Although her path through life had toughened Rosie, beneath her often intimidating exterior there beat a passionate heart for the underdog, a legacy of her own underprivileged beginnings. She had been named well. There were thorns for those who crossed her, but a kindness that bloomed with full-petalled beauty for those whom she took to her ample bosom. And Dinny Fitzgerald knew of the good woman behind the brusque exterior. He often stayed at her establishment in between his prospecting forays and, as a fellow escapee from the Belfast working class, sometimes she would spoil him with a little bit extra on his dinner plate when he was down on his luck. She often extended him credit for his lodging too, knowing as soon as he had a little good fortune he would settle his bill, and he always did, generally finding enough payable ground to allow him to be fed and briefly housed. But that was the limit of his success as a gold hunter; rarely did he bring anything but hunger out of the wilderness, and this time he was bringing another mouth for Rosie to feed.

It took several days for the party of three to reach Menzies. In that time Ngatji had gone from the almost convulsive fear of being placed on a camel, to positively enjoying the ride, where she could see above the stunted trees and far off into the distance. She even began to speak a little, although Jimmy could not understand enough of her words to work out who were her people. But as much as Ngatji had begun to feel confident that the two men meant her no harm, when they finally entered the outskirts of Menzies, the dust and the noise of gold digging quickly brought back the young girl's fear. She stared around in terror as she was carried into the bustling centre of a place filled with the white people, some of whom stared back at her in a puzzled way and yelled out in their strange language.

The wisecracks flowed thick and fast as Dinny rode through the various claims of the diggers.

"What's that, Dinny… supper?" one man asked when he spotted Ngatji's small form seated on the front of the saddle. Another shouted, "Looks like ya've been out too long this time, Dinny. Bit young though, aint she?"

Ngatji stared wide-eyed at the incredible scene before her, where strange people were turning the earth upside down, inside out. There must be plenty of lizards here, she thought, as she watched the men digging into the big burrows.

"Ohhhh, would ye be lookin' at the poor darlin'!" came Rosie's reaction to the girl with the big, brown frightened eyes. "Bring her in and we'll clean her up and feed her. Den we'll see what's to be done."

What was to be done was what Rosie had done before. Already a mother to a stolen child, she became so to the lost one. She took Ngatji in and looked after her in the same caring manner as she did all other strays that found their way to her door. She fed and clothed her, gave her the name of Lizzie and taught her the basics of her own very basic English, liberally embellished with the curse words of the Irish working class. The three females soon became an unlikely but close-knit family group, the two adopted daughters growing to love each other and their mother as much as any blood-related ones could, Gladys and Lizzie Kilpatrick becoming sisters in spirit as well as name.

Happiness had come to Lizzie under the protection of the big-hearted white woman with hair the colour of the earth, and the three years of her desert history and the trauma that brought them to an end soon withdrew to the inner recesses of her memory. But the desert blood still coursed through her veins and sometimes, in the first light of morning, when only the sighing of the east wind could be heard, she would leave her bed and follow its voice, going far enough away from the town not to see or hear anything but the bush. Then she would sit down and listen to the song of the wind as if it were being sung directly to her.

*

With the population and wealth that flooded into Menzies during the gold-rush era, Rosie's enterprise soon became a profitable one.

After just a few years of hard work she was able to purchase a two-storey brick building in Kalgoorlie, moving into the former hotel in 1899, and with the help of Gladys and Lizzie eventually turned it into the best lodging house in the Eastern Goldfields. It was a prosperous time for the three of them and their appearance reflected it. Dressed in the best of fashion, they could often be seen out around the town, apart from the obvious disparity in colour, looking just like any other well-heeled mother out for a stroll with her daughters. There was plenty of sneering of course, although none would dare say anything that might be heard by the formidable woman. Their unspoken resentment was apparent to Rosie but she simply dismissed it as a disease of the small, mean minds she had often encountered on her struggle upwards. One day, however, several years after she had moved to Kalgoorlie, someone came who would not be dismissed.

On one fine Sunday morning, as Rosie was strolling down the main thoroughfare with her girls, a down-at-heel, half-drunken man recognised her as the woman who had humiliated him nearly a decade before, chasing him out of Menzies with a double-barrelled shotgun. He followed the three at a discreet distance until they reached a building with a large painted sign that read: 'Kilpatrick's Lodging House – The Best In The West.' He slipped into the shadows of an alcove that led to a doorway of a closed store opposite, his anger flaring as he compared his sorry lot in life to the signs of the woman's obvious affluence.

After Rosie had run him out of Menzies, the history of Jeremiah Hudd had been of one failure after another. Others had pegged the payable ground that he, Blunt and Morgan had found near Eucalyptus after they were locked up over accusations cast at them by Arthur Jennings who, instead of taking up his share in the find had taken his guilt-stricken conscience to the authorities. Normally, the police wouldn't have bothered with a case that involved the killing of Aborigines, having scant resources and almost as little desire, but Jennings' story was so horrendous that one trooper was sent out with him to look for evidence to verify it. Although they found what was left of two bodies, the scavenged and scattered remains minus the skulls did not provide conclusive proof as to how the Aborigines had been killed. The accused men were then released and all quickly left the goldfields, Jennings already on the run from the others, while the digger's telegraph spread the story of the gruesome murders far and wide, ensuring that none of them would be comfortable in that part of the country again.

After leaving the goldfields, Hudd headed north, ending up in Broome under an assumed name, where he eventually developed a career as a buyer of stolen pearls, paying the thieves a pittance for the baubles then selling them off at a much higher price to his contact down in Perth. It was a business that proved to be very profitable at first, but once again the nature of the man would rule the day, and during an argument over the low prices he was paying for the stolen gems he stabbed a man to death. He fled Broome and made his way south again to the goldfields, travelling the least used tracks, to arrive in Kalgoorlie a few months later, under a third assumed name. He tried to find work down the mines before his dwindling reserves of cash ran out, and after two weeks of unsuccessful searching and constant drinking he spotted Rosie through the haze of a Sunday-morning hangover. Now, as he surveyed the boarding house, the man who had unknowingly brought the three females together by his previous heinous behaviour began to consider some more.

A few minutes after the three females had entered the building they emerged on the balcony of the top floor and Hudd scowled as he watched them chatting and laughing over morning tea. Twenty minutes later they went inside again and he sauntered across the street and down the lane that ran alongside the premises, quickly inspecting the back of the building before making his way out to his bush camp on the outskirts of town. There he would sleep most of the afternoon away waiting for darkness to come so he could carry out his plan. He figured there must be money kept in the lodging house and he would go there and rob the woman who had made such a fool of him. It would be some recompense for the humiliation he had suffered in Menzies. Then he would head south, maybe catch a boat to the eastern states and find a new life there.

Hudd made his way into town late that night. He waited until just before twelve o'clock when all the lights of the building had been out for over an hour, then sneaked around to the back of the building, prised open a small window and eased himself in. Taking a candle from his pocket, he lit it and crept through the kitchen area and into a hallway then up a flight of stairs. When he reached the top landing he moved towards the rooms at the front, where he assumed Rosie's living quarters would be. There were three doors at the end of the hallway; one facing him and two at right-angles either side. He made his way quietly there, then slowly and carefully turned the doorknob of the right-hand door and opened it. Inside was a bed against a wall; he crept over to see who lay in it.

Hudd leered at the teenaged girl lying in the bed, her dark, shining skin contrasting starkly with the clean white linen and arousing a strong desire in him to partake again of some dusky flesh. But it was money that he had come for, and he finally backed away from the object of his lust and moved carefully towards the door, candle in one hand and six-inch dagger in the other. Just as he reached it, the girl suddenly tossed and turned in her bed then called out a word, twice repeating it in a small, high-pitched voice. Hudd dropped the candle and dived at the bed, placing a grubby hand tightly over her mouth.

His actions instantly woke Lizzie from her troubled sleep and in a startled reflex she kicked and struggled to get away from the foul-smelling intruder, frantically trying to call out for help.

"Shut up... or I'll cut thy throat!" came the hissing command.

Rosie was woken by that small voice calling out from Lizzie's sleep again and lay there wondering once more about the Aboriginal word. She could only surmise that it belonged to some early trauma, for Lizzie couldn't recall anything about it when asked. Then suddenly her thoughts gave way to alarm, as through the thin partition wall she heard the sound of a rough, muted voice and a struggle coming from Lizzie's bed. She hurriedly got up, took a small pistol from under her pillow, lit a candle then went to investigate. As she cautiously opened the door to Lizzie's room, a foul odour came wafting to her nostrils. She pushed it wider and peered in, the gun raised in readiness.

Hudd had been waiting for her. As soon as he heard the door opening from the adjoining room, he had pulled Lizzie out of the bed and held her in front of him, his hand still pressing hard over her mouth, the knife blade now indenting its threat against her throat.

"What are ye doin' here? What do ye want?" Rosie challenged, holding the candle up, trying to make out the face of the man.

"What I want is yer money! Throw gun on floor and be quick about it, or nigger'll get cut!"

Having no choice, Rosie dropped the gun to the floor and then backed away at the man's motioning hand.

Pushing Lizzie across the room, Hudd reached down and picked up the weapon then threw her roughly back towards the bed, where her head banged against one of the heavy posts, knocking her unconscious.

Now he stood with the gun barrel touching Rosie's forehead.

"How does it feel, bitch? Havin' gun pointed at *thee*?" he snarled.

Rosie's mind spun in confusion, trying to make a connection, but she still attempted to appear calm.

"Well, now. So ye'd be wantin' some money den, would ye?" she asked.

But Hudd was not going to let go of the matter that had burned him for ten years and became even more enraged when she appeared to have no recollection of the incident that stood so prominently in his mind.

"So, ye don't remember me! Well, take thy mind back to Menzies and t' little matter of stickin' shotgun in me face, and all because of bloody nigger!" he spat, the menace in his voice rising.

Now it all came back in a rush for Rosie, although, in the dull candlelight there was still nothing that could bring recognition of the heavily bearded and shabbily dressed individual before her. Except perhaps for the stench he brought with him, now reminding her of having to twice wash the bedclothes he had used in her Menzies establishment before she could use them again. The thought flashed through her mind that she should have used the shotgun back then, but she fought the urge to tell him so and remained silent as the man continued to vent his anger.

"I saw thee today, strollin' 'round like madam muck in thy 'igh falootin' manner, niggers in tow. What dost thou think thou be doin'? Thou canst make 'em white, no matter 'ow much thou dresses 'em up! No more 'n thou can make lady of scrubber from Ireland!"

While Hudd spoke, the first wisps of the desert wind kicked up small puffs of red dust as it drifted into town, sighing along the streets and alleyways, rustling through the leaves of the trees. It was a hot night and Lizzie's window was open as usual, waiting for the first breath of relief from the cooling breeze, and it came in softly to her, wafting through the room, brushing past the light net curtains and caressing her unconscious form. She stirred and sighed at its cooling touch and Hudd kicked her hard in response to the sound.

"Get up, nigger!" he growled.

"Leave 'er be, ye bastard!" Rosie protested, as she moved to step in between the man and Lizzie.

Hudd roughly pushed her aside. "I'll take no orders from thee, *bitch*! In case thou 'asn't noticed it I'm 'oldin' gun this time. Now take me t' where thou keeps money or I'll use it!" He gave up on the attempt to wake Lizzie and shoved Rosie out through the doorway.

Rosie led him towards her bedroom, but just before they were about to enter it, Hudd jabbed the gun in her back.

"Hold it!" he said, as he looked at the door directly opposite Lizzie's room. "Who be in there?"

Rosie moved her head away in reflex to the foulness of the man's breath and when she didn't immediately respond to his sharp question the barrel of the pistol was rammed harder into the small of her back, making her cry out with pain.

"Shut up! I'll only ask thee one more time. *Who be in there?*"

"Gladys," came Rosie's subdued reply.

"Gladys? Now Gladys wouldn't just 'appen to be nigger-girl thou stole from me back in Menzies, would she?"

Hudd dressed the question with an evil smile, confident that he knew the answer. The young woman he had seen earlier that day was about the right age and had similar features to his former sex slave.

"Stolen by you, saved by me... and from a fate worse dan death, I'd say," came Rosie's unwise reply.

Hudd grabbed Rosie's long hair and dragged down savagely on it, causing her to grimace with the pain, but she held it in silence.

"Don't clever-mouth me again!" he said, as he tugged her down to her knees. "Now open door and wake 'er up. I'm sure she'll be pleased to see me."

Rosie gave a small moan as her hair was used to drag her to her feet. She opened the door and was prodded across the room to Gladys's bed, where she leant down and placed her hand softly on the young woman's shoulder, gently shaking her awake.

Gladys stirred with Rosie's touch and blinked at the light of the candle.

"What... what is it?" she asked groggily.

"Sshhhh, dearie... be quiet," Rosie said comfortingly, while her mind struggled desperately to find a way out of the situation that was building.

"Bring 'er wi' thee!" came the growling command.

Gladys suddenly gasped when she heard the man speak. It was that terrible voice, the one that had so often echoed through the nightmares that resurrected her abuse. She hoped she was dreaming now, but soon realised it wasn't so. It was all too true. The man had returned, the familiar stench of his presence confirmed the fact, the rank odour more a reminder to her than the rough and ugly image hovering in the shadows beyond the candlelight.

Rosie picked up Gladys' dressing gown from a chair and wrapped it around her shoulders, holding her protectively as they were herded out of the door and into the front room.

Hudd stuck the gun in Rosie's back again and shoved her through the doorway.

"Get the money!" he ordered, as he pushed the door gently to behind him.

Rosie moved over to some shelves against a wall, lifted a hidden latch and then swung them back on their hinges to reveal a small steel door behind. She quickly worked the black combination dial and opened the safe.

"Stand back! Hold candle up!" came a gruff command.

Hudd stepped forward and pulled the contents out, discarding what he considered to be worthless before stuffing some gold coins and thick wads of paper money into his coat pocket, his eyes constantly flitting back and forth between the safe and Rosie.

Whilst it was a substantial sum, Rosie cared nothing about the hundred-odd pounds the man had just pocketed. She was more concerned about what else was on his mind and soon her fears were realised.

Hudd waved the gun at Gladys. "Take thy clothes off and let's see what thou've got now," he said, a leering grin spreading across his face. "Let's see if thou can remember what I taught thee."

Rosie stepped in front of Gladys, her face blazing with defiance. "Leave 'er be! Ye've got yer money. Now away wid ye!"

"Stand away, bitch! I've 'ad enough of thy bloody mouth!"

Hudd brought the gun savagely down upon Rosie's skull sending her crashing to the floor, blood quickly flowing from the gash that opened up on her forehead. He picked up the candle she dropped and lit the oil lamp that stood on a table nearby, before turning his attention back to the cowering Gladys. Reaching out he pulled her dressing gown away then ripped the front of her nightdress, revealing a flash of naked breasts. He smiled evilly as Gladys quickly drew the torn clothing back across her body

"Well now, thou 'ast grown, 'asn't thee? And what a pretty sight thou be... I could do wi' some more o' that," he said, and stepped forward to grab savagely at the nightdress again, quickly tearing it all away.

Hudd stared at the naked, shaking female for a moment before reaching out with his gun hand and gesturing threateningly for her to move the arms she now held across the private parts of her body.

Head held down, Gladys slowly complied, and when she fully revealed herself Hudd let out a lustful, grunting moan. With his foul breath heaving in her face he ran his free hand over her breasts and then down across her stomach to her thighs. He then plunged his rough and dirty fingers between her legs, but just as he did so, a powerful gust of wind suddenly howled through an open window at the other end of the hallway and blasted the door to Rosie's bedroom wide open.

Hudd jumped with fright as the door crashed against the side of a wardrobe. He stepped away from Gladys as the wind threw open the French doors that led out onto the balcony, smashing panes of glass as it went, but as quickly as it exploded out of the night it suddenly died down to a gentle, moaning breeze. It was then that Lizzie appeared at the doorway, blood seeping from the cut to her head and moving into the room as though sleepwalking.

Hudd looked at the figure coming through the doorway, but the person he saw was not the girl he had earlier tossed to the floor. He stared with confusion and fear at the familiar sight of the woman drifting towards him, as though she were being carried into the room on the wind. It was the same vision of the naked Aboriginal woman and she was holding out both her hands again as she always did at the beginning of his nightmare. And, as it always followed, she lifted her arms to show him the mutilated remains lying there. He looked back up into her dark brown eyes and was drawn once more into her gaze of infinite sorrow, the mournful sound of the wind drifting through the building adding an eerie soundtrack to what he could see. But this was when it usually ended and his mind began to struggle against the imagery. Any moment now he would wake up. He closed his eyes tightly then opened them again, but still the apparition moved inexorably towards him, reaching out to him with its grisly reminder of the past, disinterring an act of barbarity. On and on she came, closer and closer, then the child's form squirmed in her hands and a chilling, pain-filled cry came from the mouth now contorting in the bloodied mess of the misshapen head. Terror took control. Hudd aimed the gun with a shaking hand, but as hard as he tried to pull the trigger, his finger remained frozen in place. The woman was almost upon him now, the child held up to his face. The scent of their death filled his nostrils and he staggered backwards, stumbling out through the French doors and across the balcony until his back hit the railing and he upended over it. The audible snap of his neck instantly silenced Jeremiah Hudd's shrieking descent as he hit the deserted street below, gun still frozen in his hand.

The wind moaned a little louder as it drifted away on its course through the town. Then Lizzie slumped to the floor and all became still again.

The slamming of doors and breaking glass eventually roused other occupants of the building. When they came across the scene in the front room a doctor and the police were quickly called. The women's injuries were soon attended to, but as the doctor stitched the gash on Rosie's head, he peered with grave concern at the glazed look in her eyes and listened worriedly to the slurred manner of her speech.

The police took the man's body away not long after, and in due course an inquest was held into the cause of his death. But the whole manner of his demise proved greatly puzzling to all concerned, not the least Gladys, who was the only one to have witnessed his strange self-destructive behaviour, and eventually there was an inconclusive finding of death by misadventure.

The thief in the night was dead and no one would be mourning his exit, but the stench of his being remained and from that time on life would not go as well for the three females. Rosie was to suffer the ill effects of the blow to her head for the remainder of her days. In the years following the incident her waking hours were plagued by severe headaches and bouts of nausea, which she tried desperately to ease by any means available. Over time the spells slowly grew worse until, after going through all the ineffective forms of panacea available in those days, including alcohol, she ended up on the opium-based drug, laudanum, freely prescribed by her doctor and subsequently sending her into total addiction. As time went on the combination of Rosie's health problems and drug and alcohol abuse changed her personality totally, first to one of listless irresponsibility then to outright aggression towards the two girls now left with the task of running the lodging house. She began shouting abuse at them, making unwarranted accusations of laziness and slovenliness, and as her unbridled bitterness grew she took to stabbing at them with the racial dagger. From her mind-altered perspective, she saw nothing but the worst of everything and attacked them unmercifully; especially when she found out they had been making visits to the Aborigines' camp on the outskirts of town.

"I bring ye up and civilise ye, and what do ye do? Like the fuckin' savages that ye are, ye go runnin' back to the bush!"

Ironically, it was Rosie who had initially encouraged Gladys and Lizzie to visit the Aborigines' camp. She understood what was ahead of the people there, as she noticed more and more of them moving to the edges of town and beginning to rely on the industry of the European to provide what the wilderness once had. Accompanied by the girls, she would take them leftover food and the worn blankets and linen that had to be replaced at the lodging house. The three of them were soon welcomed in the camp, Gladys and Lizzie feeling especially comfortable there, instinctively detecting a graciousness that came from somewhere beyond the Aborigines' rough manner and poverty-stricken existence. So, as Rosie's changing persona began to make the young women feel unwanted and alone, they gravitated towards the companionship and friendship they found with the fringe dwellers.

Eventually, the lodge's income diminished, due to its growing reputation as an undesirable place to stay, where boarders had to put up with a ranting, raving person stamping around upstairs at any time of the night or day. Then, as Rosie's mental state deteriorated to one of total paranoia, the shortfall in the income inspired her to accuse the girls of stealing from her. One day in a drunken rage she kicked them both out, banishing them from her life with the accusing and damning words 'Yer all thievin' bloody niggers! Yer all fuckin' savages! Go back to the desert where ye belong!' In the same state of mind she changed her will, writing them out of the ownership of the lodge she had previously bequeathed them. Just a week later, the blood clot that had taken nearly three years to reach the killing-place in Rosie's brain finally ended her earthbound misery.

Eight

"It's time ta rest now, Rosie," were the last words spoken by Lizzie to her adoptive mother, as she placed a bunch of flowers against the headstone in respect for the good woman she knew lay beneath it. Then she turned from the grave and walked with Gladys into their uncertain future.

Rosie had gone and soon the lodge would go too: the principal beneficiary in her last will, her only surviving brother, put it up for sale immediately after inheriting it, and the building was quickly snapped up and turned into a pub again. Lizzie and Gladys separated and went into domestic service at other boarding houses in the town, quickly hired because of their experience, but not rewarded for it. The comfortable existence they had enjoyed at the lodge then gave way to the realities of their true place in early twentieth-century society. Food and a bed as far away from the rest of the occupants as possible was now their lot, with long hours of work that gave little chance of rest or recreation.

After a couple of unhappy years, Gladys eventually gave up working in town and went to live with the fringe dwellers for a while, before taking up with a young man who had employment on a sheep station, a day's cart-ride out of Kalgoorlie. She ended up settling with him there, keeping house for the station owner while her man herded sheep, with food their only wages and blankets for bonuses. But it wasn't an unhappy life and they managed to produce three children who were brought up in the native workers' camp that became their home.

Lizzie would travel a harder road. She persevered in service for over six years, moving from one ordinary job to another, her relationships with men more in the way of fighting running battles with them than finding a partner. A pretty woman in her early twenties, all she had known was the snatch and grab of lodgers and owners alike, who presumed to see the fondling of the black maid as part of the services she was poorly paid for. It was another sour part of her reality, forcing her to leave employment and subsequently leaving her with no desire at all to take up with a man, until she found a job at Windsor Rooms.

It was late 1914 when Lizzie started working at the small boarding house in Boulder, just a few miles from Kalgoorlie. This establishment, which offered bed and breakfast for three shillings and sixpence a night, was not the worst of places to work in, although its owners, Fred and Margaret Gardiner showed the usual indifference towards her. No more so, however, than they did to each other and to their only child, a raw-boned sixteen-year-old lad named Johnny. In fact they hardly appeared to be a family, a situation mostly generated by the mother, whose cold demeanour had managed to construct a triangle of separateness between the three. But as long as Lizzie did her work properly she was left alone, and after her years of unhappiness elsewhere she found some contentment once more. The essential warmth in her personality began to emerge again, her mischievousness and bright humour finding a responsive partner in Johnny. She became his older sister, the only person he felt comfortable going to for advice, until he grew older and everything changed.

Lizzie had worked at Windsor Rooms for over two years when her relationship with Johnny moved indiscernibly from easy friendliness to mutual desire, the boy's growing physical maturity stirring the sexuality in both. For a while they managed to keep a lid on it, giving no indication to each other of what was building beneath their good-natured banter, but temptation was almost constant, as they often came across one another at work: Johnny now responsible for the building's maintenance. The inevitable happened one Saturday afternoon when they found themselves alone there, with Margaret Gardiner away at a church meeting, Fred on another of his regular benders and everyone else at the races.

They were working in the kitchen area, Johnny not so busily building some shelving in the pantry and Lizzie distractedly setting tables in the dining room and preparing vegetables for the evening meal. Their usual light-hearted conversation was replaced with furtive glances, the air between them crackling with sexual energy.

It was Lizzie who became the lightning rod; going into the pantry to get some vegetables she didn't need, squeezing past Johnny when she didn't have to, front-on, pushing her full breasts firmly across his chest. Twenty minutes later they both lay exhausted on the floor, stretched out amidst a confusion of dismantled timber shelving, pots and pans, canned goods, jars of preservatives and the vegetables Lizzie had gone to collect. They began to giggle then laugh, joyous after their frantic union, unconcerned about the demolition job they had done on the pantry, when their desperate lovemaking had shook clamps from the unfinished shelving and sent goods from those on either side toppling to the floor. They were virgins no more and ecstatic about it; yet, while the man was experiencing the warm relaxation that followed penetration, the woman was suffering the discomfort of her first time, and when Johnny eventually saw the result of taking his pleasure he suddenly ceased laughing.

"Gawd, Lizzie... I've rooned ya!" he cried out at seeing the stains on her dress and on him.

"Don't worry... the bleedin'll stop soon," Lizzie said with assurance, courtesy of the education Gladys had given her.

They lay in each other's arms for a quiet half-hour until they realised that people would soon be returning and began to quickly clear everything away. The clean-up finished just as Johnny's mother walked in the front door. Her comment that he hadn't done much on the shelving nearly caused another outburst from the two workers, now going about their tasks with a united furtiveness in their smiles.

Over the following weeks the two of them revelled in their new relationship, taking every opportunity to be together whilst making every attempt to keep their illicit affair secret. But eventually they were found out when Johnny's mother, feeling unwell and returning early from a Sunday church service, heard the giggling and sighing coming from her son's bedroom.

Margaret Gardiner may not have been feeling well that day, but what met her eyes when she pushed open the door almost sent her to hospital. The sight of her son, bare-buttock naked and wrapped around an equally naked Lizzie, brought instant apoplexy. After a few seconds of open-mouthed shock, there came a stream of invective which would have sounded more at home with drunken miners in a pub brawl than a respectable churchgoer. What followed for Lizzie was instant banishment. Jobless and homeless she ended up in the only place that would accept her – the fringe-dwellers' camp. As for Johnny, the formerly cold relationship with his mother became a total freeze-out, only just falling short of banishment for him too, whilst amidst all this disgrace his father just drank some more.

But separation just strengthened the forbidden union and when his old man was sleeping off the booze, Johnny would sometimes take his bike and ride out to the ramshackle bush camp that now served as Lizzie's home. She would then sit on the cross bar and they would head out to a place they had claimed as their own, a rocky outcrop a few miles from the camp. There they would make love then lie talking until the sun went down, before racing the darkness back through the bush to separate and wait longingly for the next stolen moment. And their passion would grow ever stronger over the following months, until one of a different kind finally brought the liaison to an end.

For Johnny, king and country had been calling since 1914, when young Australians first began lining up to fight in World War I and, after nearly a year of reading the drum-beating articles in the newspaper and listening to town gossip, his blind hatred for the Hun finally sent him to the queue. But he didn't even make it to the recruiting desk before a pair of hands removed him from the line and told him to go home and grow for a couple of years. He had done so, waiting impatiently until he turned eighteen, ignoring the messages that the growing casualty lists in the newspapers were sending, before eventually enlisting. In June of 1917 he headed to Perth for basic training then in July boarded a boat to Europe. His journey ended six months later, lying amidst the churned up mud and carnage of a bloodied battlefield in France, his body riddled with bullets from a German machine-gun.

Lizzie received only one letter from her soldier at the front. As arranged between them before he had left, it was sent to the Kalgoorlie post office, and was waiting there for her about three months after his departure. In it he described the horrors that a young man had discovered about war and the deep desire he had to get out of it, back to her and the peace and quiet of the goldfields. But events would fall so that she was never to hear of his end and he was never to know of the new life gestating inside her.

Johnny now had his peace and quiet, to lie forever under a headstone gleaming white upon the manicured greenness of a French war cemetery, but back in the goldfields Lizzie's battle continued. She now held a very poor hand in the card game of life. She was an Aboriginal woman in love with a white man whom she didn't know was alive or dead; she was pregnant and without a proper home for her baby, and living in the worst of times in Australia to be giving birth to a part Aboriginal child. But still she glowed with the idea of being a mother, even if at first the only person she felt close to besides Johnny hadn't shared in her joy.

"Bloody 'ell, girl! I told ya what would 'appen if ya kept messin' 'round with that white fella!" came Gladys' response to the news.

"What? Ya reckon it wouldn't 'ave 'appened with a black fella? They've both got the same pistols ya know! But then ya would know, wouldn' ya? If I'm not mistaken there's three little results of *your* messin' 'round, right over there now, tryin' ta turn that dog into a pony," Lizzie said, as she pointed towards a group of children fighting over whose turn it was to ride on the large animal's back.

Her words brought a brief chortle from Gladys, but then came the warning. "Ya know what I mean. I told ya what happened ta the one Daisy had by that miner. No more 'n two-years-old and the bastards just took 'im away… gunna grow him up in a proper place was all the copper said. The poor little bugger was Daisy's only kid and she went mad from not knowin' what 'appened to 'im. Went walkabout and no one's seen 'er since. You stay 'ere and the bastards'll come fer yours too. There's no other way for it…you'll 'afta come with us ta the station. I c'n look after ya when yer time gets near, and there'll be a better chance of 'idin' the baby out there afterwards."

"What about the owner?" Lizzie asked.

"The boss 'ardly ever comes to the camp. Anyway, as long as there's enough slaves to work the property, that's all that matters to 'im."

That afternoon Lizzie went with Gladys to the station and the following months she spent there would be mostly happy ones; the living standards, although bordering on the primitive were far superior to the fringe-dwellers' camp, where she had a constant battle to keep herself and her surroundings clean. Now she had a permanent soak nearby which allowed her to have a regular wash, and the atmosphere of the camp was relaxed and friendly, everyone giving each other a hand when needed. It was there also that she began to get back something else, when the women from the camp would take her out hunting for bush tucker, an important supplement to the flour, sugar and salt that was given in payment for their labour on the station, with the rare bonus of a sheep thrown in. She felt a sense of peacefulness out there in the bush, digging up grubs and roots and occasionally wandering off on her own to feel the country, where the warm sand flowed like blood into her bare feet and the wind whispered to her through the trees.

But there were unhappy times, whenever anyone returned after a journey into town, coming back empty-handed from the side trip to the Kalgoorlie post office. It had been a long time since she had sent a reply to Johnny's first letter telling him of their coming child and she couldn't understand why an answer would be taking so long, although most at the camp already knew. They would be saying nothing, however, of what they had heard around town until the child was born and Lizzie had gained some strength.

*

The war department had sent the telegram almost as Lizzie was moving out to the station and at first Fred and Margaret Gardiner received it with dismay and disbelief, followed by varying degrees of grief. As the couple had lived together in a separate way, so they reacted to their loss: after the initial shock abated, their farce of a marriage eventually disintegrated in a blaze of accusations, guilt and recrimination.

The telegram had been delivered in person by the local police sergeant, leaving no doubt as to what it contained, and Margaret had opened it in an almost detached way. After reading it, she folded it up neatly and placed it on the dresser in her husband's room, then for the rest of that day proceeded to run on automatic, engaging a lifetime habit of emotional restraint, until late in the afternoon she found herself standing in a daze, frozen in some half-completed task. The tears finally began to tumble down her cheeks, flowing for her as well as her son, his death bringing out the old guilt she had carried in not wanting a child in the first place and hardly accepting his presence when he was alive.

For Fred's part the news brought as much anger as sorrow. He had never wanted his son to enlist. He held no patriotic feelings toward the mother country; to him it was Britain's war and Australia would be better off out of it. He also believed that it was Johnny's lonely home life that had helped inspire him to go, and he figured he knew who was to blame for that. So, after a day of drinking and stewing over the sorry news, he confronted his wife.

"If you had been a proper mother, he wouldn't have run off to war! If you had shown the slightest affection towards him, he wouldn't be dead now!" he slung at her from his drunkenness after barging into her bedroom late that night.

"Of course, the fact his father is a drunkard and a whoremonger wouldn't have had anything to do with it, would it?" she coldly countered, keeping her gaze firmly fixed on the Bible she had been reading.

Fred's face grew red with rage and he leaned down close to his wife and screamed at her, "If you were half a woman I would never have needed to go elsewhere! But since you bring it up, I will tell you that those women have more honesty in their little fingers than you have in your whole body. They sell themselves but they don't pretend about what they do. But you... you hung out the shingle and when you got the buyer you took the goods off the counter!"

Tears began to form in the corner of Margaret's eyes, as her hand mechanically turned the pages she was no longer reading. But Fred continued the savaging, purging the feelings kept hidden for so many years and now set loose to rampage through what was left of their relationship. When he spoke again, it was in a quieter way, although with no less anger.

"You know, it's not surprising to me that Johnny fell for the first female who would give him some affection. And God knows he must have been desperate to seek company from a nigger servant. Just as desperate as I was when I first went down to Hay Street!"

"Get out of my room! Get out of the building! *Get out of my life!*" Margaret finally screamed.

Fred complied, walking out of her room, out of her life and out of Kalgoorlie. The boarding house was put on the market and sold a month later, with Margaret leaving the town just as her grandchild was about to enter the world a day's cart ride to the east.

*

When Lizzie's time came, Gladys sat with her all through the final hours of her labour. She had known the blinding agony of it three times and calmly responded to the groaning and screaming with the knowledge that there would be an end to it, but she wouldn't be prepared for the one that came. At first all had appeared well; the midwife had cut and tied the umbilical cord and placed the baby on Lizzie's chest; the mother was happy; the child healthy and suckling strongly, but after a while, Gladys noticed that blood was still running freely from Lizzie and she called the midwife back.

The elderly woman frowned when she saw what was happening and beckoned to Gladys to follow her. "Somethin's wrong inside Lizzie... better get the doctor," she said quietly, as they stood outside the brushwood humpy.

Gladys dreaded the consequences of bringing someone of white authority to the camp, but there was no choice and no time to waste. She ran up to the big house and asked the station owner's wife to call the doctor.

The doctor arrived an hour after Lizzie had passed away, and couldn't have saved her anyway from the haemorrhaging caused by the uterus that had failed to retract. But he did what he considered the best thing for her child, although not without resistance from Gladys, who had hidden the baby away in anticipation, telling him that it had been stillborn and buried. The medico demanded to see it. Gladys refused, but finally capitulated under the threat of police action. She produced the child then pleaded desperately with the doctor to let her keep him. But when the man saw its pale colour, after a brief and unsuccessful quest to find out who the father was, he wrapped the baby in a towel, placed him on the back seat of his car and took him back to Kalgoorlie. There the baby boy would enter a laundering process unofficially begun some years before, when those who ruled the land had decided the best place for part Aboriginal children was in a white environment, where it was expected that education and breeding would eventually wash their colour away. His travelling papers were marked 'Child abandoned – parents unknown' and after a few weeks in the care of the local hospital he was handed over to Jack and Madge Arnold.

*

Gladys stood watching tearfully until long after the doctor's vehicle disappeared from view, then went back to sit by Lizzie's side. She stared at the contented smile on her sister's face and again a conflicting sense of mystery and faint celebration began to push through her sorrow.

It was about half an hour after giving birth that Lizzie had turned her loving gaze from her son to Gladys. "Feelin' a bit tired Sis... think I'll take a nap," she said, before closing her eyes and drifting away, a hand gently holding a tiny one of the baby's as he slept contentedly on her chest. But about a minute later, just as a light breeze suddenly picked up out of the still morning air and sighed its way through the brush walls of the humpy, Lizzie's eyes opened wide and a smile came to her face. She reached out as if to someone standing at the end of the bed. A word was spoken and the baby stirred, opening his eyes before quickly closing them again, his body pushing into Lizzie's, the fingers of his free hand working in a feeble grasping motion on a swollen breast.

Many times, Gladys had heard Lizzie call out that word, but this time it had come not in the small, troubled voice of a child but in the tone of a woman's; not called out from sleep but sung as if by the wind. *Mungatjarra*, the voice had sighed, fading away as Lizzie's hand fell to the bed.

The thought of that mystical, bittersweet moment clung briefly to Gladys, before she bowed her head again and began to sob once more for the child. "I'm so sorry, Sis," she blurted out. But a few seconds later, her heaving body suddenly stiffened. She lifted her head and looked at Lizzie, then smiled faintly as the wisp of air that had swirled around her like caressing fingers drifted away.

Nine

The dying breeze wisped across Smiler's face, carrying that cracking sound again, still far away, but slightly sharper now and followed by the faint chorus of human voices. He stopped in his weary tracks and sniffed the air. He still couldn't detect anything beyond the scents of the bush, but when he moved on he did so with renewed energy, his hearing telling him that his journey would soon be over.

Since the night of the crash ten days before, Smiler had travelled over a hundred kilometres through the blazing heat of late summer, the pain from cuts, bruises and a badly torn shoulder slowing him to a stumbling and shuffling gait. Thirst slowed his progress further, the constant need to quench it sometimes taking him well away from the route his homing instinct had mapped out. One of those detours came on the first day, when he saw a small flock of sheep and attempted to fall in with them in the hope they would lead him to water. They couldn't accept him as a sheep, however, and trotted away every time he came near, eventually disappearing from view as his lameness prevented him from keeping up. But his nose was still in working order and after spending another miserable night curled up under a bush he managed to follow the flock's path the next morning. About midday he came across the windmill they had been heading for, where he hobbled into the long concrete trough and lay down in its soothing coolness, lapping the water up regularly as he rested. He remained near the water source for several hours and then in the late afternoon set off again, no longer thirsty and with some strength regained, but still very hungry.

Incapable of chasing anything down, food became anything that scurried, scuttled or slithered across Smiler's path, and he could only gaze with a drooling mouth at the occasional passing kangaroo. But one he came across on the third day didn't inspire such appetising thoughts; it wasn't even the right colour, all green, black and blue after lying dead in the sun for days. It was definitely past its prime, even for his ravenous state, although some crows and an eagle didn't seem to think so, as they dived eagerly into the inside of the carcass.

Smiler stood there surveying the decaying remains, the stench of putrefaction offending even his toughened nose, but with his strength rapidly fading he knew that he needed more than the small creepy-crawlies he had been snacking on. He stepped tentatively forward, sending the scavenging birds flapping and complaining into the sky. He nosed the disgusting mess and then took a first cautious nibble from a haunch. He chewed on the small piece of dried meat and then swallowed it. *"Mmmm... not too bad actually."* If he kept his eyes closed, his sense of smell shut down and ignored the clouds of blow-flies; he might just be able to pretend it was a meal. He proceeded to chew and pretend for as long as possible then retreated, some form of sustenance now in his stomach but only just managing to stay there in defiance of the foul odour clinging to his snout. He rubbed his face with his paws and brushed his nose in the dust, but still the smell remained. Finally he gave up and moved off again, feeling stronger but thirstier now.

Later that afternoon the screeching sound of pink and grey galahs took him once more away from his path. It sounded to him like their bath-time conversation and, after travelling half a kilometre and climbing slowly up a ridge, he looked down the other side to see them gathered in and around a small water hole at the base of some rocks. He eased his way down towards them and when he came near, they rose from their ablutions in a pastel cloud of squawking surprise, to gradually regroup on the ground a safe distance away.

Smiler quickly stuck his muzzle into the muddied liquid and greedily slurped away, the birds' sharp complaints gradually growing louder until they reached an almost deafening pitch. By now he had had a gutful of his Odyssey and he turned suddenly and barked.

"Shut up, ya crazy bastards! A dog can't even 'ear 'imself drink!"

The birds lifted as one again at the sound of the sharp rebuke then landed a little further away, still grumbling to each other about the smelly intruder but less loudly now.

After drinking to a swelling capacity, Smiler moved off, snarling at the feathered gathering as he walked past, *"Just come a little closer ya bloody lunatics and yer feathers'll be fuckin' toothpicks!"* After a few more shambling steps he added a sharp postscript. *"Fuck it all!"*

The days that followed were much the same as before, patterned by thirst, hunger and the constant hammering heat, his pads cracked and bleeding, his shoulder throbbing and his wounds festering. It was a trail of misery, occasionally embellished with a flash of danger, like the morning he awoke with a tickling sensation on his nose, to stare cross-eyed into the beady little eyes of a scorpion, its tail coiled and ready for action. He shook the creature off with a yelp, retreating almost as quickly as he did a day later, when attempting to share a cave with a King Brown. The large and very poisonous snake lashed out at him with lightning speed and sent him scrambling back out into the relentless heat. Yet he had some good fortune nearly a week into his trek. Following a fence line, he came across another windmill and found the carcass of a sheep next to the water trough. It was not long dead and he consumed the mutton with great relish, crunching joyfully on a leg bone and carrying a piece of it with him when he finally moved on the next day.

But that had been two days ago. Now he was struggling for survival again, so weak that he had to stop every ten minutes or so to rest, with each breather becoming progressively longer and each travelled section shorter and shorter, until he was barely able to manage a hundred metres before having to seek the shade of the nearest tree. There he stood on trembling legs, too frightened to lie down for fear of not being able to get up again, his smile having long since been wiped off his face, his body fast approaching capitulation. Then he heard that first faint sound of leather on willow.

*

"Out!" called Professor, holding his finger up with stern authority immediately after the wicket-keeper appealed for the catch.

"Whaddya mean?" cried Claude. "That ball hit the bloody pad!"

"What I mean, my fine fellow, is that you have been given leave to exit the arena. That you are excess to requirements and your incompetence with the willow now presents someone else with the opportunity to have a go. So, with the full power vested in me, I now repeat. You are *out*!" Professor swung his finger up again, this time accompanied by an evil smile.

This was one argument that Claude couldn't win, but that had never stopped him before and he glared at the umpire as he shuffled off towards the pub veranda, where his name was having a zero chalked up next to it on a scoreboard made of old timber planks painted black. "Bloody bullshit, Prof!" he finally protested.

Professor answered with a satisfied smile.

Charlie passed Claude halfway across the gravel playing area. "Piss poor, Claude! I suppose *I'll* 'afta get us outta the shit now!" he declared, as he headed towards the crease, resplendent in his freshly washed red and white beanie, heavy work boots and long khaki shorts, his face clean-shaven for the occasion. On his legs he wore a pair of tattered old pads with the stuffing sprouting out here and there along the seams: protection of a kind, but for what Charlie was about to receive, next to useless. On his hands he wore a pair of the leather gloves he used when sorting out the rubble on the dryblowing trays and, as the outgoing and incoming batsmen passed each other, Claude offered him some protection for the tender region of his anatomy.

"I strongly recommend that ya take this," Claude said, stopping to grope into his trousers and pull out a smelly, sweat-drenched crotch protector, about to have its eighth home for the day.

"Be buggered I will! I'm not stickin' *that* next to me jewels, mate,"

Charlie retorted. He was as rough and ready as any human could be, but when it came to testicles he preferred his own company.

"Good luck… don't say I didn' warn yaaaa," Claude sang out, waving the box in the air as he trudged away.

Charlie made all the initial moves of appearing to be a batsman, after all he had top-scored with fifteen runs the year before, even if they were made against some innocuous off-breaks that had only taken on the qualities of thunderbolts as his year-long bragging progressed. He placed his bat in front of the stumps and called for 'middle and leg', then, taking a very correct stance, he faced up; and that was about the limit of his skill as a batsman.

The first ball from Leonora's secret weapon whistled past Charlie's nose to only just be stopped by the outstretched hand of the wicket-keeper, who cried out in pain, threw off his glove and wrung his hand.

"Jeeesus Christ, mate… it's only a social match, ya know!" Charlie squealed.

The bowler smiled all the way back to his mark nearly forty metres away, then turned and came galloping in again.

The sizzling delivery cracked into Charlie's right shin, treating his batting pad with total contempt. He hurled the bat down and hopped around in a circle, howling with pain.

Reg, backing up at the other end, couldn't stifle his amusement and snorted with laughter.

Charlie got angry. He grabbed the bat and faced up again. "All right ya bastard… give us yer best!"

The next delivery came down in direct compliance with Charlie's request, fizzing straight through his elegant defence to catch him right in the head office, the sickening sound of the hardened leather ball thudding against an unprotected crotch bringing an instant silence to the field. Faces grimaced with pain and legs were mentally crossed. Then came the first low sound, starting a little like a cow in labour, before quickly building into a very good impression of an air-raid siren, followed by a gasping not dissimilar to a death rattle. Charlie dropped to his knees and the bat fell out of his hands and knocked off the bails.

"Je-e-es-us Chr-i-i-st. I'm roooned!"

It was almost with apology that Professor declared Charlie out, and the unfortunate victim was chaired back to the pub veranda by two fielders, where he was placed next to Claude, now sipping contentedly on a can of beer. In deference to Charlie's pain, he waited just a little longer than usual before singing out, "Told yaaaa."

"Shut the fuck up, Claude, or some time tomorra mornin' you'll be *shittin'* that can!" Charlie snapped, and then pulled out the top of his trousers to inspect the damage. His gear looked the same but it still felt as though a medium-sized gorilla was swinging on it.

"I believe you'll be needin' this, mate," Jim said, as he passed a glass of beer through the open window.

Charlie drank it in two gulps, and requested another. After a third glass, things began to feel a tiny bit better.

"Who is this bloke anyway? Takes it a bit serious, don't 'e?" he asked, as all eyes were trained on the bowler, raring to go again from his mark. Klaus was now facing up, the cricket bat lifted over his shoulders like a baseballer and the hygienically suspect protector firmly in place between his legs.

The young fast-bowler, who just happened to have played more than a few games of first class cricket in Perth before being recently transferred to Leonora in his job as a telephone linesman, smiled when he saw Klaus's stance, and added another few metres to his run-up.

"Arrogant bastard. We'll 'afta make sure 'e gets the man-o'-the-match award," Charlie added. Knowledge of what was in store for the recipient of the trophy brought a ripple of laughter from the others on the veranda.

"Ground the bloody thing, Klaus, or 'e'll go straight through ya!" Reg called from the bowler's end.

"Neffer you mind... I vill show him. Fucking rink-in bowler," Klaus declared bravely.

"Strike one!" a fielder called out, as the ball flew past Klaus's savage swipe and barely missed the top of the stumps.

The bowler followed through and stopped only a couple of paces away from Klaus, his hands on his hips and grinning broadly. "Next one, mate!" he threatened, before turning to stride back to his mark.

The next ball came hurtling down with added velocity, rising up from a short length in a direct line towards Klaus' head. He let loose with a swing and a prayer, closing his eyes as he followed through, but this time he connected, sending the ball flying by the hands of a fieldsman straight to the boundary for four runs. A loud cheer erupted from the gallery, the sound echoing down the hill from the pub and out into the flats, filtering through the bush and drifting faintly into the ears of a lone traveller struggling along on his last furry legs.

Klaus was ecstatic at his success. This was the first time he had ever played, only being chosen because they were a man short. Usually he would just sit on the veranda, get drunk and laugh at the stupid pommy game, but now, after that sweet hit, he believed he could get to like it.

"Next one, mate!" he mocked the man now glaring down the pitch.

To everyone's surprise, Klaus continued to hit the ball, his confidence growing with each run, the young fast bowler rapidly losing his, as his best efforts came back with interest and the heat began to take effect. The partnership between Klaus and Reg, who was the only batsman with any ability and had been there from the beginning, began to head towards what was a record for the Jimblebar cricket club, forty runs and building, Klaus having swatted twenty-five of them. Only four more runs were needed to break the record and Klaus did it in style, smashing another short-pitched delivery high into the air, this time beyond the boundary for six, sending the ball racing down the main street towards the railway line where it slowly rolled to a stop at the bottom. Reg shaded his eyes as he watched the ball go, then he saw the shape of the animal struggling across the line and heading in a slow, painful way up the road.

Smiler saw the ball bouncing down the road towards him, before it rolled to a halt a few metres away. He looked at the round leather object. Dog – ball, ball – dog. Somewhere in a fading part of his memory there was a faint command being issued. 'Fetch, Smiler, fetch!' He shuffled wearily up to the ball, then collapsed before it, his nose almost on it. *"Be buggered I will!"* he wheezed.

"What's that?" Reg called out.

"Looks like a dog," someone replied.

Reg put his bat on the ground and quickly walked down the hill. Halfway there, the fieldsman who had gone to retrieve the ball called back. "It looks like one *stuffed* dog to me."

It took Reg a little while to recognise Smiler; he was all skin and bones and coated with red dust, but his earlier suspicion was confirmed when he tentatively called his name.

"Smiler?" he queried, and saw the limp wagging response of the tail. "Jesus Christ, mate! What the bloody 'ell 'appened to you?"

"Ya wouldn' wanna know, mate," came the faint, whimpering reply.

Reg picked Smiler up and carried him to the pub veranda, where a wife of one of the station owners became his nurse.

"Ohhhh, you poor thing! You poor fella," she cooed, as she stroked Smiler's head.

"Aaaah, from hell ta heaven in just a few strokes," he sighed at the touch of the soft hands.

"Someone get some water," she requested.

"Beer would be better," came the snuffling, unheard request, but when his bowl was produced and filled with water he drank the cool fluid with almost the same relish.

"He's filthy! And look at these cuts… they're festering. They've got to be cleaned up, maybe even stitched. Bring him around to the laundry. I'll give him a wash and take a proper look there."

"Laundry? Wash?" Smiler's tired and drooping ears began to struggle into their normally pointed appearance. He knew the procedure. After every trip into the desert he had lain on the cool concrete floor watching as his partner's clothes went round and round in that machine. Now he had visions of getting the same treatment, stuffed into it, soaped and cleaned beyond recognition and then tumble dried. As for the word 'stitched', it had a certain ring of pain about it, and he'd had enough of that commodity for now. He struggled to get up and make a stagger for it, but the legs would not respond. Then he

was scooped up and carried around to the back of the pub, laid on the floor and given a gentle sponge bath by his doting nurse. "*Mmmmm, I could get used to this,*" he sighed, until the stinging of the antiseptic solution being applied to his cuts and raw feet snapped him out of his comfort. He squirmed against the burning pain, but those gentle hands now held him strongly and a firm voice told him to be still.

Jim Donnelly appeared from inside the pub. "Here ya are, mate... get this into ya," he said, as he threw a hand-sized piece of prime steak onto the floor in front of Smiler's nose. The meat disappeared as quickly as it hit the ground.

"You shouldn't have given him that yet! It might make him sick," the woman protested.

"*Every dog should be so sick,*" came the snort.

"Just crush up a few dog biscuits, and feed him that for awhile," she added.

A faint moan came from the floor.

Smiler was carried back to the front veranda after his clean up. Although his cuts were infected, once cleaned they appeared closed enough not to need stitching, and Reg, who had claimed ownership of the dog, nodded at Jill's instructions for them to be bathed with salty water each day and treated with antiseptic until they healed.

The cricket match continued for the rest of the day, with Smiler contentedly sleeping the afternoon away. He didn't even wake when loud cheering erupted from the Jimblebar team, in celebration of a win by two runs, albeit with the help of the runs that came from Bosun the galah. The bird that had been amusing and abusing everyone on the veranda for most of the afternoon had hopped onto the top of the scoreboard near the close of play and added to the score line by leaving a white, streaking dropping next to Jim Donnelly's two. At the end of the day, however, with most of the players under the weather from the ten-minute drink breaks taken every half-hour, no one noticed or even cared about the birdseed in the twelve runs that were ultimately credited to Jim.

There was a barbecue after the game, and it was then that Smiler stirred from his sleep, his nose commanding his body to rise and follow it to the front of the hotel, where the meat was sizzling on a hotplate placed over a halved forty-four gallon drum. The dog-biscuit diet went by the board over the next hour or so, as he settled himself strategically in the middle of the throng and preyed on their sympathy, hardly able to believe his change of fortune. This morning he had been near death and now he was in doggy heaven, where scraps of meat and bone rained upon him.

As the sun went down, everyone adjourned to the bar for the trophy presentation. The Jimblebar cricket team had retained the perpetual trophy, having their name inscribed on the goat's skull with a marker pen for the fourth year in succession. For the man-of-the-match however, the trophy was a little less permanent, and at first there was a little discussion as to who should get it, Klaus, with his match-winning thirty-two runs, or the bowler that Leonora had snuck in under Jimblebar's guard. He had taken eight wickets for thirty-five runs and, although the lad was on the losing side, Charlie's pleading support for him won the day, and he insisted on presenting the trophy.

"And now we come to the elite award of the evenin', folks. It gives me great pleasure to announce that the man-o-the-match trophy goes to Brian Thompson from Leonora." Cheers rang out in the bar, followed by a chorus of chuckles.

Charlie stuck his hand out to congratulate the young man, who came forward a little tentatively, suspicious about the laughter and the look of eager anticipation on most of the faces.

"Jim?" Charlie requested.

Jim turned around and took a large glass jar from a bottom shelf and shook its contents energetically before placing it on top of the bar. Then he unscrewed the lid, placed a whisky glass next to it and stood back, as if frightened of what might come out of it.

"Bottoms up, mate... and congratulations again," Charlie said cheerfully, as he slapped the lad on the shoulder. The room rang out with laughter again.

An uncertain smile formed on the face of the man-of-the-match, now fighting to cover up a look of undisguised disgust. Standing before him was a container full of brandy with the remains of a very old King Brown coiled up and pickled within, bits of its body floating around in the milky liquid, its glazed eyes staring up from the bottom of the jar, dulled but still intimidating.

Charlie dipped the glass in, filled it up and pushed it across. The contents had a strange odour, not foul but, in combination with the knowledge of its origin, most definitely stomach-turning.

"I'm not gunna drink *that*!" the young one protested.

"Ya 'ave to. It's an 'onour," Charlie stated, pushing the glass closer.

"What are you… a schicken?" Klaus called out, bravado sprouting from the relief that he hadn't won the trophy.

Everyone laughed and then started up a chant. "Schick*en*… schick*en*… schick*en*."

The chorus rolled around the bar like an ambulance siren and the victim could see he had no choice. He suddenly grabbed the glass and swallowed the contents in one gulp, followed immediately by the rest of the beer he had been drinking. But his face still contorted from the after-taste of the embalming fluid. He grabbed someone's whisky, threw that down and then looked around for more. Anything would do to kill the strange taste that clung to the inside of his mouth. His eyes darted around the room in a panic but everyone held their drinks a little closer, before Jim put him out of his misery by pouring a large brandy from a bottle without sediment.

"What's the matter with ya, son? There's nuthin' wrong with this!" Charlie crowed, and with that comment, dipped the whisky glass in and had a snort himself. "Aaaaaah," he sighed in feigned appreciation, as he put the glass back on the bar.

A brief silence descended on the room then laughter erupted again as Charlie dived for a Jim Beam bottle and swigged out of it.

"Jesus… it's gone off a bit since last year!" he sputtered. "Wouldn't fancy bein' next year's winner!"

"I dunno, that just might be you, mate!" Gary Armstrong called out. "Anyone who's been chaired off a cricket pitch has gotta have a fair bit of potential. How are they hangin', by the way?"

More laughter burst out in the room.

"Cast iron, mate. It'll take more than your secret weapon to put a dent in 'em. You'll 'afta bring a tank next time if ya expect to put me outta action," Charlie declared, in defiance of the dull throbbing still coming from below.

Jim leant down under the bar and pulled out a bottle of Bells ten-year aged whisky, holding it out to Brian. "Here's the other half of the trophy, son."

Everyone demanded that the winner share it around and within five minutes it had all gone.

At about ten o'clock the party began to wind down. It was Sunday and most of them had to work the next day. The Leonora team began to reluctantly file out and climb into the bus that had been borrowed from one of the mines. As Gary Armstrong was leaving, Reg stopped him at the door.

"Find anythin' out about the road'ouse fire?" he asked.

"Not a lot. It looks like an accident at this stage. There appears to have been a fuel leak from one of the bowsers. Anyway, that's what the experts said. But how it caught fire is still a mystery. They found what was left of Elliot lyin' in the driveway, but there wasn't enough of him to tell anybody anythin'."

"Crispy fried bacon… couldn't 'ave 'appened to a nicer pig," Charlie declared from his place at the bar.

The comment brought a wry smile to both men. Then Reg remembered something. "It looked like 'e was fiddlin' with one o' the bowsers when we were comin' back from seein' you the other day. One o' those in the middle island."

"Yeah? Well that's about where they tracked it to, but it still doesn't give any answers as to why it happened. Truth is we'll probably never know. What I can say is that we found his safe and the gold you told me about wasn't in it. But then, if he took it, he probably wouldn't have put it there. And if it was on the premises it's gunna be hard to find anyway. Junk has been sprayed all over the place. They even found a couple of bowsers about forty metres away from the building. It could be anywhere. Maybe some lucky tourist will beep it on a metal detector some day. I've sometimes seen them sniffin' around those old shafts out the back of the roadhouse."

Charlie's ears pricked up at the comment as he walked past the two men and onto the veranda, where he yelled out to the departing opposition.

"Don't forget ta come back now, will ya? *Losers* are always welcome."

"Who's that? Is that *you*, Charlie?" a voice enquired from within the bus. "Sorry, mate... couldn't recognise ya voice. Sounds a bit higher than usual."

Loud laughter trailed out of the windows as the bus rumbled off down the hill and Charlie knew that this one wouldn't be lived down for a while. But he didn't care. His mind was already on something else.

Reg walked to the end of the veranda to pick Smiler up from where he had been sleeping off his feast, noting the added weight in the dog as he carried him to the ute. He laid him down in the back and began to climb in the driver's side. As he did so, Jim came out onto the veranda, waving an envelope above his head.

"'Ang on, Reg, I nearly forgot about this. It came in on the truck yesterday afternoon." He walked towards the vehicle and handed the letter to Reg.

Reg put his glasses on and held the envelope up to catch the light coming from the pub window, faintly recognising his daughter Carol's handwriting. He placed it in his top pocket. "Thanks Jim. See ya when we see ya," he said, and then climbed into the cab.

After returning to camp, Reg brewed up a cup of tea then sat down under the light of a gas lantern to read the letter.

"Who's it from?" Charlie enquired, as he stood stripped down before the fire, having a quick wash before getting into bed.

"Carol," Reg answered, and read on without offering any more.

"Good news? Bad news?" Charlie pestered a minute later.

"If ya let me read it, I'll tell ya!"

Reg spent another five minutes slowly reading the three pages before putting them back into the envelope and going into the hut to file it away in his suitcase cupboard. Then he went back outside, stripped down and took his turn in the washing basin, pouring cold water over his head from a jam tin dipped in the small bucket by his feet. He shivered and complained with the shock of the water, as he quickly lathered his lean and still firm body, before repeating the shower. He towelled down, took the waste water over to their two-metre-square vegetable patch, lifted up the shadecloth insect cover and poured the soapy liquid around the two spinach plants, one tomato bush and a healthy looking brush of young shallots; then he climbed into bed.

"Vegies are lookin' good," he said, as he stretched out.

"Well! What's in the bloody letter?" Charlie blurted out.

"We're gunna 'ave a visitor," came the casual reply. "Me grandson Kenny's been gettin' inta a bit o' trouble down in Perth. 'E's inta the booze and the fightin', and now the cops 'ave picked 'im up fer stealin' a car. 'E's got off with a fine and probation for this one, but 'e's been warned that next time it's gunna be detention. Carol's asked if she can send 'im up 'ere for a while, to get 'im away from the crew 'e's been mixin' with."

"How old's 'e now?"

"'Bout sixteen."

"Sounds about the right age fer trouble," Charlie assessed. "Yeah... send 'im up here. We've gotta dog now... might as well 'ave a kid as well."

"I 'aven't seen 'im since he was about seven. From all accounts 'e's been okay 'til the last coupla years," Reg added.

"Aaar... the fireworks 'ave gone off, mate, the 'ormones 'ave been lit up. Not a lot ya can do about that. Tell Carol not to worry. We'll sort 'im out. A while on the end of a shovel and 'e'll be too tired for anythin' but sleepin'."

The two lay there in silence for a few minutes then Charlie brought up the thing that had been on his mind ever since they had left the pub, "Whaddya reckon we take a sniff around the roadhouse with the detectors?"

"No."

"Why not? That big piece at least has gotta be worth a few grand," Charlie protested.

Reg began counting off the reasons. "Because, one: I'm not goin' sniffin' 'round there like a ghoul. Two: we still don't know for sure if 'e took Johnno's gold. An' three: even if it is there somewhere, there's so much rubbish around that spot, ya could be searchin' for a year before ya found anythin'. If ya wanna make a mug o' yerself, go an' do it. I'll be quite 'appy ta stick ta where I know there will be gold."

"Yeah, tooth fillin's, mate. Don't ya ever get sick of breakin' yer back fer bugger all? I know I do."

"It's enough fer me. I'm gettin' a regular feed and puttin' a bit aside, and I've got me freedom. What more can a man want?"

"What 'appens when yer too old to swing a shovel or a metal detector? What then? I don't wanna end up rottin' away in some old fogies 'ome, 'avin' me arse wiped by some girl young enough to be me granddaughter!"

"Oh, I dunno... doesn't sound too bad to me."

"Joke about it all ya like, mate, but that's where we're 'eaded if we don't get somethin' more substantial together."

"It doesn' matter 'ow much dough ya've got... we all end up on the same mulch 'eap. Ya never know, ya might zap a hundred-ouncer one day and drop dead from the shock of it... then that'll solve all yer problems."

"Yeah... well, more gold will buy a bit o' comfort at the end, that's all I know, an' I don't see why we shouldn't be tryin' every angle to get it."

Reg closed the matter with no reply and the two men eventually drifted off to sleep but, lying on the ground next to Reg's bed, a certain dog was still awake, thinking about what he had heard, and remembering. His survival test was over and life had suddenly become pretty cushy, but memories of his former partner and the fate he had suffered were still fresh in his mind. He missed Johnno. He had been a good mate despite all the arguments. And it had all come about because of those bloody stones. Suddenly he got angry.

"I wouldn't go chasin' those fuckin' stones if I were you!" he barked loudly at Charlie.

Charlie was suddenly snapped out of his snoring nirvana. "Jeeesus *bloodee* Christ!" he moaned.

Reg's hand flopped down and clumsily patted Smiler's head. "She'll be right, mate. Go ta sleep."

Smiler raised his jowls from where they had been pushed into the dirt. "*Thanks fer that… I feel so much better now,*" he snorted, sputtering the grains of sand away before lowering his head again.

The snoring soon resumed and Smiler sighed in resignation as he prepared to join the sleepers, but something in the sound of the wind drifting through the camp caused his ears to prick up. He thought about barking again, but if the two-legged ones didn't seem capable of hearing what he had to say when he was on full throttle, he doubted if they could hear what was whispering through the camp now. Indeed, he had often wondered if any of them could ever hear anything.

Ten

Cassie stood at the front door of her house and watched vacantly as the two policemen walked back to their patrol car. She was shocked by the news, but somehow not surprised. Two nights ago she had felt something was wrong. It was the twin thing again. Usually the connection came like a faint memory, something intangible, intruding on her thoughts like a flash of déjà vu and nearly always before one of her brother Kevin's infrequent letters or telephone calls. But this time it had come in the form of a terrifying nightmare.

On the night of the dream, Cassie had come home early from her late shift as a barmaid with a local hotel, finally capitulating to a prolonged dose of summer flu, and, after washing down two headache pills with a shot of brandy, she had taken her misery to bed. The medicine had worked, quickly drugging her to sleep, but the potent combination eventually dragged her down into a darker level, where the demons of nightmare waited to claw at her from the shadows.

The woman's voice had come faintly at first, drifting to her on a hot, dry wind that blew from a strange, pink-coloured, flat and desolate landscape, the wailing of the wind breaking up the sentence and making it sound like an interrupted radio signal. "*It's...ti... re...now... sie,*" the broken message came. She walked towards the voice as it called out again, the tone growing louder but the words still remaining unclear. She saw a figure up ahead and felt compelled to run towards it, but stopped as she drew closer. Now she recognised her brother Kevin, but something was terribly wrong. All she could see was the upper part of his body protruding above the pink sand, and on his face a look of horror.

The wind blew stronger and again the voice spoke those broken words. Then she saw something moving under the sand. Like a giant worm the unseen thing came on, moving swiftly and rhythmically, leaving a trail of mounded dirt in its wake as it snaked towards her brother. But just before it reached him it suddenly disappeared. The nightmare hung in a moment of terrible anticipation, then the dirt suddenly exploded behind Kevin. She drew back in horror as the form of a giant golden serpent rose out of the earth, its mouth agape and eyes blazing red. It hissed evilly then, almost comically, began to bark like a dog; a sharp bark that hurt her ears, before its huge fangs closed over the top of her brother's head and sunk into his eyeballs, sending blood spurting all over her. "*It's...ti...re...now...sie,*" the woman's voice repeated, just before the serpent coiled its golden body around Kevin's and dragged him into the earth, his arms thrashing about wildly and hands slapping and clawing at the dirt as he disappeared.

Cassie heaved loudly as she emerged from the dream, frantically trying to wipe the blood away from her face as she sat up in bed. She turned on the bedside lamp and looked at her hands, snorting with relief to see only sweat there instead of fingers dripping crimson. But her consciousness was stained and her mind would constantly resurrect the terrifying imagery until a visit from the police put any sort of meaning to the dream.

Dreams. There was not a night went by when Cassie didn't have them and subsequently try to analyse them, shuffling through their jumbled messages attempting to find the logical source. Mostly the connection would be obvious, flashing familiarly from a recent incident or image, but sometimes they were more than just the confused record of her existence. Sometimes they appeared to link up with incidents years after she had dreamt them, as if there were some other channel open out there and her dreams were the tuning knob.

As she watched the police car drive off, she felt she now understood the message the most recent one had sent. Her brother had died the night of her dream. She had looked at the clock not long after being shocked into waking. It was 10 o'clock at night in outer suburban Sydney, which meant it was seven o'clock in the west; according to the police, about the time that her brother's car had run off a deserted country road and slammed into a giant boulder. But what was the golden snake with the crazy bark all about, and the woman's voice that seemed to be calling her name?

As sibling relationships went, she and her brother were not very close. He was a drifter, a loner, and she hadn't heard from him for over two years; hadn't seen him for ten. But in the way of their genetic relationship, he always seemed to get in touch with her whenever there had been some trauma in her life, such as the divorce, or when her daughter had left home to go pot-smoking and tree-hugging in a Queensland rainforest. Then there had been the time she was very ill with pleurisy. Yet, although he cared enough to respond to the mysterious news service that sometimes ran between them, she could not claim to know much about him. What she did know, however, was that he hadn't made much of his life, wandering around for years in a West Australian desert, chasing gold and finding very little. That was something they did have in common. She couldn't claim to have had any more success in her assault on life either. Right at this moment her path felt as though it had taken a detour into a rubbish tip. She was divorced, alone, working in a poorly paid job, renting a pretty ordinary house and driving a twelve-year-old Ford Falcon that kept breaking down. The balance of her bank account currently stood at the grand total of three hundred and seventy-one dollars and sixty-two cents, two hundred of which was soon to be ripped out for the next fortnight's rent, and she still had the rotten flu. She sniffed as she reached for another tissue, the natural sadness at losing a brother mixing tears with the phlegm of her affliction.

Now she had another problem. She would have to go over to Kalgoorlie and organise the burial. But she had little finance; and would the car make it? It took her about an hour to decide what to do. She despised her occupation, having to serve up alcohol, cigarettes, fat snacks and bright, cheerful conversation to the drivelling ones on the other side of the bar. After ten years she felt she had heard and seen it all, and the thought of going in there every afternoon to breathe that sickly stale atmosphere of alcohol-shampooed carpets and smoked furniture had simply become nauseating. She had nothing to lose by tossing it all in. She would sell her car and the furniture, and there was also the bond money on the house. Of course there was little hope of getting any of the several thousand dollars she had lent to her daughter over the years. She hadn't heard from Julia for a long time and after their last conversation she doubted if it would be anytime soon. On that occasion she had hardly recognised the voice when she first picked up the phone, and the rest of the call had gone accordingly, as if she was talking to a stranger.

"Hiiiii... Muuuum," the greeting had drifted dreamily through the receiver.

"Julia... is that you?" She had to ask, even though there was no one else on the planet that would be calling her 'Mum'.

"Nooo... Muuuum, it's Pixie now. I changed my name."

"What!"

"Don't get stressed out, Muuuum. We all decided to change our names to be more in tune with the environment. I was given Pixie Green Leaves. I think it's a great name, don't you?"

"I'll tell you what I think, Julia. I think you've been smokin' too many dried bloody leaves! Please tell me that it's just a nickname! Please don't tell me that you've done something official about it!"

There was a short silence on the other end before her daughter's dreamy monotone came again. "We all went into Cairns a few months ago and changed our names by deed poll. It's what I wanted to do. Don't get upset, Muuuum... names don't mean a lot"

"Then why didn't you keep the perfectly good one I gave you?" Cassie yelled down the line.

There was no answer, so Cassie continued, "What is it you rang about, anyway? I'm sure it wasn't just to tell me you've changed your name. You obviously didn't think it was important enough to tell me earlier."

"I wanted to know if you could lend me some money, Muuuum. Our car's broken down. Jai said it's gunna cost five hundred dollars to fix. He said it's somethin' to do with the gearbox... or somethin'."

It took a second for Cassie to explode again. "You tell this bloody Jai... Great Bugger of the Forest, or whatever *his* name is, to get off his arse and go and earn the money! I'm not your bloody piggy bank! I'm already payin' for you and your shower of dole-bludgin' buddies through the tax they take out of my wages! There'll be no more! And I don't care what you've changed your name to. As far as I'm concerned it is Julia. I didn't spend five hours screamin' my guts out in a labour ward to deliver a spaced-out garden gnome! Goodbye, Julia... ring me when you've returned to planet Earth!" With that, she slammed the phone down.

That had been over eighteen months ago, and since the aunt and uncle who had brought her up died several years ago, she no longer had any close contact with any blood relations. So it was not difficult to decide to leave. Hopefully, after the liquidation of her scanty assets, she could get enough together to pay for a train fare, the burial expenses and some accommodation. Maybe she would go on to Perth afterwards and try to find a job there. She began planning the trip and started to become excited about it. It was a sad thing to be burying a brother, even as distant as he had been, but she felt like it was giving her a new direction.

A fortnight later Cassie set off, all her possessions now contained in two medium-sized suitcases, the car and all of her furniture sold through an auction house for about a third of their worth and her refunded bond money only half of what she expected because she hadn't given the required month's notice. But she figured she had enough funds to get her there, pay for the funeral, and survive for a little while. After that she hadn't a clue, and as she stepped onto the Indian Pacific and made her way to her seat in the second-class section, she found that she didn't really care. She suddenly felt wonderfully free.

*

Cassie sat in room twenty-two of the Golden Mile motel, Kalgoorlie, staring at the small ceramic jar she had purchased at a local op shop. Inside it was her brother's ashes, and next to it stood a cardboard box of all that remained of his worldly goods. The long train trip over had been relaxing, but now that sense of freedom had gone. Her financial calculations hadn't quite worked out the way she had hoped and she was nearly broke again, after having to sell off all her brother's tools and prospecting gear to help pay for his cremation. She had taken it to a store that dealt in used mining equipment and, judging by the amount she received, suspected the manager was related in some way to the owner of the auction house in Sydney. After the trauma of having to officially identify her brother in the local hospital's morgue, something she could only do by a distinctive tear-shaped birthmark on an underarm, there was the guilt of not being able to pay for a proper funeral, or even the simplest headstone. All she could afford was just a cremation without ceremony, although her guilt about that was alleviated a bit by the knowledge that Kevin was a loner and would have preferred no fuss. The police had given her directions to where he died and to a place called Jimblebar, where they said he had some contact with other prospectors. She wanted to visit both places and scatter his ashes somewhere in the country he seemed to love, but all she had left now was enough money for a couple of nights at a cheap motel – then what? A stroll through the town that evening soon provided the answer, but it was not the one she desired.

'Barmaid wanted' said the words chalked up on a small blackboard outside the old hotel. She looked at the sign with dread, but knew at this moment she had no alternative. She entered and ten minutes later had a job, with the same poor wages, same stale atmosphere and the same old clientele.

She moved into cheaper accommodation at a caravan park, and her days began to follow the pattern they had back in Sydney; afternoon shift at the pub, come back to her caravan, sleep in till late morning, have something to eat, read a bit, then go to work. Depressingly, nothing seemed to have changed for her, if anything things had become worse, having to wake up in an oven every morning, and put up with the noise that went with living in a caravan park: kids screaming around the place; raging domestics between those who had succumbed to the claustrophobia, and the ignorance of others who wanted everyone else to hear their taste in music or television. The one bonus was that she was managing to save a little money, her only expenditure on anything besides food and accommodation being the purchase of paperbacks from a second-hand bookstore. Like Kevin, she had a strong reading habit and it was this that eventually changed her direction.

Interspersed with reading the books, Cassie had also begun perusing her brother's diaries, and day by day she would get closer to the last words that he wrote, learning about his hatred of the heat, but of his love for the isolation and the beauty of the desert wilderness. She began to understand a little more about the type of person he was, and a lot about the character of a dog called Smiler and the pub at this place called Jimblebar, but it wasn't until two weeks later that she got to the ecstatic declaration on the last page of the last diary. Kevin's jubilant words about the gold instantly took up residence in her mind and began to dominate it completely. By then she'd had more than enough of her new job and the revelation in her brother's diary seemed to be the only way ahead; the only hope of escaping a life destined to be spent shrivelling up behind hotel bars.

Her brother's meticulously kept records were almost like painting-by-number directions to the gold, but Cassie knew that she would need help to find it and her mind eventually drifted back to one of the entries in an earlier diary. She searched through them and found the page. It read, '*Ran into Reg Arnold today, way out near the salt lake country. We talked all arvo. Learnt he was an orphan too. Loves the desert. Good bloke.*' It was a typical entry, short and sharp, but it gave her enough of a lead. After reading those words, Cassie tore the page out and added it to the one she had taken out of the last diary, along with the map. Now she had another reason to go to Jimblebar.

Cassie didn't quit her job; instead she took a couple of days off during the next week, hired a car and drove up north on a reconnaissance mission. She needed to find out what type of person Reg Arnold was. She had come to the conclusion after years of listening over the bar, and through her own marital strife, that there weren't many men who could be trusted, especially when it came to money. It wasn't as if she was completely sour on the male of the species, but they weren't going to get her again.

Eleven

"That must be 'im," Reg said, as he swung the ute around in front of the Kalgoorlie railway station.

It was Saturday afternoon, two weeks after Reg had received the letter from his daughter, and his grandson had finally arrived on the train from Perth. The boy was sitting on the pavement with his back against the wall of the station building, looking the part, surly after a run in with a self-important railway employee who, upon seeing the figure with legs sprawled out on the footpath, had immediately assumed that he was drunk or doped out.

"Ya can't 'ang 'round there!" the man had snapped.

"Go an' get fucked! I'm waitin' for me grandfather!" young Kenny Edwards had snapped back.

"Yeah? Well you're an obstruction to people usin' the footpath and if ya don't move, I'll get the coppers to move ya!"

Kenny slowly drew his knees up in a compromise and the man stared for a moment then let it be. But as he walked away, Kenny switched on the portable boom-box sitting next to him. The heavy metal sound of Def Leppard came roaring out of it with head-banging volume.

The man stopped, turned around and stared at the defiant boy for a few seconds, then yelled, "There's a law against that too! Turn it down!"

Kenny eyeballed him intensely for a few more seconds, then

reached over and hit the stop button. "There oughta be a fuckin'
law against you!" he called out, as the man turned and walked away
again.

The little intrusion into Kenny's sour frame of mind had just added
to the growing resentment about where he was heading, out into the
dust and the heat and the flies. He didn't have to come of course; but
he had given in to his parent's pleading and had decided to give it a
go, the threat of detention next time leaving him something to think
about. It was his last chance and he knew it, coming as it had at the
end of a long string of warnings, and he had to admit that, at first,
the thought of going gold digging had given him some slight interest,
but right at this moment he was inclined to tell *everyone* to go and get
fucked.

Charlie stared at the boy with some confusion, his mind running
through a personal colour chart. He'd never seen him before but
he had once met his part Aboriginal father, and Don was as light-
skinned as Carol, yet the person sitting there looked almost like a full
blood. As usual, he couldn't contain himself.

"Jesus… 'e's a bit dark, mate. Either Carol picked up the wrong
baby at the 'ospital or the kid's been spendin' a lotta time down the
beach."

Reg didn't say anything, he just cast the usual hard look in response
to the less tasteful levels of his mate's humour, but he had to admit
to a little surprise himself at the lad's extra duskiness, even though
his daughter had mentioned it in one of her letters. It was unusual,
but it seemed that something extra from the past had found its way
through.

The ute came to a stop in front of the station building and the two
men got out. Smiler stood up in the back of the vehicle, walked to the
side and stared curiously at the teenager.

"You'd be young Kenny," Reg said. "I'm yer grandfather."

The boy stood up slowly. He was tall for his age, well built and reasonably good looking, although his face was erupting with the plague
of the teenager. He lightly shook the hand that was offered. Then he
eyed Charlie sullenly: the clash with the station employee was still

sitting resentfully in his mind, and what he detected in Charlie's eyes instantly resurrected it.

"Who's 'e? Nobody told me a honky was gunna be part o' the deal."

"What!" Charlie exclaimed and stepped forward aggressively, until he was halted by Reg's hand.

"Oh, *yeah*... this is gunna be *real* good!" Charlie groaned, as he turned around and got back into the car.

Reg stared at his grandson, his smile gone, totally taken aback by the overt animosity. "That's no bloody way ta speak ta people! Charlie's a mate o' mine... but you'll be callin' him Mr Anderson until yer manners improve!"

"I'll call him nuthin'!" the youth sneeringly replied, placing the boom-box with care in the back of the ute before roughly throwing his bag in and climbing on.

Reg got into the cab and it was about one second before Charlie spoke, "Never mind the chip, mate... there's a 'ole bloody wood 'eap there."

Reg didn't answer. He could've made a wisecrack about the fair-sized chip he knew his partner also carried around, no matter how much he tried to disguise it with humour, but he was preoccupied by this stranger in their midst. Blood relation or not, he was now beginning to feel distinctly uncomfortable about the disruption he could see coming to his peaceful existence.

Smiler sat on his haunches, eyeing the stranger closely as the car sped off up the highway. His injuries had healed well, but his fur still remained patchy around the abrasions, giving him a distinctly ragged appearance, and it drew a snarling comment from the newcomer.

"What are *you* grinnin' at, ya mangy lookin' mongrel?"

Smiler's head turned quizzically to the side. *"I dunno, son... I left me 'uman book back at the camp,"* he snorted, and then lay down on the floor. After a minute or so, he felt a hand come down and affectionately rub his ears, only for a moment, but it confirmed what he had seen in the boy's eyes and his tail slapped a brief, lazy acceptance on the floor of the ute.

They got back to camp in the late afternoon, and there the city dweller entered the first phase of culture shock when he was shown the rough timber bunk he had to sleep in, lovingly crafted by the two men in less than half an hour and covered with an old foam mattress, a sheet and a couple of blankets. More shock followed when he was directed to the kamikaze loo, and then informed that he would be sharing in the cooking duties.

"Don't even know 'ow ta fuckin' cook," he complained.

"That's all right... Mr Anderson doesn't know either," Reg replied.

Another moan of complaint came when he was told that reveille was usually at around four in the morning, when he would be getting up to go digging with them but, tomorrow being Sunday, he could sleep in.

"Big fuckin' deal!" came the reaction; then he didn't speak for the rest of the afternoon, even after Charlie took off to go to the pub. He just wandered around the camp then went and sat on the top of the hill for a while staring out on the horizon; no city noises now to drown out the teenage questions in his head; no mates to come and pick him up for another adventure in the night. He felt homesick and alone, except for the animal that had been dogging him all afternoon, and which now sat next to him staring into the bush as he unconsciously stroked its fur. His hand withdrew suddenly when Reg came to get him for dinner.

For most of the meal they sat in silence, and Reg didn't ask any questions about the trouble that had brought his grandson there; his daughter had told him enough of that in the letter and the build up to it in the others sent over the last couple of years. They had all read the same: teenager troubles, nothing that most parents hadn't experienced. But the problems were exacerbated by their son's seething resentment about where his colour had placed him in society, seeming to want to take it out on nearly everyone around him; not only on whites, but also on any of his own race who appeared to be in union with them. Carol bemoaned her inability to set him straight, fighting a constant war with him since his early teens when the police first started turning up over his petty thieving, brawling and vandalism. It was even more frustrating for his father, the experience Don had gained from his work with homeless Aboriginal kids proving useless in the effort to sort out his own son. Kenny had simply refused to go back to school at the beginning of the year, and the last letter was full of the fear that he was heading for a lifetime of crime and prison, just like so many others who had been unable to remove the swaddling cloth of prejudice wrapped around them at birth.

"How's yer sister gettin' on?" Reg asked, as he poured out two cups of tea. The last he had heard of his granddaughter, Sylvia, was that she had passed her matriculation and was intending to go to a technical college to study journalism.

"Yeah, she's doin' okay... turned into a good little girl, she has. Looks white... thinks white."

Reg drank his tea and then got up from the table, poured a little hot water into a small basin and began to wash the dirty dishes. After he had finished the first one he pulled a tea towel down from the rafter above him, and then threw it at the youth.

"You wipe!" came the curt command.

Kenny retired to bed soon after his silent wiping of the dishes and a very nervous visit to the toilet, where he had listened with concern to the creaking and groaning of the floor under him and flashed the torch around constantly, looking for snakes or whatever else might be crawling through the darkness.

Reg sat up by the fire for about another hour. For some silly reason he had imagined his grandson would be sitting next to him, watching worlds crumbling and being rebuilt in the glowing coals, relaxing and pouring out all his problems. Instead he found himself wondering if he could ever get Kenny to speak about anything. The kid didn't even bid him goodnight, just sounded out his last statement for the day and what seemed to be his general attitude to life, by farting at it before he quickly went to sleep.

Three hours later the camp was aroused by the noisy arrival of Charlie's ute skidding to a halt outside the hut, sending a cloud of dust over the two sleepers. He got out, singing loudly and badly.

Reg groaned as he awoke. Putting up with a drunk when you were sober was one thing, suffering one when you were trying to sleep was unbearable. He listened to his partner stumbling around for a couple of minutes, howling like a banshee, before he heard a splashing sound on the leaf litter under the willow, followed by a short trumpet solo, a groan of relief, then silence. He began to relax. Then the singing started up again.

"Aaar, fer Chrissake… shut up and go to bed!"

Charlie took the comment as an invitation to talk. "Ya wouldn' guess what I found out tonight, mate. I was drinkin' with Klaus and ya wouldn' believe it! The beautiful Anna he's always cryin' over… well, she's a *dog*! She's a bloody *dog*!" A fit of laughter followed from him.

Reg lay there waiting, suffering, while Charlie laughed his way into bed.

"Whaddya mean… a dog?" he finally asked, fully awake now and mildly curious. "That's no way to speak about a bloke's woman. No one's ever seen 'er, so 'ow do ya know?"

Charlie sputtered out the news in between his laughter, "He showed me a photo. She's a… she's a bloody *dog*! A bitch! A bloody great, woolly German Shepherd! We'd been arguin' all night about which dog breed was the best an' then 'e finally pulls out a picture of this thing with a blue ribbon slung around its neck. It won first prize at some bloody dog show!"

Charlie's words brought a subdued snigger from Reg, a lustful sigh from Smiler, but an angry response from young Kenny.

"Fuck this!" he cried out, after impatiently waiting for everyone to shut up. "I'm gunna sleep inside the hut!" He then picked up his bedding and tramped off.

"Yeah, you go in there, son… yer braver than both of us. We won't sleep in there durin' the summer. It's because of the snakes, ya see," Charlie said quietly.

Kenny returned a few seconds later, slammed his bedding back on his bed, climbed in and pulled the blankets up over his ears.

Charlie giggled, and then leaned over towards Reg.

"Has 'e met Cedric yet?" he whispered.

"Naah, 'e wasn't around tonight," Reg replied, smiling a little at the thought of the city boy meeting their resident dragon, a two-metre long bungarra lizard that often prowled around the hut looking for meal leftovers. Charlie had named it Cedric because it reminded him of an uncle of his, although he found more to like in the reptile than its now deceased namesake.

"Coupla bits o' bacon should work," Charlie suggested, before quickly falling asleep.

*

The next morning a sound came roaring into Charlie's ears like a Harley Davidson starting up next to his bed, the drum solo of Dire Straits' *Money For Nothing* opening the way for a guitar riff that exploded like hand grenades inside his head, blasting his eyelids open and appearing to lift his body off the mattress.

After recovering from the initial shock, Charlie raised himself up slowly, straight-backed, like Frankenstein's monster in the first realisation of life, although the mad scientist would almost certainly have knocked this effort on the head. He was wearing the ever-present red and white beanie and, this being Sunday morning, he carried the regulation seven-day growth upon his face. He closed his eyes against the glare of the sun and swivelled his head slowly from side to side in the morning ritual to loosen up his spine. His mouth was agape like one of those clowns' heads at the Royal Show waiting for a table tennis ball to be fed in, except that a fly entered his, and as he breathed it in he shivered with disgust, coughing, choking and sputtering in the effort to get rid of it.

It was not a pretty sight from where young Kenny was seated, feet up on the meal table and cigarette in hand. At first he had been amused by his provocative little act in cranking the boom-box up to maximum; it was the first time he had ever witnessed the miracle of human levitation, but now he looked on with awe at the thing that had risen from the nearly dead.

The machine-gun guitar kept firing and the words of the pop song ricocheted like bullets around the inside of Charlie's head.

"What the bloody 'ell!" he finally croaked, after giving up and swallowing the fly. He peered at the boom-box then shifted to the side of the bed, rubbed his face and stood up unsteadily, before leaning down to pick up his trousers from where he had dropped them in the dirt. He took out his wallet and shuffled over to the source of the noise.

"Ow much do ya reckon this'd be worth, son?" he asked, switching the player off as he spoke.

"Dunno... 'bout fifty bucks," came the reply dressed with a questioning scowl.

Charlie opened his wallet and counted out the correct amount. Then he picked up his purchase, put it under his arm and walked off up the hill.

"Where the fuck are ya goin' with that?" Kenny yelled out alarmingly.

"I'm just goin' ta install a music system in the ol' Laxative," Charlie casually replied.

"Bring it back ya bastard!"

The helpless cry followed Charlie as he disappeared inside the loo, where he promptly dropped the boom-box into the sinister darkness below and listened with satisfaction to the cracking and crunching of plastic as it went on its way. Then he sat down and carried out a satisfying finishing touch.

When he came back about five minutes later he was greeted by a very unhappy teenager and a glum looking Reg, just returned from gathering kindling.

"I oughta smash ya fuckin' head in, ya crazy bastard!" Kenny threatened.

"Easy, breezy... ya've got a long way ta go," Charlie calmly replied.

"That was a bit rough. Ya coulda jest turned it down," Reg said.

"The kid needs to be brought into line. 'E needs a bit o' discipline an' I jest gave 'im some. Ya don't walk inta someone else's 'ome an' jest take over. I'm not gunna put up with listenin' to that crap first thing in the mornin'!"

"Better than the fuckin' crap you were singin' out last night... ya fuckin' white cunt!" a seething Kenny fired back.

"What! I'll give ya white cunt... ya fuckin' black bastard!" Charlie yelled.

With that the two of them rushed at each other, almost coming to grips before Reg stepped in between. Then Smiler got into the act, barking out loudly in remonstration, and making the three of them stop and look at him in puzzlement as he did three-sixties in his excitement.

"Shut up, Smiler, ya crazy bastard!" Charlie finally shouted.

"Crazy is as crazy does, mate! I'm not the one who's fightin' over the colour of a bloke's fur!" came the instant, loud reply. Smiler then turned and walked away, barking another rebuke that tailed off into a complaining growl.

The canine interruption seemed to work, and the two who were about to take to each other, separated, Charlie wandering off to have a shave and Kenny slumping down at the table again, to stew in his miserable situation. He had begun to think that a detention centre mightn't be such a bad option compared to this place, and was further convinced when he saw what was now slowly making its way across the ground towards him.

"Jesus *Christ*! What the fuck is that?" he yelled.

Cedric had finally come out of his hole to be introduced, reptilian body slowly swaying from side to side, tongue darting out and clawed feet making a scraping sound on the ground as he approached, his small dark eyes appearing to fix Kenny with a hungry stare. Then Cedric suddenly made a rush towards him, knocking over a chair as he made for the bacon that Charlie had quietly removed from the gas fridge and dropped just behind the boy.

Kenny screamed and jumped up. Charlie roared with laughter.

"Fuck it all! I'm gettin' outta this mad'ouse!" Kenny declared. He stormed inside the hut, grabbed his bag and started to stride off down the track.

"See ya, son. We'll come down and pick ya body up some time tomorra," Charlie yelled after the fast-moving figure.

Kenny dropped his bag and came charging back. This time Reg had no opportunity to break it up, as the teenager laid into Charlie, fists going like pistons, blows raining in from all angles.

"Ya fuckin' old bastard! Ya fuckin' white prick!" he screamed as he flailed away.

A few punches caught their mark but, despite his advancing years, Charlie was a tough nut and he easily absorbed the punishment as he waited for the opening. It soon came and he quickly stopped the enraged youth with two vicious blows to the stomach and a jabbing uppercut that sent him crashing to the ground. It was all over in less than a minute, but he remained standing over the winded Kenny, ready to knock him down again if he tried to get up.

"What's the matter with ya?" Reg shouted, as he roughly pushed Charlie away. "Whaddya think ya doin' beltin' a bloody kid like that?"

"Well, the bloody kid belted me first... and it was only a bloody joke! 'E's gunna 'afta lighten up a bit if 'e's gunna stay 'round 'ere," Charlie declared, feeling a little guilty about what he'd done, but determined to defend a position he felt was under threat from the first time the kid had opened his mouth.

Kenny got to his feet. All he had suffered was a slight cut to his upper lip, but there was a large bruise on his fighting pride. He used to think he was pretty good in a scrap and was always trying to prove it, but a pensioner had just whipped him and he felt a strange sense of shame and embarrassment; of not being in control any more. The wind and the confidence had been knocked out of him and he realised now that no one was going to take any crap from him out here, including his grandfather.

Kenny sat down again at the table and Reg sat opposite, tapping the top of it forcefully as he began to lay down the law.

"Right! Let's get a few things straight 'ere. Yer parents 'ave given me the job of tryin' to 'elp keep ya outta trouble. So while yer 'ere, what I say goes. I'm not sendin' ya back until the three months are up. An' the first thing you'll be doin' is ta start showin' some respect, or what 'e gave ya'll be nuthin' ta what I'll 'and out!"

"As fer you, mate," he called out to Charlie, who was now replacing the shaving foam wiped off in the scuffle, "Try an' tweak the timin' o' that 'ilarious sense o' 'umour. Ya know... so we c'n actually get a laugh out of it."

"Wood 'eap mate," came the casual reply, which fired up Reg a little more.

"Yeah... and it doesn't need any o' yours added to it!"

That one stung Charlie into silence, but Kenny had the bad judgement to have a moan again.

"He chucked me blaster down the fuckin' shit 'ole!"

Reg leant across the table, lined him up and gave him a measured backhander across the face, the action inflicting as much shock as pain.

"That's another thing! You'd better start learnin' ta talk without usin' that sorta language every time ya draw breath, or there'll be more o' that! He shouldna done it, but 'e's paid ya, so that's an end of it!"

"He hasn't paid fer the fu... fer the tape," Kenny replied, grimacing as he rubbed his cheek.

"'Ow much?" Reg snapped.

"Dunno. Mum got it for me." Kenny's head turned slightly towards Charlie before adding loudly, "It was a goin' away present!"

Charlie calmly continued with his shaving

"Right. I'll sort that out with yer mother," Reg said. "Now that's an end of it!" He stared straight into the boy's eyes as he spoke, daring him to say something else.

Kenny nodded sullenly and the camp grew quiet once more, the rest of the day following suit, with Charlie spending a large part of it lying on his bed recovering from the night before, while Reg read a book he had picked up in Kalgoorlie about vegetable growing. But, despite the seemingly peaceful resolution, something had been set in motion that day and neither partner felt comfortable about it.

There was a pile of old magazines in the hut and Kenny flicked through them for a while before taking a nap. Then he awoke late in the afternoon and decided to go for a walk.

"Don't go far." Reg advised. "Even experienced bushmen c'n get lost in this country. Take a bottle o' water and some matches. Keep an eye to this 'ill and don't go near any old mineshafts."

Kenny set off with Smiler in tow, the severe heat of the day now waning as he and the dog walked down from the camp, heading in an easterly direction. Strangely, after the blow up that morning he had begun to feel a little better about being out here. A boundary had been set, but within it he began to feel a sense of freedom, and he strolled along almost resigned to his immediate future, soaking in the wilderness around and feeling more at home in the environment.

As instructed, he kept a constant eye to the hill, until Smiler spotted a mob of kangaroos slowly hopping by, starting to move around again as the day cooled down. The cattle dog couldn't help himself and took off. As he disappeared from view, a concerned Kenny followed, hurrying along as Smiler's barking grew fainter, then starting to run when he could no longer hear it. Eventually he had to stop to regain his breath, but when he looked in the direction from which they had come, the hill where the camp stood had melted into the rolling landscape, an indistinct, dull green vista that stared back in silent indifference to his plight.

Kenny stood wheezing and panting as he scanned the horizon. Where there had been one hill there now seemed to be several, all appearing like the same little bumps in the low canopy of the scrubland. He knew enough to head into the setting sun, which was now starting to sink below the horizon, but he had no specific direction to follow, and in the first uncomfortable realisation that he may be lost, he yelled out loudly for Smiler; but there was no sound or sign of him. He took a drink from the water bottle and set off, still calling the dog every minute or so as he unknowingly headed in a north-westerly direction away from the camp. Soon the sun dipped below the horizon and dusk spread across the land. Half an hour later it was dark and Kenny no longer had any indication of where to go, which was fortunate for him, because it stopped him going even further from the camp that was now a few kilometres away to the south. He did the only thing he could do. He walked to the top of the nearest hill and prepared to build a fire, picking up the abundant dead branches that lay around then placing them against a tree. When that caught he hoped it would be enough for someone to see. And it would have been, except for the two larger hills that stood between him and the campsite. He lit the kindling and sat down nearby as the flames quickly took hold. The light and warmth gave him some security, but there was still the fear of the darkness beyond the flames, and of being alone. He took his pack of cigarettes from his shirt pocket and found the fat one with the twisted ends. It was his last joint and he figured that this was the perfect time to smoke it.

*

"Kenny... Kenny!" Reg bellowed out from the side of the hill, his eyes scanning the scrub below. Dusk was about to fall and he was getting worried. Some start to the kid's rehabilitation, he thought; lost in the desert on the second day. He turned to Charlie. "Bugger this... you light a bonfire 'ere and I'll take a drive 'round. Fire off the shotgun occasionally."

Charlie nodded glumly at the instructions, irritated now at having to help save the newcomer who had got up his nose from minute one. Some *boong*, he thought, couldn't even find his way back to a hill.

Reg headed off into the scrub as the sun dipped below the horizon, with the ute's headlights on full beam as he carefully steered it around the razor-sharp stakes of eroded tree stumps and bushes. There was a spotlight on the roof of the cab for whenever they went out to shoot a roo for the pot, and when darkness fell he stopped every now and then to swing it around, but all he could pick up was the occasional red-eyed glare of his usual quarry. He hit the horn as he went, and a couple of times got out to stand on the roof and yell a few coo-ees. Then, after nearly an hour, he staked a tyre and had to spend twenty minutes changing it, cursing through the task, while concern over his grandson's welfare rapidly grew. The boy had matches, some water and a dog with him, but that was going to be of no use if he had been bitten by a snake, or had fallen down one of the old mineshafts that dotted the countryside.

After he replaced the tyre, he headed back to camp, planning to go to Jimblebar and get some help for the search, dreading the thought of having to tell his daughter that the son she had sent up to him for straightening out had gone missing and could possibly be permanently straightened out somewhere in the bush. It was his responsibility. He shouldn't have just let the boy wander off like that. What was he thinking about to allow it? He drove into the camp in a very worried state. Then Smiler ran out to greet the car and he saw Kenny standing by the fire, drinking a cup of tea. The relief came first then the anger quickly followed.

"Where the *bloody* 'ell 'ave you been?" he bellowed.

"A mob of roos sidetracked me. Smiler started chasin' 'em an' I followed. Before I knew it I'd lost sight o' the hill," a chastened Kenny explained.

Smiler had settled on the ground with his head on his paws, and when he heard those words his eyes rolled upwards and glanced at Kenny. *Yeah, that 'd be bloody right... blame the dog!*

Reg didn't push the boy any more. He looked genuinely upset by the experience, distracted even.

"Okay... at least yer back. But there'll be none o' this wanderin' off on ya own again. Ow *did* ya find yer way back any'ow?"

"Oh... I just 'eard a gunshot and then I saw the fire," Kenny half lied, still trying to come to terms with what had happened out there.

*

The fire had quickly died down from its initial burst, the hard timber of the branches only holding the flames in the tree for about ten minutes before they snuffed out, leaving just the dry wood burning at its base. Kenny got up and started to pile up some more wood against another tree, but as he did so he thought he heard a muffled voice. He stopped and strained his ears to listen. "Smiler?" he called out then started giggling at the thought of the dog answering him, but shut up quickly when he heard the voice again.

"Burra," it said softly, the feminine tone coming clearly this time, drifting to his ears as if on the breeze that had begun to rustle through the tops of the trees.

Kenny froze, his mind unable to comprehend what he had heard, his nickname sounding out of the darkness almost as if it had been spoken by the wind, just like the first time it had come to him. Only his mates in Perth called him by the name he had adopted in his early teens, although he didn't really know where the word came from or what it meant. It had just popped into his head one summer's night as he sat by the Swan River waiting for his father and a mate to pull in the prawn net they had been dragging through the shallows for half an hour. His father had called out from the shadows of the river, 'Bugger it! Let's give it away. The easterly's in. All we'll be catchin' now'll be jellyfish!' After the warm breath of the summer wind had carried his father's voice to him, he had vacantly scribbled the word in the sand below the gas lantern. He stared at it for a while, before pronouncing it to himself. It seemed to have a familiar ring about it, but he couldn't think where he had seen or heard it before. A few minutes later his father spoke again. 'That's funny... the wind's died down again. Let's give it another lap and then head in.'

It was not long after that night that Kenny's dreams started; the ones where he kept waking in fright, trying to escape from something, someone, his legs still pumping madly away as he woke. Somehow he felt the word was connected to those dreams and it would eventually follow him everywhere. Whenever he drifted away in the classroom he would end up vacantly doodling it in his schoolbooks, outlining it in different coloured ink, so that most of the books ended up looking like a version of the graffiti tag he would later take delight in spraying around the neighbourhood. That was until the police found out whose name it was and, after being made to clean it off all the fences, windows and walls where he had proudly left it, he dropped it as a signature to his street art. But he still retained it amongst his friends; rejecting the name his parents had given him as a mark of his growing rebelliousness.

"Burra," the voice came again, although a little further away this time. He shook his head. He knew he wasn't doped enough to be hallucinating. Then he heard the voice a third time, a little bit further away again, and he suddenly felt compelled to follow it, a full moon now providing enough light for him to make his way through the bush.

Smiler finally caught up to his companion halfway back to the camp. He had been tracking his scent for nearly an hour and when he finally spotted him in a clearing up ahead he trotted quickly to catch up. As he got closer, he saw the figure that was standing on a rise just ahead of the boy. He slowed down now, the cold chill of an unwanted memory closing on him as he surveyed the shadowy presence. It was the woman again. But the boy didn't seem to notice her and just kept on walking. Smiler followed, but he hung back until, about fifteen minutes later, the woman suddenly disappeared.

Kenny stopped and looked closely at the horizon. He had heard the boom of a gunshot and could now see the faint glow of a fire up ahead. Then Smiler came up next to him.

"There ya are, ya bugger! Where did *you* get to?" the relieved youth enquired.

Smiler didn't answer. He could have told the boy how stupid he had been; that, if he had stayed where he was, his doggy nose would have found the way back long before now. But his canine mind was on other things. He knew there was something different about this kid the first time he had eyeballed him, but that little episode with the woman would take some figuring.

Twelve

"Don't shovel so fast! The dirt's just runnin' off the top! You'll never recover anythin' that way!" Charlie yelled above the noise of the dry-blower's motor. "Couldn't ya see 'ow yer grandfather was doin' it! Take it slow and easy. Don't go at it like a bull at a gate!"

It was the first day on the job for Kenny and, while Reg was taking a breather under the shade of a tree, he had taken over the job of shovelling the dirt on the dryblower instead of breaking up the ground with a pick, as he had been doing for hours. There was an uneasy truce between him and Charlie, and when the shouted advice came it was greeted with a halt in production and a cold stare.

Reg snorted at the 'bull at a gate' comment that came from the man with a patent on the approach, before calling out some calmer advice to the boy. "Listen to what 'e's tellin' ya. Put less dirt on the shovel and let it run down the trays slowly."

Kenny took heed and slowed down into a steady rhythm, cutting out a neat channel through the broken soil that lay below where the old dryblowing heaps had been. Charlie stood there in a cloud of red dust, concentrating on his job too but still annoyed by the presence of the third person.

The three had been working since five-thirty that morning, shov-elling the old dryblowing heaps through and clearing the way to the virgin soil underneath. As usual, they were concentrating on the outer borders of the alluvial area where the original workings petered out, the ground given up by the old timers as not payable enough. But it was where Reg and Charlie often found their best gold, and this patch had proved to be a relatively good one; hence Charlie's anxiety to see that it was done properly.

The whole process was hot, dirty, noisy and tiring; not much different to the conditions of the past, except that the modern dryblowers were many times more efficient and managed to pick up most of what the primitive contraptions of a hundred years ago had left behind. The latter-day prospector also had the advantage of the metal detector to scan over the treated dirt, sometimes finding gold in the occasional piece of quartz or detecting the odd nugget lying hidden under the bed of a trench they had finished cleaning out. Once, Charlie had found a ten-ouncer embedded in soft coffee-coloured rock only a few centimetres below the level they had been working, the sound through the earphones nearly blowing his eardrums out. They had eventually sold it to a collector for eight thousand dollars and lived on the thrill of it for months, but now it was just hard graft for ordinary wages and, with a third body to share it with, Charlie was not pleased. But the drop in income didn't bother Reg. He had always found most of his rewards in the lifestyle and he hoped that it would bring some peace to his grandson too, even though he could see the opposite effect the kid's presence was having on his partner.

Reg peered through the cloud of dust, watching the two figures toiling away. He didn't have to be a keen student of body language to see the changes; Kenny working away methodically and purposefully, appearing to be genuinely interested in what he was doing; his partner standing at the dryblower, his back a little stiffer than usual, eyeing the youth critically, his sense of humour gone. What a difference twenty-four hours had made. Yesterday the boy had spent most of his time in the same sullen mood with which he had arrived, but there had been a distinct change in his attitude after his little night stroll in the bush. He had even peeled a few spuds for dinner without being asked and, although he remained quiet for the rest of the evening, he did say goodnight before he went to bed.

Reg watched Smiler get up and follow Kenny to the water bag. The boy took a long draught of the cool liquid and poured a little into the dog's bowl before walking back to his task. Smiler quickly drank his share then followed Kenny back to the trench again. It appeared that even the dog had changed from the independent soul that he was. He had adopted the boy and now stuck to him like a shadow. Animals are supposed to know, Reg reflected, as he slowly began to feel better about the individual who had entered his life like a willy-willy and turned everything upside down.

"Too much!" Charlie snapped, as a larger shovelful than required slammed against the grate and half of the soil ran straight off the top and landed on the pile of rocks and stone at the base of the trailer.

Reg got up and walked over to Kenny. "Take a break. Yer doin' okay," he reassured, and when the boy and the dog went over to rest under a tree, he spoke quietly to his mate.

"Give it a rest will ya. Can't ya see the kid's makin' an effort?"

A muted grunt was the only reply.

Although still very hot it was relatively mild for a March day and they had decided not to drive the ten kilometres back to camp for their usual midday rest. They had heard on the car radio that there was the possibility of showers heading into their part of the goldfields overnight. That meant they wouldn't be able to work the ground until it dried out again, so they had decided to put as much dirt through as they could while they had the chance. They took their rest under a nearby tree instead and had a lunch of canned mackerel in tomato sauce, slapped between thick slices of the bread they had purchased in Kalgoorlie two days before. The bread's relative freshness quickly disappeared as soon as it was taken out of its wrapping and introduced to the dry desert air, but it didn't bother the hungry workers, or Smiler, as he quickly devoured any corners thrown his way.

Later in the afternoon Reg gave Kenny a quick lesson on how to use one of the detectors and directed him to ground that might produce something. Then the greenhorn proceeded to spend the next two hours wandering around digging up the leftovers of the past: nails, bits of rusted cans, wire and the occasional flattened lead of a bullet. His only win was a coin, not an interesting or valuable one dropped by a prospector nearly a hundred years before but a recently minted 1981 two-cent piece. Reg, however, reckoned that he had done all right to find that. He calculated that for every nugget he had ever found there was an average of at least fifty pieces of rubbish, so any financial gain was a bonus.

Kenny was disappointed about not finding any gold, but he had savoured the one thing that drove all prospectors, the anticipation, the impending thrill that the next sound would lead to a nugget. The dirt going through the dryblower inspired the same feelings and that afternoon, as they loaded the two drums of concentrate onto the back of the ute for panning back at camp, all three of them were looking forward to seeing what the day's hard yakka would turn up.

After arriving in camp, the usual ritual was followed. The billy was put on the coals and after ten minutes the tea was poured. Charlie sat down on a stool, leaning over a cut-down forty-four gallon drum. It contained just enough water for him to submerge the large gold pan he held between his legs. He picked up two handfuls of the concentrate and began his work, to him the only enjoyable part of the dryblowing process.

Kenny sat nearby, watching eagerly as Charlie shook and settled the dry soil in the pan, before dipping it into the water and beginning to expertly swirl it around. He quickly removed the larger and lighter material from the top, swirling the water again, shaking the pan, removing more of the useless material, repeating the process rapidly until all that was left was a thin sliver of black sand running down to a trail of grainy gold about as long and as wide as a matchstick.

"Not bad," Charlie said, as he handed the pan up for Reg to inspect.

"Mmmmm," Reg agreed, and showed it to Kenny, who got up quickly from his seat to look. Reg then took a cotton bud and picked up the tiny pieces of yellow metal and tapped them off into a small medicine bottle half-filled with water. Some of the gold was so fine it floated on top; the rest dropped quickly to the bottom, settling on a two-centimetre layer of gold and black sand, the results of the previous two weeks hard work.

Kenny looked closely at the bottle and asked how much was there, disappointed to be told that it was only about five hundred dollars' worth, and even less impressed when told about how long it had taken to retrieve it. He did a quick mental calculation and worked out that the two men had been working for less than forty bucks a day. Not much future in the dryblowing game, he reflected. But he was still intrigued by the panning process and watched closely as several more pans were washed, some producing less, some a little more, and others hardly any at all. After about an hour Reg took over and did about another half a dozen, before he turned to Kenny, who had now moved his chair closer to the drum.

"D'ya wanna 'avago?" he asked, and then gave up his seat as Kenny nodded enthusiastically.

"Aaar... Jesus," Charlie moaned. "There's little enough without a beginner washin' it all away!"

Reg gave Charlie a quick cold glance and then picked up an empty bucket and placed it next to Kenny. "Put all the stuff ya take off the top in 'ere. I'll give it a double check when ya've finished."

Suitably dismissed, Charlie walked off to start preparing the meal. It would soon be too dark to be doing any more panning anyway, and they didn't have much water left either: the rain tank was at the moment very close to empty; the partial refill from a brief thunderstorm two weeks before had been quickly used up. Tomorrow, if it rained enough, they would have the water and the time to finish the panning job and wouldn't have to drive out to a bore a couple of kilometres away to replenish their domestic supplies. They hoped it would be so, not only because of the work entailed in getting the bore water, but because, even after being boiled, it felt as though it was putting its claws out as it went down the throat.

Charlie glanced to the west and briefly studied the advance scouts of the front rolling in across the sky. "Rain could be 'ere tonight," was his hopeful assessment, before he started savagely chopping at some onions and carrots.

Kenny had washed through three pans by the time the fading light made it difficult to see, not really getting the knack of it until the last one, when the results of his efforts glistened back at him in the form of a match-head sized piece of gold. Then he was hooked, and wanted to keep working by lamplight, until Reg explained that the gold was hard to see in false light and he would have to wait until morning. He was disappointed, but it was something to look forward to. As the cooking smells began to drift from the fireplace, his mind focused instead on the food he had been craving since early afternoon, the hard day's work magnifying his already large teenage appetite.

It was the first time Charlie had cooked since their guest had arrived and when his idea of a meal was served up about half an hour later, Kenny instantly lost his appetite. He stared at the plate of unrecognisable goo before him with undisguised disgust then looked across at his grandfather, who was now trying very hard to hold back a smile.

"It's okay mate… it'll protect ya from snakebite," Reg said casually. "Just close ya eyes, 'old ya nose and swallow… quick."

Charlie sat down, glum-faced. He hated cooking and his efforts had once again reflected it. His style had developed over the years into a sort of can-opener-meets-greasy-spoon cuisine in a head-on collision which left nearly every meal unrecognisable – except for baked beans on toast; and sometimes even that was only faintly familiar. Usually, however, he could laugh off the jibes that came with his efforts, but right now he wasn't up to his mate's humour.

Despite the disappointment, hunger ruled and Kenny took a tentative mouthful, then spat it straight back out. "What *is* this shit? Ya tryin' ta poison me or somethin'?"

They were the first words he had directed at Charlie in over a day, and they had almost the same effect as the ones that had preceded their dust-up.

Charlie stood up, grabbed Kenny's plate and hurled it at the willow tree; the meal's gluey and elastic consistency stuck to the trunk for an inordinate length of time before it slowly released and plopped to the ground.

Smiler couldn't believe his luck and made a beeline for the remains, intent on getting the windfall before Cedric made his usual dinner-time appearance. He wolfed it down hungrily.

"If ya don't eat that… ya eat nuthin'!" Charlie bellowed, before he sat down again.

Reg looked at his grandson and smiled. "Don't worry, mate… that's just the tenderisin' process. You'll 'afta wait a bit now until the dog brings it up."

The calm words had the hoped-for effect; the first twitches of a smile began to work at the corners of Kenny's mouth. Then he finally burst out laughing when Reg piped up again.

"My biggest worry is, who's gunna give the dog mouth-ta-mouth if 'e *doesn't* bring it up?"

The two of them snorted and chuckled, but Charlie's mood kept darkening. He picked up the tomato sauce bottle and angrily whacked the bottom, sending a great dollop spurting all over his creation.

Reg put his hand up, shielded his face from Charlie and then spoke in a clandestine way to Kenny. "That's another secret, mate. Ya gotta drown the bastard!"

Kenny laughed again, but Charlie finally exploded.

"Stuff the both o' ya! I'm goin' ta the pub!"

With that, Charlie threw the contents of his plate towards Cedric's home. The gargantuan lizard quickly emerged out of the shadows and into the arc of the lamplight the moment it hit the ground. But the illumination did nothing to help the reptile make out what lay before him and, after peering at it for a while, tongue darting out in inspection, he thought better of consuming it and slowly strolled away.

It was a damning indictment from a creature that consumed almost anything, but the verdict had no effect on Smiler, as he saw his chance and dived in again.

"I dunno what the problem is… but I do wish you'd stop throwin' the bloody stuff in the dirt. I've gotta perfectly good bowl over there," he snuffled, as his teeth crunched on pebbles, sand and the odd twig. Then his ears pricked up alarmingly at the next words he heard.

"Go an' 'ave a look in the pantry. There's plenty o' canned dog there. Take ya choice," Reg said to Kenny, as he carried on eating, his stomach hardened to years of ordinary cooking, while the chef who had provided it disappeared in a huff of red dust as his ute rattled off down the track.

Reg watched the vehicle go. There was no doubt the arrival of his grandson had fired up the resentment in his mate; but he sensed what was going on was more than just getting the hump with a surly teenager. Charlie's thin veneer of humour was beginning to lift and expose what Reg had spent a lifetime mocking.

For the surly teenager, however, there had never been any veneer to lift. The first day he had seen Charlie he had instantly detected in his eyes what he had spent most of his young life railing against. He had been getting that look from whites ever since he was a small kid; mistrustful, judging glances; he called them the shopkeeper's stare; the sort that followed you around the stores and supermarkets, as though any minute you were going to steal something, start a fight, or abuse people. And, as whitey constantly expected trouble, eventually he had given it to them, taking every opportunity to get up their superior, sniffing noses, even if it also meant trouble for himself. But as he watched his grandfather sitting quietly by the fire, head bowed and staring into the flames, he began to experience an uncommon feeling of guilt over the unease he had brought to the old man. Something about this place was beginning to work on him, soften him and, unlike back in the city, he didn't feel much like fighting it. He finished his plate of canned spaghetti and meatballs and started to wash the dishes. His grandfather turned at the sound, and Kenny pulled down the tea towel and threw it at him. "You wipe!" he said, with a faint hint of a smile.

"Can't ya let an old bastard 'ave a rest," Reg complained happily, before dragging himself over to the table.

After the quick wash-up they sat around the fire for a couple of hours, not saying much but enough to keep the ice thawing. Mostly the conversation revolved around prospecting, but later, just after they had gone to bed, Kenny brought up the subject that had been bugging him all day.

"Grandad?"

"Yep."

"Somethin' funny 'appened last night when I was out in the scrub."

"Oh, yeah… what was that?"

There was a short silence while Kenny wrestled with what he had to say, and how to say it without looking stupid.

"Years ago I gave meself a nickname… Burra. All me mates back in Perth call me that," he said, before hesitating again.

In the brief silence, the vaguely familiar word rolled around Reg's mind seeking connection.

Kenny carried on, "Don't laugh, but what I was gunna say was that I… I thought I 'eard someone callin' it when I was out there last night. It sounded like a woman's voice. I'm sure I 'eard it a few times. It was like the wind was speakin' to me. I followed it and then I saw the fire o' the camp."

It was Reg's turn to hesitate. The mystery he thought he owned was now being described to him. Of course, the kid could have been frightened enough out there to imagine anything and, as much as he wanted to share his own tale of voices in the night, that knowledge tempered his response.

"There's plenty who'd laugh… but not me. Sometimes when the wind's blowin' through the sheoaks, I swear I c'n 'ear voices too. Could be senility of course, but what I do believe is there's more ta this country than what meets the eye."

A slow nod greeted Reg's mystery-coated reply and a long silence followed before either spoke again.

"Where did ya get that nickname from, anyway?" Reg finally asked.

"Oh… it just popped into me 'ead one day."

"Mmmmm… it's gotta good ring to it. Rather be called that would ya?"

"Yeah."

"Okay. It'll be Burra from now on."

Nothing more would be said of voices in the wind and soon both succumbed to sleep, only to be awoken by the wind wafting in from the west, carrying misting rain that drifted in under the lean-to and forced the two sleepers to decamp to the inside of the hut.

Half an hour later the affronted cook returned from the pub, staggering into the hut after being informed that his bunk was inside. Then, apart from the snoring and the gentle, satisfying sound of rain pattering on the roof, all fell silent again.

Thirteen

The next morning broke on a different world. Gone was the bright hello from a wide blue sky; a grey one now hung like a misty quilt upon the land, and the rain that drizzled all night long had painted the scrub in darker shades, bringing a certain sense of claustrophobia to the camp's surroundings.

The sun had risen over an hour before, but it hung diminished in the shrouded sky, the air at ground level bitterly cold, with no one feeling inclined to leave the warmth of their beds until Reg finally got up and started a fire in the large fireplace that stood at one end of the hut. Fortunately, he had thought to stack some firewood under the lean-to the afternoon before and he soon had it blazing away, bringing warmth and the smoky atmosphere of winter to the interior.

Burra couldn't believe the change in the temperature outside, from bloody hot one day to freezing cold the next. But he was happy that the flies had decided to sleep in. He was finding it difficult to deal with them, fighting them all day long as they relentlessly sought out sustenance in his eyes and nose. Even when he went to bed at night, he could hear their constant buzzing in his ears, their soundtrack imprinted on his brain. His grandfather had said they would be going to pick up some supplies in Leonora sometime during the next few days, and first on his shopping list was going to be some insect repellent, and he didn't care how much of a wimp that was going to make him look.

The weather didn't improve during the day, and most of the time was spent panning the gold just inside the door of the hut, where there was warmth and enough light to see properly. Burra's skills with the pan improved, but the values that came from the concentrate remained pretty much the same as the day before, except for a two-gram piece that showed up in Reg's shift. When they had finished early in the afternoon they had added about a hundred dollars' worth of gold to the bottle, a better return than usual, but still pitiful when matched against the labour required to retrieve it.

"Same old slog. Same old pay packet," Charlie complained.

Charlie had been quiet for most of the day, not bad-tempered, but definitely discontented. He had been so even before the extra body had turned up, and the boy's arrival had only served to exacerbate his unsettled state of mind. He figured that with the way things were at the moment it was as good a time as any to take a break. He had virtually decided in the pub last night to go down to Kal' for a few days. Go to the two-up. Have a few bets at the TAB – and ponder his immediate future.

It was the usual situation; the need for a bit of space had arisen again, but this time for a different reason, although the ground being saturated and unworkable was the one Charlie used.

"Okay, mate." Reg responded to the news. He stood and stared pensively as Charlie's vehicle rumbled off down the track, the short conversation preceding his departure tinged with more discomfort, both men hardly glancing at each other before swapping a simple 'See ya'.

As the sound of the vehicle faded away, Reg suddenly snapped out of his reflection and turned to his grandson.

"Well, young Burra. I reckon it's about time to put in the winter vegies."

The rain had eased off during the afternoon and, now that the ground was soaked, it was the perfect opportunity to plant the seeds he had picked up when in Kalgoorlie a couple of days before. He had decided to expand his vegetable patch this year and had already prepared the ground and built a bigger shadecloth cage for the broccoli, cabbage and cauliflower that he would be pampering for the next few months.

Burra and Smiler followed him to his treasured market garden, which was located behind the hut and conveniently near the water tank. There stood a shadecloth-covered frame covering a strip of soil about three paces long by one wide. It had been constructed out of drilling pipe, using Jim Donnelly's welder, and on each end it had two overhangs for use as handles.

"Grab the other end, mate," Reg said to his now slightly amused offsider.

"Jesus... whaddya tryin' ta do, keep elephants off the patch?" Burra groaned, as he took the weight of one end.

"Nuh... just the goats. They grow pretty big out 'ere."

They moved the frame to reveal the strip of rich brown soil liberally mixed with the sheep manure that Reg had dug out from under a shearing shed on Nandee station, the other side of Jimblebar. He visited the station not long after every shearing season had finished and filled up half a dozen sugar bags with the valuable fertilizer, digging it in around his vegetables every few weeks.

After moving the frame, Reg sat on its edge, pulled up the reading glasses that were hanging on a piece of string around his neck and peered at the instructions on the packets.

"Right. Ya need ta dig furrows about one 'and span apart."

"Me?" Burra asked.

"Yeah. Don't forget I've gotta do all the plantin'," Reg said with a faint smile.

"Get Smiler ta 'elp ya, 'e's good at diggin' things up."

"Yeah ... very good, comin' from someone who's dug up half the country lookin' fer funny rocks," came the whimper.

"There ya go. See... 'e agrees with me. Don't worry, they only 'ave to be about an inch deep. Use that stick there."

Burra picked up the piece of mulga branch and ran it along the broken ground, with Reg following, sprinkling the seeds liberally then lightly covering them with soil.

"Right, now that the babies have been put ta bed we've gotta make sure they're fed three times a day. The tank's nearly full again so we should 'ave enough ta do that for a while. Bit o' water and anythin'll grow in this country." He picked up a small watering can and filled it from the tank, lightly watering the rows, before the two of them lifted the shadehouse back over the patch.

By late afternoon the clouds were drifting away like the last guests at a party, and the setting sun, not wearing its usual veil of heat haze, was dropping into its slot in the horizon like a newly minted golden coin. It was then Reg decided to take Burra up to the top of the hill to share something with him.

They both sat there with the dog between them, nothing said until the lengthening shadows started closing on the breakaways, moving across the land like a horde of paintbrushes dipped in gold, reaching out to put the grand finishing touch on the day.

"Look over there," Reg said, pointing at the coffee-coloured cliffs.

Burra stared towards the horizon not knowing what he was supposed to be looking for; then, like magic, the cliffs began to glow, pale yellow at first, but changing by the second, running quickly through all the tones of the colour to finally finish in a blaze of gold.

"That's fu… that's bloody wicked!" Burra enthused, as the last strokes were applied; then, almost as quickly, the shadows began rolling up the canvas and taking the fleeting masterpiece away.

"Wicked?" Reg queried.

"He means it's fu…he means it's bloody great," came the sighing voice from between them.

"It's bloody terrific," Burra translated.

"Well… I was nearly right."

Reg patted Smiler's head then stood up. "Okay, mate. I'm 'ungry too. Let's go an' eat."

"That's not what I said!"

"Yeah, Smiler… let's go an' eat," Burra yelled, and then began to run up the hill.

"That's not what I bloody said, fer Christ's sake!" Smiler protested as he got to his feet.

"That's right, mate, *food*! And if ya don't 'urry up I'm gunna beat ya to it!" came Burra's taunt as he raced away.

"Gaaawd, why do I even bother?"

Smiler sprinted after Burra, passed him halfway up the hill then stopped at the top and looked back.

"Well… smart arse? Are we eatin', or what?"

*

The next couple of days were spent detecting, reading, resting and regularly watering the vegetable patch, keeping the small strip of soil moist as they waited for the still ferocious early autumn sun to do its job and render the rest of the country dry enough to proceed with the dryblowing. One morning Reg took Burra to a patch of ground a few kilometres from camp, where he and Charlie had always managed to find a nugget or two. Reg, the veteran, found a couple of small pieces after clearing away the collapsed remains of a dead tree, searching ground where previously low growing branches had made it difficult for metal detectors to reach; but the greenhorn continued his role as a garbage collector.

"That's okay," Reg stated, when Burra emptied his pocket of the useless items he had earlier dug out with still enthusiastic anticipation. "If ya findin' that stuff, sooner or later you'll crack it. There's been times when I've gone days without findin' any, and that's when there was still plenty lyin' around. Sometimes it all comes down to luck, but perseverance is the main one. Ya gotta keep at it… like anythin' else in life."

Reg cringed the moment he said those last words. The one thing he hadn't intended to do with this troubled kid was to start throwing pearls of grandfatherly wisdom at him. He wanted him to untangle his own fishing line and was confident the bush life could help him do that if given enough time. As he had learned with his own teenagers, well-intentioned lectures usually fell on resentful ears and Burra's glum and dismissive reply of "Yeah," reaffirmed his resolve to play the patience game.

That afternoon they took off to a dam about twenty kilometres away. It had originally been built to supply water to Jimblebar, but not long after its construction a good supply of underground water had been found in the middle of town and the dam was never used for its original purpose. Instead, it had become a bit of a recreation area and picnic ground for locals and tourists alike; a place to go for a swim or catch the yabbies that some thoughtful soul had introduced years before. It was the proverbial oasis in the desert; its levels varied a bit from year to year but none of the locals could ever remember when it had run dry.

It was the first time Reg had been to the dam since early summer and he was pleased to see the water as high up the wall as he had ever seen it in the dry season. "Level looks good," he said, as he parked the ute near the shallow end and scanned the surrounding countryside. "An' it looks like we've got the whole place to ourselves. You can go fer a swim if ya like. I'm gunna set up these drop nets."

Burra didn't need any more encouragement to cool down in the inviting waters. He instantly set off for the wall with Smiler following, walking along to where the crumbling remains of a small brick tower stood. Then he climbed up to the top of it and with a celebratory shout jumped up and out, holding one knee crooked as he executed the perfect 'bombie', disappearing back-first under the surface and sending an explosion of water cannoning up and out from his point of entry. His smiling face appeared above the water a few seconds later.

"Eh... Grandad! Come an' 'avago at this!"

By now Reg had finished placing the nets for the tasty crustaceans he was hoping to have for their evening meal, baiting them with some leftover meat from a goat he had shot the week before and settling them in the shallows. He had entered the water for a sedate little paddle when Burra's invitation came.

"Ask me forty years ago," he replied, as he quietly enjoyed the cool luxury closing around him.

Burra swam energetically back to the end of the wall and climbed up, before racing the exuberant Smiler along the top.

"You wanna come in too, do ya mate?" he said, as he ruffled Smiler's fur.

"Not bloody likely, mate!"

Smiler didn't mind a bit of a stroll through the shallows with his feet firmly on the ground, but as far as going in at the deep end, the humans could have it. However, as usual, the message didn't get through and, just before they reached the tower again, Burra suddenly picked Smiler up and stood on the edge of the wall.

Smiler looked down at the water with undisguised fear, growling menacingly as he struggled to free himself, but Burra held him firmly and jumped.

"Yahoooo!" came the ecstatic cry from the human, followed by a loud shrieking kind of a sound from the canine.

They hit the water in a mass of flesh, fur, thrashing paws, bubbles, swallowed water and exploding ear drums, before Smiler broke the surface, already paddling furiously and heading straight for dry land.

Burra laughed uproariously as the furry torpedo sped for shore. "Chicken!" he yelled out.

"Shithead!" came the short, sharp response, as Smiler made the muddy shallows and struggled out, vigorously shaking the moisture away, before lying down to sulk.

Smiler watched as, with unremitting energy, Burra made his way along the wall and climbed up the tower again. But as the boy steadied himself to jump, the dog's radar suddenly kicked in and he stood up and ran along the edge of the dam barking out loudly across the water.

Reg looked at him with surprise. "It's okay mate, he's not gunna throw ya in again."

But Smiler kept barking and racing back and forth along the shore, causing Reg to turn and look at Burra. Just as he did so a cry came out from the human bombshell, as the brickwork he was balancing on gave way. His feet went out from under him and he banged and tumbled his way down the wall to land clumsily in the water.

"Jesus!" Reg cried out, then dived into the water and swam furiously towards the wall.

By the time he had reached it, the boy's body had disappeared under the water, and he took a deep breath and dived. He caught up with the sinking form a couple of metres from the surface. Hooking one arm under Burra's he struggled frantically back towards the surface. He shifted his grip to under the boy's chin and backstroked hard to the shore. He pulled the heavy weight of Burra's unconscious form as far as he could up the bank and, when he saw the blood on the back of the boy's head, quiet man suddenly became panic man. He urgently tried to recall that first-aid lesson: Clear the mouth of obstruction. Give mouth-to-mouth and then lay the head to the side. Or was it the whole body to the side? Do you lie him on his front and push his back to get rid of the water? His mind spun with the search for lost information, but he had to start. He held his thumb and forefinger over the boy's nose and breathed heavily into his mouth, watching the chest rise and fall with each breath. The seconds passed like minutes and there was no response. He sat astride him and pushed upwards on his chest, almost crying now from frustration and helplessness. He slapped the boy's face. Then he gave him mouth to mouth once more. Still there was no response. Time was running out. He quickly felt for a pulse and was encouraged to find it faintly beating along his neck. He carried frantically on, swiftly alternating between mouth-to-mouth and applying pressure to Burra's chest.

Smiler looked on, whimpering and whining, his head cocking from side to side in puzzlement at the sight of the panicked human until, just as a small willy-willy spun around the dry, dusty edge of the dam, he suddenly burst into a loud, frantic barking.

In his frustration, Reg opened his mouth to scream abuse at Smiler, but the whirring cylinder of dust and debris soon closed it. He covered his face with his hands as the mini tornado spun around him, hovered for a moment then roared away again. Then he took his hands away and squinted through the thick dust still hanging in the air, only to be shocked by what confronted him.

Reg had been sitting astride the prone Burra when the willy-willy hit, but now the boy was sitting upright, staring at him, his eyes wide open with fear, his face looking different somehow, younger and, as Reg peered at it, a voice in a much higher pitch than Burra's broken one yelled out something in an Aboriginal tongue. The boy's legs began moving in a mad panic, as if trying to get away from something, bucking Reg off in the process, before he fell back again, sputtering, coughing and finally releasing the water from his lungs.

"Thank Christ fer that!" Reg cried out, his confusion momentarily replaced with relief.

He turned Burra on his side as the water dribbled out, ecstatic to hear the boy moan then speak.

"What's goin' on?" Burra asked dopily, as he raised himself weakly up on one elbow.

Reg's calmness returned. "Oh, ya've just been playin' submarines… that's all. 'Ow's yer 'ead?"

Burra put his hand up and winced as he felt the grazed lump on the back of his skull.

"'Ow'd I get that?"

"Ya took a tumble down the wall. Nearly drowned. If it wasn't fer Smiler's barkin' I mightn't 'ave got ta ya in time."

Reg held out a hand to the dog sitting on his haunches a little distance away now, uncharacteristically quiet and with his eyes fixed on Burra.

"C'm 'ere, Smiler."

But Smiler remained where he was, still trying to work out what was going on. He had seen the woman of the willy-willy again; that was strange enough, but stranger still was seeing a human sitting up and lying down at the same time. He shifted his feet nervously as Burra turned around and looked at him, but now he could see nothing of the other one in his eyes.

"C'm 'ere, mate," Burra said quietly, and Smiler complied this time, wagging his tail slowly as he came forward. Then he lashed the boy's face with a sloppy tongue.

"This is fer chuckin' me in the water, ya bastard!" he growled playfully, worrying the boy's neck and ears with his slobbering face, until he was affectionately pushed away.

Concerned that Burra might have suffered concussion, Reg made the decision to pull the yabbie nets and head back to camp. The catch total was just three of the small freshwater crayfish so instead of the feast they had been looking forward to, they would later become just one tiny appetiser each for the two humans and the dog. What followed was the usual canned fare adorned with the last of the fresh spinach from the old vegie patch, but what didn't follow was the usual quick slide into sleep once they hit their bunks. Each one would lay there with troubled minds; Smiler, recalling the image of the woman and the even stranger one of the double human; Reg, with the mystery of that voice, coming out of what he was not even sure was Burra's mouth; and Burra, thinking of that dream he hadn't had for quite a while. It had descended upon him sometime during his unconsciousness at the dam and had only lifted when he coughed himself awake. He had been running away again; from something terrible, something unseen that had quickly closed upon him, before he felt once more that smashing blow across the back of the head. Then, as he awoke, there was a brief sense of a comforting presence nearby, the same sort of feeling he had experienced when nearly lost in the bush a few nights before.

"'Ow's the 'ead?" Reg asked for the sixth time that night, still worried that Burra might have concussion. The boy didn't seem to have any of the nausea that he knew from his football experience would often follow a bad knock on the head, but sometimes it took a while to set in and he intended to keep checking.

"Don't worry. I told ya… me 'ead's okay." came the slightly irritable confirmation.

Then all went quiet, apart from a last troubled snort that came from under Burra's bed.

"Yeah… but which 'ead?"

Fourteen

"'Ow's the 'ead?" came an echo of the night before.

Burra was leaning over the fire attending a fry pan when he heard the voice. He turned around to see Reg lying with hands behind his head and a wide grin across his face. "Jesus, Grandad! Haven't ya gone ta sleep yet?"

"Well, 'ow is it?"

"I'm fine. Get up. Breakfast'll be ready soon."

By the time Reg was up and dressed, there was a plate of bacon and eggs waiting for him, with a large cup of steaming black tea sitting next to it. He could get used to this, he thought; unlike the breakfast Charlie normally served up he could actually see what was bacon and what were eggs.

"When will we be workin' again?" Burra asked as they ate.

"We'll 'afta give it another day I reckon. Still looks a bit damp in places. But if ya want to, ya c'n take the detector down ta the slope below the Laxative. We've occasionally found somethin' down there. Try amongst the thicker bush. It's 'arder work, but we 'aven't covered that area thoroughly. I might come down later. I wanna take a look at the carby on the ute first. It's been playin' up fer a while now. Needs ta be pulled apart and cleaned, I reckon. An' I've gotta water the vegies."

"Did it before ya woke," Burra casually stated. "An' I can strip the carby and clean it up if ya like. I'm always messin' around with motors back home."

"I'll tell ya what. I'll take it all off, and then ya can clean it and put it together again. Ya gotta leave the ol' bastard with somethin' ta do."

Burra smiled. "Yeah... okay."

He grabbed one of the detectors, a water bottle and a small pick then wandered off barefooted with Smiler following.

"'Ang on!" Reg called out with concern. "Where's ya shoes? Ya can't go wanderin' around the bush in yer bare feet!"

"It's okay. It feels more comfortable. Anyway, I am a *boong* arn' I?" he yelled out without turning.

Reg chuckled at the comment. He'll be back as soon as he gets sick of pullin' prickles out of his feet, he thought, as he headed over to the ute and lifted the bonnet.

But Burra wasn't back soon, and an hour passed before Smiler, thirsty and bored with watching him wave the detector, wandered back to the camp for a drink, walking quietly up to Reg, who still had his head down in the engine of the ute.

Reg had removed the carburettor and was peering at some corrosion around the water pump, unaware that Smiler had returned, when suddenly the dog let out an ear-piercing bark right next to him. A loud bang came from the bonnet as he straightened in fright.

"Jesus *Christ*, Smiler!" he cried out, as he tried to rub away the pain.

Smiler ignored the complaint and kept barking as he stared towards the top of the hill.

"What the bloody 'ell is it now?" Reg queried irritably, shading his eyes as he peered in the same direction.

The sun had risen halfway into the morning sky, shining directly from behind the image of the person standing on the hill and holding a hand up as if in a greeting.

"Burra?" Reg called out uncertainly.

The figure called out something in reply and began to move out of the blurring halo of bright sunlight and down the slope.

Reg closed his eyes tightly, doing a swift double take, stunned by what he thought he had heard and what he had seen, but in the time it took to blink, the image of a naked Aboriginal boy carrying what appeared to be a spear had been replaced by a familiar one.

Reg watched Burra walking towards him holding up his hand in victory, the spear he thought he had seen now visible as the extended shaft of the hip-mounted metal detector.

"Guess what I found?" Burra cried out in triumph.

Reg remained silent in his confusion; Smiler was as silent as he ever could be, his barking dropping into a troubled growl. He moved away a little as Burra approached them and held out his hand to Reg.

In his palm was a small piece of gold about the size of a pea but, according to the grin across Burra's face, it could have been a two-hundred-ounce nugget. Reg looked at it without responding, his mind still struck by the image and the word he had heard, sounded out in the same nasal high-pitched way that Burra had yelled after his hit on the head at the dam. Maybe that was Reg's problem right now; banging his head on the bonnet had stuffed up his sight and his hearing for a moment. But it seemed so clear.

Burra's excitement finally faded as he noticed Reg's distracted manner. "What's up? It *is* gold isn't it?"

Reg began to emerge from his confusion. "Yeah... yeah, that's gold... all right." But he had to ask. "What was that ya yelled out ta me at the top o' the hill?"

Burra looked at Reg in slight confusion now. "You called out me name, so I just asked what was the matter. Why?"

What's the matter? *Mungatjarra*? It sounded similar, Reg thought. "Aaah, nuthin'. I just couldn't quite understand what ya said. Me 'earin' must be goin'."

"*No it aint, mate,*" came the snort from behind Reg's legs.

Reg took the small piece of gold out of Burra's hand and tossed it up and down.

"About two weights, I reckon. Where'd ya find it?"

"Where ya told me... amongst the bushes. What's a weight?"

"It's the old measure. Twenty weights make an ounce. In your lingo it's about one an' a 'alf grams. So what you've got there's about three grams. That's about forty bucks with the silver taken out. Not much, but it's worth celebratin' with a counter meal at the pub tonight."

Reg handed the nugget back. "Yer buggered now. There'll be no rest for ya now ya've found a piece."

True to that prediction, Burra decided to do a bit more before lunch and walked quickly back over the hill again. The dog and the old man watched him as he went, both still unsure.

Three hours later, a weary Burra made his way back to camp; the enthusiasm from his earlier find worn down, waved away, his feet almost stumbling as he made his way into camp to slump down in a chair.

"Welcome back to reality," Reg said, with a smile. He had the carburettor spread out in pieces on the table and was cleaning them with an old toothbrush dipped in a can of petrol.

"Gotta get a new filter when we go in fer supplies. There's 'eaps o' dirt comin' through from the tank. I've managed ta clean this one out a little, but it's only gunna keep givin' trouble if it's not replaced. Get somethin' ta eat, then ya can put all this back together again."

Burra ate, and then started on the carburettor, impressing Reg with his dexterity as he quickly re-assembled the pieces and, after checking part of the worn linkage, went over to the wreck of a third ute that the two partners kept for spare parts and found a replacement. Late in the afternoon, Reg started the ute up, and it revved like a beauty, just in time to take off to the pub.

Halfway down the track Reg spoke in a serious tone. "Ya mother told me yer a bit fond o' the turps. Yer too young fer it, but now that you've started, while ya with me ya gunna learn some control. Ya gunna be on dog's rations. Smiler gets one can and that's all you'll be gettin'. And just to be fair about it I'll stick ta the same… okay?"

"Yeah… okay," came the subdued reply, then the curiosity. "Smiler gets a can?"

"Yeah, it's the 'ighlight o' goin' ta the pub, watchin' 'im get stuck inta 'is can o' beer. Isn' it mate?" he asked as he rubbed Smiler's ears.

Smiler just stared ahead with almost wild-eyed anticipation, not responding until Reg spoke again.

"Watch this. *Beer*, Smiler!"

Smiler started whining, *"Aah, Jesus, do we 'afta go through this every time we go ta the bloody pub?"*

"*Beer*, Smiler!" Burra encouraged.

"Grrrrr, okay… Beer! Beer! 'Appy? Now let's get into it."

Reg and Burra broke out into loud laughter.

"Dickheads!"

Reg pulled the ute up next to a familiar battered old Toyota ute, which stood beside a late model Landcruiser and a small white Holden sedan. He didn't know the other vehicles but was glad to see that Professor was there.

Loud laughter echoed out of the front bar as the three of them made their way along the veranda. When they entered the small room, Reg was surprised to see a woman sitting up at the bar next to Professor. She looked familiar, attractive, in a slightly plump sort of way. Along the other end sat three men. One was grey-haired and in his mid-fifties, the other two much younger, late twenties maybe. They were all dressed in dirt-stained khaki shirts and shorts, and shod in the solid work boots of the mining industry. The two younger ones were doing all the laughing, the older one seeming a little bemused, but when Reg, Burra and Smiler entered, the two men stopped laughing and stared. One of them whispered privately to his mate, "Jesus, they'll let every man and 'is dog in 'ere. Maybe there's gunna be a corroboree tonight!"

More laughter came and Jim looked at Reg with a pained smile. "Geos… been here all arvo," he murmured as he leant on the bar. "But I don't know whether it's worth all the dough they're spendin'." He craned his neck over the bar and spoke to Smiler. "Beer, mate?"

For once, Smiler couldn't be baited, his attention too taken by the woman as he crooked his head and stared quizzically at her familiar-looking face.

"Speak of the devil," Professor said, as he turned around to Reg. "This lady has just been asking after you. This is Johnno's sister,

Cassie… his twin sister no less, and here madam is the very person you seek… Mr Reginald Arnold himself. And who would this young man be?" he asked as he spotted Burra standing behind.

Reg smiled at Professor's manner, his exuberance indicating that he had been in the pub all afternoon, too.

"This is Burra, me grandson. He's come up ta stay fer awhile." Reg said, almost vacantly, as he looked at the woman, his curiosity growing with Prof's introduction.

"And a fine young fellow he looks too." Professor held out his hand to Burra. "How do you do Mr Burra, Arthur Pitman's the name, and digging out gold isn't my game. You can call me Prof… everyone around here does. It's on account of my knowing more than the whole lot of them put together."

Burra smiled thinly at the verbiage as he shook the man's hand.

Reg held out his hand to Cassie. He was the only one around Jimblebar who previously knew that Johnno had a sister and he now felt a responsibility to say something on behalf of them all.

"'Owyagoin', Cassie… just like to say that we were all sorry ta hear about Johnno. We didn't see much of 'im 'round 'ere, but 'e seemed a decent bloke."

"Yeah, thanks Reg. I hadn't seen much of him either over the last twenty years. But that was Kevin. Never needed much company. Can I get you a drink?"

"Its okay, I'll get it. You?" Reg responded, pointing at Cassie's near empty glass.

"I'm fine at the moment, thanks."

"Prof?"

"I never thought you would ask, my good man. I'll have a shot of the finest whisky you have, Innkeeper… and hold the icebergs."

Jim gave Reg a resigned smile. Then he took Professor's glass and pushed it up against the dispenser of the hardly-aged rough he had been serving him for most of the afternoon. "What about you, Reg?" he asked, as he put the glass before Professor.

"Three beers thanks."

Jim didn't even question the obvious underage status of Burra.

Around here, any drinker that wanted a drink got served, including the dogs, and as soon as Jim took the bowl out and placed it on top of the bar, Smiler staked his claim, going immediately into his routine.

"Bout bloody time!" came the ear-shattering bark, causing the three men at the end of the bar to jump in their seats.

"An' ya can get off me bloody seat, too!" he directed aggressively at the one against the end wall.

"What the fuck's up with ya mongrel, mate! Call him off, will ya?" the young man requested with alarm as he backed up against the bar.

"It's okay... yer in his seat. Just move up one and you'll be right," Jim calmly stated, and then smiled at Reg and Professor

"Piss off! I'm not shiftin' fer a bloody dog!" came the protest.

Smiler went off his brain again. *"You'll shift, mate, if ya wanna keep yer legs!"* Then he made a move for the man's feet.

"Aar, fer Chrissake, get out of his seat and let's have some peace," the older man intervened.

The young man grumbled; but he shifted, and Smiler immediately jumped up onto the stool and sat with his body against the wall, paws resting on the bar and looking like a regular. But they still didn't get any peace. As soon as Jim opened the can, Smiler started up again, barking his approval as the foaming liquid poured in. Then he started slurping at it, suds and fluid flying along the bar and over his reluctant drinking companions.

The three of them jumped from their seats in a flurry of protest, and Cassie and Burra laughed out loud at the spectacle. Two of the men saw the joke and chuckled as they scrambled away. But the young one unseated by Smiler had drunk his way beyond the humour stage and cursed out loudly before giving Burra a poisonous look as he followed the other two out of the room.

"C'mon Heckle and Jeckle," the older man said, as he walked around to the room on the other side of the bar. "Let the yokels have their bit o' fun. I'll give you young'uns another lesson in how to play darts."

There, the three eventually settled into a loud game of 201, but the unhappy one still occasionally glanced dirtily at Burra and Reg.

Smiler polished off what was left in his bowl and hopped down to wander out onto the veranda.

"Yeah, that's right, mate. Go and sleep it off and leave me ta clean up the mess," Jim called out as he wiped the bar down.

More laughter came from those in the front bar, but Smiler growled. *"Yeah, bloody 'ilarious! I'd like you lot to start drinkin' with ya tongues and see 'ow ya go!"*

Before heading out the door he stopped at the woman's feet, wagging his tail as he looked up at her. He could see a lot of his former owner in her face and a small faint flash of the thing that had led him to his death dancing in the back of her eyes. He hoped it wasn't so, but he felt ill at ease as she leant down and patted him, detecting an underlying tension in the soft perfumed touch and the assuring voice.

"Don't you take any notice of them, mate," Cassie said sympathetically, while the memory of that sharp bark played darkly through her mind.

"Smiler was yer brother's dog," Reg said, as he watched the four-legged patron stroll a little unsteadily through the doorway.

Cassie nodded her head in a distracted way. "Mmmm... I know about Smiler. Kevin wrote about him in his di... in his letters."

Reg caught the correction and a small flush of excitement passed through him, but he gave no indication of it. "Lucky to 'ave survived the crash 'e was. Didn't turn up 'til over a week later. 'E's a tough bugger," he concluded.

"Yeah, he must be. I saw the boulder that Kevin hit," Cassie replied, the vision of the painted rock standing in her mind like a comical but sinister monument to her brother's death. The police were right, you couldn't miss seeing it, and when she stopped the car that afternoon and walked over to it, it seemed to be staring back at her as if it were alive; a giant malevolent frog that gave her the distinct feeling it was still watching her as she walked back to the car and drove off, its big yellow eyes following her up the road. For a while it even seemed to be keeping pace with the car and she began to form crazy images of it bounding over the flats, chasing her. Her last thought of it as it disappeared in the rear vision mirror, was that someone should remove the paint, simply as a mark of respect.

Burra sat inside for a while chatting with Professor, until the constant questioning from the inquisitive man drove him out onto the veranda to keep company with the snoring Smiler. He didn't want to speak of the trouble he had got into back home and that was where the interrogation was leading, as Professor began probing like a dentist with the hook, digging into the nerves of Burra's Aboriginality and releasing the mistrust the boy had for all whites.

He handed his half-emptied can of beer to his grandfather before he went out. "You 'ave this, Grandad. I don't really feel like it. An' don't worry about dog's rations, have as many as ya like."

Somehow he had lost the desire to get drunk, or doped out. After a few days out in the scrub he just didn't see the point any more, and he didn't even feel like a legitimate smoke either, after hanging out for one ever since his last drag a couple of days ago. He had intended to stock up here, but instead he ended up buying a bag of potato chips and a can of Coke.

"Don't go stuffin' yerself with that, mate. Remember we're 'avin' a meal 'ere tonight. By the way, Jim, what's on?" Reg asked the barman, who was now busy keeping the booze up to the rowdy bunch in the other bar.

Just then another Landcruiser utility pulled up in front of the pub and three young men from one of the nearby stations jumped out, quickly moving up the steps and through the front door.

"I got some nice snapper in on the truck the other day, but if the place keeps fillin' up like this, ya might 'afta knock it up yerself," came the harried reply.

"I can help out in the bar if you like," Cassie chipped in. She had been only too happy to get away from for her job for a couple of days, but somehow, here, she didn't feel that it would be work.

"What's on the menu, Jimbo?" one of the station workers called out as they stomped into the bar and greeted the others with friendly abuse.

Jim turned towards Cassie. "Do ya know what to do?"

"Unfortunately… yes. I'm workin' down at the Royal in Kalgoorlie at the moment. Until I can escape," she replied, sardonically.

"Okay, it's all yours. I'll go and play chef now."

Alan Prescott, the middle-aged geologist, who had been eyeing Cassie since she had walked into the pub, heard the information she gave Jim and filed it away. Then he spent the next hour or so trying to get something else out of her, joking with her in the same old barspeak with sexual overtones that he had used many times before. What he needed right now was a distraction from his problems and, as he watched Cassie bend down to take a tray of glasses out of the washer, he figured a night of hot sex might help, although he was fast drinking himself beyond the ability to participate. But the buxom object of his desire had obviously heard the foreplay of the drunk many more times than he had used it and she treated it accordingly, dismissing his every hint with practised humour. Oh well, he thought, if she wasn't interested, there was always Hay Street. In the end it didn't really matter to him which way you got it, you always had to pay for it, and at least with a hooker the price was set, although where to get the money was fast becoming a problem.

Prescott ran a freelance geologists outfit and had spent the majority of his working life in the outback of Western Australia and, at the moment, his services were much in demand. 1985 had brought the beginning of an exploration rush in the goldfields and it had gathered pace in the first couple of months of '86. The work was pouring in and he should have been doing well – but he was broke. The floodgates of his gambling habit had finally opened wide and let everything run out. Now he was using contracts just to pay his debts – the second mortgage on his flash City Beach home; the back rent on his suite of offices in Kalgoorlie – and at the same time trying to keep up the lifestyle that his high-maintenance wife and two spoilt children expected. Then there was the alimony for his first wife and the three offspring from that union.

A vision of his current young wife, with one of her arty-farty male friends up to the hilt in her, flashed through Prescott's mind. It wouldn't surprise him. She had started to go cold on their relationship about the time she started mixing with the arts fraternity, buying paintings that didn't look like anything and always from good-looking young male artists. She had even started talking about setting up an art gallery. That would be handy for her, he figured, being able to promise a hanging in return for the favours of the well hung. He mentally shrugged his shoulders. It may as well be someone, he thought. He couldn't go there any more. She didn't want him there; didn't really want him in her life. She had made that all very clear the last time she had bawled him out over his gambling losses. It was the classic case of the money running out and the age difference raising its wrinkled head. He was wondering how long it would take and now it was almost here. Maybe he should just call an end to the farce; make it official. But she was still such a horny woman to look at.

He sighed within. He wished that they had never built that bloody casino in Perth. It was hard enough to keep control with the two-up and the horses, and fight the urge to fly to casinos in the eastern states and overseas, but once he had walked into that mugs' paradise right on his doorstep, it was like the proverbial kid in the candy store. Within a month he had gone from a hundred-dollar-a-card on blackjack to a thousand, and sometimes much more. He had blown so much and in such a short time that right now he was wondering where he was going to find the money to pay the two featherweights loudly competing over a game of darts behind him.

He turned around and stared at the two men; the embarrassing remnants of his worth; the clear evidence of his downfall from a time when he had a dozen geologists and their crews working for him. Back then he was able to leave the fieldwork to others and enjoy the high roller's lifestyle, but now he had had to go back to it, unable to find anybody of quality to work for him because of the money he still owed to some of those he once employed. His name was mud, and he was stuck in it with two constantly chattering assistants, the nicknames he gave them fitting almost perfectly, except that the two cartoon crows were infinitely more intelligent. But their dullness of mind had its advantages when delaying them over payment for their time. He had been suffering them out in the field for several weeks now, core sampling at various drilling sites, but the money from those contracts wasn't due for weeks, and to pay them he would probably have to go cap in hand to the bank again, or have a sudden change of luck.

He took another mouthful of scotch and stared longingly again at the woman behind the bar then, in a poor trade-off, asked her for three serves of the fish and chips and salad everybody else was getting stuck into.

About an hour after the food service had been completed, the three station hands left and Cassie was relieved of her post when Jim reluctantly vacated his seat on the customers' side of the bar.

"Thanks. And don't worry about the tariff fer tonight," Jim said as they swapped places.

"I didn't do it for that."

"I know, but that's how it'll be."

It was only a few minutes after she sat down with Reg that Cassie decided to speak to him about the diaries. She had been observing the calm and well-mannered man for over two hours now, assessing him with a barmaid's skill and, after a couple of sips from the brandy and Coke Jim had placed before her, she asked him quietly if he could step outside for a minute.

Reg nodded casually at the request then got up and sauntered with the woman through a side door that led out into the yard where a windmill stood, now creaking slowly with the first hint of the desert's breath.

The two entered the pitch-black darkness of the yard and, when Cassie thought they were far enough away not to be heard, she stopped and spoke.

"Sorry that it's taken so long to get to this, Reg. But I had to pick my moment."

"That's okay... what's up?" Reg asked, his casual manner belying his anticipation.

"My brother mentioned you in one of his diaries. I got them from the police along with all his other stuff. What he said in one of them makes me think that you can be trusted."

"Oh, yeah… well, I always found Johnno to be pretty genuine, too."

Cassie hesitated for a moment, before the words came out in a rush.

"I found somethin' else out from his diaries. In the last entry he made he spoke pretty excitedly about findin' gold."

The news that Reg had been expecting brought the glint of Johnno's gold shining more sharply from his memory, but he still managed to contain his excitement.

"Oh, yeah… what'd the diary say?"

"It shows the area where he found it out in the desert. It's marked on a map he kept with his diaries. I'm tellin' you about it because I'm goin' to need someone to take me out there, and you're the only person I've got any sort of a handle on around here. I don't know if what he found is worthwhile or not, because there were no more entries after that one, but if you help me in this, I'll give you twenty percent of whatever we find. But you must excuse me for not showin' you anythin' just yet," she finished, feeling a little silly about the secretiveness of something she was not totally sure existed. Whilst she was excited about the prospect of finding the gold, the thought had also occurred to her that Kevin might have gone crazy out there. He had mentioned getting a dose of the sun not long before the entry about his discovery, and there was no gold amongst his things. She might just be chasing hallucinations. But Reg immediately wiped out any doubts from her mind.

"Oh, I think it'll be worthwhile all right. I saw some of it not long before 'e died. Me and me mate were 'ere when 'e came through that day. 'E was tryin' to keep it from us, but 'e dropped a bit of it outta the bag 'e had it in. What I saw tells me that 'e found somethin' big."

Reg described the piece he had seen and explained where they suspected the gold had ended up, telling her what he had said to the police and finishing with an account of Elliot's demise.

"Well, that explains one thing, but I wonder why the coppers didn't tell me anything of what you've just told me."

"They didn't 'ave any real proof of its existence. They didn't find it at the roadhouse so all they 'ad was what I told 'em, which was nothin' about the big piece. Fortunately for you it appears that they didn't bother reading the diaries too closely either."

"Fortunately for both of us," Cassie said, smiling in a knowing kind of way. She was pissed off about the loss of the gold, but her annoyance was quickly overruled by Reg's obvious shrewdness and calm manner. He was just what she needed. She was excited too by his certain assessment of what her brother had found. Now she was beginning to believe that she really had been given the big break; the chance to escape from the drudgery of her existence and finally enjoy the sort of life that a lot of money could bring. She had been study-ing the map so closely now that she could almost point the way to the gold by memory, but even though all the indicators showed that this man could be trusted, she still added a little insurance when Reg asked her approximately how far out in the desert it was.

"It's located in some lake country, oh, about two hundred and fifty k's from here as the crow flies, assumin' that Kevin followed the scale on the map closely enough, of course," was her deliberately vague and misleading reply, which had added about fifty kilometres to the distance.

Reg smiled knowingly at the mild subterfuge. She was shrewd too, but the next question she asked reminded him that she was a townie and, as such, more than a little naïve about the bush.

"Can we go soon, Reg?"

The eager question sealed the partnership, but without consid-ering the organisation required for their journey together, or that there would be any complications, such as the next thing Reg was to say.

"Well, there are a coupla things first. I know that Johnno spent a lotta time out there, even in the 'ottest part o' the year, but as far as I'm concerned, it's no place ta be until it cools down a bit. There's a spot on the map that ya might have seen, called Linger and Die well, and that's only 'alf the way out ta where we'd be goin'. It might give ya a little idea of 'ow dangerous the country is. I reckon we'd 'afta wait another month or so before attemptin' it. Besides, it'll take a while to get properly organised. And there's another thing. As well as me grandson, I've got a partner. If I get involved, then they'll be comin' too… that's the way I always work. Of course if ya agree ta that, their share would be comin' outta mine. That's if we find anythin', of course."

Cassie was a little disappointed, but not because of the extra bodies or the last thing Reg said. It was the waiting that she didn't fancy, stuck for another whole month working in that bear pit of a bar in Kalgoorlie. She wondered if she could last that long.

"Okay… you know this country best. I'll leave it to your judgement. I'm stayin' at the pub tonight and goin' back in the mornin'. When you want to contact me just ring the Royal Hotel or Gateway caravan park."

They turned and walked back into the hotel but, not long after they disappeared inside, a figure moved in the shadows not ten metres from where they had been standing.

A couple of minutes before Reg and Cassie had walked out into the yard, Alan Prescott had wandered out there searching for a place to relieve himself after finding the inside toilet engaged. He had just started to do up his fly when he heard the voices, and had remained fixed in place, his fingers frozen on the zip until they had walked back into the building. Now the information he had heard was pinging madly around inside his head. He didn't go back through the side door, but found a gate in the corrugated iron fence and walked around to enter the rear of the hotel, quickly moving back into the bar to join his colleagues. The two he had heard talking in the yard were now innocently engaged in conversation with the others in the front room and he stared at them intently, enjoying the fact that he knew their secret, and slowly working through a plan to find out more. He knew where the woman worked and lived, and that she would be there for another month or so; that should give him time to figure out something. For now, he decided to socialise.

"Anyone want to challenge us to a game of darts," he called out, looking directly at Reg as he did.

Reg thought about it for a few seconds and then called to Burra through the open window "C'mon mate, let's show these blokes 'ow ta play the game." He had been glancing over occasionally at the three men and their form looked less than impressive.

"Never played," came Burra's uninterested reply.

"Doesn't look as though that'll be a 'andicap. C'mon, I'll show ya."

Burra got up and slowly walked through to the back room.

"Look out, mate! We're in trouble now. Here come the spear chuckers!" Jeckle cried out.

The young man smiled just enough to get it by as a joke, but the words still seared into Burra's mind, taking residence with the sour look the other loudmouth had given him earlier in the night.

The darts went well for Reg and Burra, the latter proving to be a bit of a natural, and after losing the first game they had proceeded to wipe the floor with the opposition over the next three. It was the fifth game when the trouble came, the losers making the suggestion that they should put a few bucks on it and, as Reg wasn't averse to taking money off mugs, he agreed. Then, halfway through the game, with his needle bouncing on a full tank, the surly Heckle lived up to his earlier promise and accused Reg of cheating.

"That's not right, ya cheatin' black bastard!" he bellowed uncontrollably, as Reg chalked up a score on the blackboard.

Burra rushed forward, only to be held back by his grandfather's outstretched arm. Then Reg turned to Heckle and went into his act.

"Aaaar, c'mon bro!" he entreated theatrically. "It's all dem dere witchetty grubs I bin eatin'. Dey mess a poor old blackfella's mind up. Sometimes I jest caarn't count. Look! I'll show ya!"

He held his right hand up before the young man's scowling face, counting off the fingers out loud as he curled them back slowly with the index finger of his left hand, "One... two... three... four... *six!*" Then he looked upwards, frowning in a confused way before the fist he had formed shot out like a piston, producing a powerful short-arm jab that caught the transfixed Heckle full in the face and floored him in an instant.

"What'd I tell ya? I'm always 'avin' trouble wid dat dere numba five."

Burra erupted in a gale of laughter; Professor and Cassie joined in, but Jim looked worried and almost immediately his fears were realised.

The other young drunk yelled out at Burra. "Who the fuck do ya think ya laughin' at, ya black piece o' shit!"

The room went quiet but, outside on the veranda, Smiler raised his head, his ears pricked in response to what he could hear coming through the darkness. Suddenly the stationary rudder of the windmill banged violently around and the blades whirred like the start-up of a light aeroplane, the warm blast of air that had given it ignition whipping through the side door of the pub and swirling through the bar.

Alan Prescott hardly registered the sudden rush of nausea that flooded through him as the gust of air hit, the sensation passing as quickly as it had come, his attention now drawn to the escalating tension in the room.

The brief silence exploded into action and this time Reg was nearly bowled over in Burra's rage to get at Jeckle.

"Oh, Jesus... 'ere we go!" Jim said with alarm, now expecting the night's takings to be wiped out in collateral damage and quickly trying to remove some of the breakables from the top of the bar.

But the bout wouldn't last long enough to do any serious damage. Burra waded in like a madman, his fists raining in on his opponent to swiftly record a knockout victory. The only harm that came to the furniture was when he picked up an ancient bar stool to confirm Jeckle's status, crashing it down on him until all that was left in his hand was a broken piece of one of the legs.

Reg stepped in and pulled Burra away before the simple fracas turned into a case of manslaughter. But he had to use all of his strength to restrain him, as the raging boy struggled to get at the curled up form on the floor.

Burra finally backed away at his grandfather's intervention, but then suddenly turned and stared fiercely at Alan Prescott, the stool leg raised like a spear.

"Do you want some o' this too, ya fuckin' bastard! I'll kill the fuckin' lot o' ya's!" he raged now at Prescott, his eyes burning with hatred, tears beginning to run down his cheeks.

For a moment Alan Prescott stared fiercely back, before he casually raised his hands as if in surrender. "Nuthin' to do with me, son. They were out of order and you fixed them up. We'll leave it at that for now, shall we?" he said, with just the shadow of a cold smile on his face.

"Ya'd better take those two and leave. I think there's been enough fun fer one night," Jim said. "I'll give ya a 'and ta get 'em out."

Alan Prescott nodded. "Come on you two… take your lumps out to the car. You can sleep it off in Kal '."

"Sorry about this, mate," he said to Reg, as he lifted one of the two off the ground and began to haul him out of the door. "They've been out in the scrub workin' for a while. This is the first break they've had in weeks, and they'll be payin' for it tomorrow."

Reg nodded in mute acceptance of the apology, but knew their hangovers wouldn't change a thing, his instinct telling him that Prescott too held something of their attitude behind his conciliatory and easygoing manner.

"C'mon, mate," he said to Burra. "I think it's about time for us ta get a move on too."

Reg bid the others goodnight then quietly told Cassie that he would be down in Kalgoorlie in a couple of weeks. He would give her some details then. She smiled and nodded.

Professor waved at the grandfather and grandson as they walked out through the door. During the evening he had quietened down into his observant state, studying the dart players closely throughout their contest and the incident that followed. A people-watcher of the earnest kind, he was intrigued by the build up and then the eruption, but he had also felt ashamed of the two who had just been dragged out of the pub. He thought of saying something as the boy walked past, but he knew that words would mean little so he did it the best way he knew how. As Reg and Burra walked onto the veranda he sat down at the old upright piano and called out through the window.

"Hey there, Mr Burra! Listen to this!"

Reg and Burra stopped to listen as Professor proceeded to play the old instrument, sending the first melodic notes of Franz Liszt's *Liebestraum Number Three* drifting out of the window, carrying its message of peace into the night. The piano was slightly out of tune and a couple of the keys were defective, but the power of the piece was still there, reaching out to the savage breast.

Reg knew that Prof could play, but it was the first time he had heard him produce anything on the old instrument beyond the popular sing-a-long ballads that the locals wanted to hear, and the rough old prospector stood captivated by the music's beauty.

So too did Mr Burra. It was far from Def Leppard and Dire Straits, yet somehow this piece of music swiftly penetrated the angry veneer to reach a quieter place. He stood listening with his grandfather, drinking in the fine sound as it wafted out through the window to join the chorus of the east wind, now singing in softer tones as it made its way through the darkness.

The music tinkled out to its satisfying end and for a few seconds there was silence. Then Prof's voice called out loudly. "That is what whitey *can* be capable of, Mr Burra!"

Burra smiled at Professor's manner. His booming voice sounded just like that of a few teachers he had known, but this time he had listened to the lesson and the message had been received.

It was late evening when the three arrived back at the camp, and Burra headed straight to the fire to stoke it up as the easterly brought the chilling side of its nature to bear. Soon the flames were lighting up the area in front of the hut and the two humans and the dog settled near its warmth, with Smiler quickly capitulating to the Labrador in his soul, snoring gently as he slept.

Little had been said on the way back from the pub and Reg and Burra fell into total silence as they sat by the fire, their meditation interrupted only occasionally by the contented voice of the dog, the sipping of tea and the popping and crackling sound of burning wood as it built the mysterious world of the coals.

Burra's quiet mood had Reg concerned that he had taken a backwards step after the blue in the pub, retreating into the surliness that he had brought with him from the city. He hoped it wasn't so. He had been thinking also of the conversation he had with Johnno's sister about their trip out into the desert and he decided to break the uncomfortable silence by telling the boy about it.

"We're goin' out inta the desert in about a month's time... lookin' fer gold.

Burra grabbed onto the words like a lifeline. He had been stewing in guilt from the moment he had recovered from his violent outburst in the pub. He felt he had let his grandfather down and the old man's silence seemed to confirm it.

"Oh, yeah! 'Ow far we goin'?" he asked enthusiastically.

"A bloody long way, by the sound of it," a relieved Reg replied. "I've been given a lead on somethin' by the woman I was talkin' to in the pub tonight. She asked me ta take 'er out there."

Reg then briefly recounted the day Johnno turned up with the gold and his subsequent death, holding Burra completely captivated by the story. It all sounded to him like it was out of a movie or a book – *The Lost Treasure of the Sierre Madre*, or *Lasseter's Reef*; he knew about them. As a young boy he had taken an avid interest in all that stuff after he was told his grandfather was a gold prospector, the old man coming alive in his imagination, even though his toddler's memories of him and the infrequent family trips to Kalgoorlie were vague.

Before meeting him the other day, Burra hadn't seen his grandfather since he was seven years old. On that occasion the old man had gone down to Perth on a rare visit and sat quietly in the lounge room, not saying very much at all, and it had been a huge let down to a young boy who was expecting a tall man with a long beard, carrying a pick and a shovel and maybe even leading a mule. What he got was a man who was still shocked by the loss of his life's partner – physically not big at all and shrunken emotionally as well, although Burra was too young to comprehend what was going on. He was just told that his granny had gone and the friendly woman with the kind voice wouldn't be speaking to him on the phone any more. She was up there somewhere, but having a good time according to what his mother told him. Truth was he had not been really looking forward to meeting his grandfather again, especially considering the purpose for which he had come to the goldfields. He was expecting the same old lectures and all the other crap that came from the oldies, but over the last few days the quiet man had grown hugely in stature, most recently earlier tonight with his calm despatching of one of those bastards at the pub. As they settled down to sleep he started giggling at the recollection.

"Eh, Grandad... 'ave ya ever eaten any o' dem dere witchetty grubs?"

"Nuh. Wouldn't even know where ta find one."

Burra's chuckling voice trailed off into the night.

Fifteen

A couple of days later Charlie turned up, lighter in the wallet and heavier under the eyes. Reg and Burra had been out on the patch working the dryblower for most of those two days and had just started the late-afternoon shift when Charlie appeared through the blinding cloud of red dust like an apparition, the machine's motor drowning out the noise of his ute's approach.

"Jesus Christ! Why don't ya scare the 'ell out of a man?" Reg exclaimed, as he turned to see his partner standing behind him.

"Missed me, huh?"

"Missed ya cookin'."

Reg's comment brought a slight smile to Burra's face as he cleared a few rocks off the screening mesh of the dryblower.

Charlie didn't respond. He looked as though he had been on a five-day bender and had still not quite returned.

"Ya look ready for an undertaker, mate. D'ya make enough to retire?" Reg enquired, already knowing the answer.

"Won a coupla 'undred on the two-up... lost it on the gee-gees. Plus a little bit more. 'Ow's the dirt?"

"'Bout the same. But I've got some news that might cheer ya up. I'll tell ya about it tonight. Me and Burra are gunna put in a coupla more hours before we 'ead back." Reg studied his mate's face for a moment then smiled. "Ya look as though ya need about twenty-four hours sleep, mate. I'll see ya back at camp."

"Burra?" Charlie queried.

"Yeah. It's Kenny's nickname. He prefers it," replied Reg.

Burra felt like saying he preferred his *friends* to call him that, and five days ago he would have said it, but he took the slight nod from Charlie when he first turned up as some sort of progress in their brief, stormy relationship.

Charlie turned to glance at Burra, who was standing there in shorts and bare feet, covered from head to toe in red dust.

"Didn't take 'im long ta go native, did it?"

"Pull ya 'ead in. 'E's okay… and 'e's turnin' inta a 'alfway decent cook. With a little bit o' luck neither of us will 'afta do much of it fer a while."

"Yeah, right. Well, I'll see ya later then," Charlie said as he wandered back to his ute.

Reg put down the shovel and followed him. He leaned down and spoke to Charlie through the car window.

"The kid's shown a lot of improvement over the last few days. Just give 'im a bitta space."

Charlie nodded. He wasn't really interested in the subject any more. His head hurt and he was tired, but curiosity over the news Reg had mentioned prompted him to seek some more information.

"What's this news ya talkin' about?" he asked.

"It's about Johnno's gold. I'll tell ya about it later."

That four-lettered word suddenly cleared Charlie's head. "Tell me now!"

"Plenty o' time when we get back," Reg said dismissively, and then walked back into the mini dust storm that Burra was creating.

Charlie drove off, not for the first time irritated by his partner's uninformative manner and when he arrived back in camp to take his much-needed sleep, he found he couldn't. He lay there like a kid waiting for Father Christmas to arrive and the moment he heard their vehicle coming he jumped up and began brewing the tea.

"Cuppa?" he yelled out enthusistically, as Reg and Burra got out of the ute and unloaded the two drums of pay dirt.

He didn't wait for the reply and quickly poured their tea, hardly allowing Reg time to sit down before he started with the questions.

"So, what's this about Johnno's gold?"

Smiler had been sniffing around Charlie's ute, searching for any alien scents that needed to be drowned and, finding a particularly nasty one on a back wheel, he had his leg raised reclaiming his territory, when Charlie's question stopped him mid-stream. He wandered over to join the humans and sat down next to Burra, ears pointed with concern.

"I met 'is sister the other day," Reg casually replied, and then began to relate the story of their meeting, his eager listeners paying close attention to everything that was said, but everyone ignored the occasional small yelp of alarm from Smiler.

"Jesus, mate! This is it! This is the one we've been waitin' for!" Charlie gleefully cried, only to react with astonishment when Reg told him it would be at least a month before they would be making the trip.

"*Whaaat*! Are ya mad? Slow and easy isn' gunna win the race with this one, mate! What if she loses patience and blabs ta someone else! Ya know what women are like! I dunno what ya coulda been thinkin' about! Do ya wanna stay on the end o' that shovel 'til ya drop dead?"

"Better than droppin' dead in the desert. You know as well as I do that this is no time o' year ta be travellin' out there. Wouldn't be at all surprised if it *was* the 'eat that drove Johnno crazy. Besides we've gotta lot o' organisin' ta do. I don't think we can risk it with both our vehicles. I figure we take one o' the utes and ask Klaus if 'e can lend us 'is Rover. 'E can use the other ute while we're away."

Charlie quietened down a bit, but he was still unconvinced. He knew what Reg was saying made sense, but the gambler in him also knew that there were times to take a risk and, with the memory of Johnno's gold glistening before him, he figured that time was now.

"We c'n take enough water with us. Klaus's vehicle has got two big tanks on it. I know it'll be bloody 'ot out there, but if we travel at the right time o' day, we could do it," he almost pleaded.

Reg sat there unmoved. Maybe if it were just he and Charlie, he might take the risk. But he had the young fella to worry about. He didn't think Carol would take too kindly to the idea of him carting her son out into the desert at one of the hottest times of the year, no matter how big the financial rewards might be.

"Just calm down, will ya. The woman doesn' know anybody else that she can trust. She took the time ta come up and see me because Johnno gave me a pass in 'is diary. She's no fool. She isn' gunna spread it around. I said I would go down an' see 'er in a coupla weeks, and that's 'ow it's gunna be."

Reg's firm statement still wasn't enough for Charlie. He tried another angle.

"And what do you reckon, young Burra?" he asked of the one person who had remained silent throughout the whole discussion.

The feigned friendliness brought no reply from the boy, but it instantly fired up Reg.

"Whaddya comin' at? Don't ask the young bloke! It's not up ta him! Christ, ya really 'ave got it bad, 'aven't ya?"

Charlie was unsettled now by his mate's tone of disgust. It was rare that Reg ever lost his temper and he had seen what could happen when he did. He didn't particularly want to be on the end of that, so he fought his overwhelming frustration and stifled the desire to let fly with things that would almost certainly mean the end of his chances of going on the expedition.

Burra's voice now temporarily intruded, trying to slip in between the trouble that he could see brewing, "I'll go with whatever Grandad says," he said, even though deep down he was almost as anxious as Charlie to be on the gold trail.

"There... 'appy now?" came the question Reg didn't want answered.

Charlie had to be, even though right now there wasn't a being in the camp that was, including Smiler, who was now lost in thoughts of his previous visit to the place his companions were arguing about, and wishing dearly there was some way he could put in his sixpence worth without being told to shut up. He knew there was trouble coming when he saw that woman the other night. If only these mugs could hear what he had to say, they wouldn't even be thinking about going – would they?

"Okay. But yer not gunna keep goin' out ta the patch now, are ya? Seems a bit pointless bustin' a gut with what's comin' up," Charlie added.

"Bird in the 'and, mate. We 'aven't found what's out there yet. Cassie said the maps are pretty clear, but we've gotta remember 'ow big that country is. If Johnno's miscalculated by a quarter of a mile, ya could spend a lifetime searchin' fer it and not find it. Anyway, ya don't 'afta come out ta the patch. Burra's doin' a good enough job. Ya can spend yer time getting' the ute up ta scratch and any of the other things we'll need to organise. I reckon we should take mine. We fixed the carby up the other day, so that's one less thing ta worry about. We'll go inta Leonora in a few days and pick up any parts ya think we'll need."

Charlie nodded at his partner's words, the flash of resentment at hearing that the grandson was doing his job well passing quickly as he started to think of the tasks ahead.

"Okay... we'll take yours. Mine's startin' ta slip a bit through first and second anyway."

*

The next few days went as planned, Reg and Burra going out to work the dryblower and Charlie pulling whatever he thought was needed for Reg's ute off the spare parts wreck, even enlisting the aid of Burra one afternoon to take off the tail shaft for use as a backup. He couldn't help but be impressed by the kid's mechanical knowledge and they both grasped upon that small common interest to ease the discomfort between them, everyone pulling their heads in now as excitement grew with the prospect of what lay ahead.

Three days later they drove into Leonora. Charlie went off to the garage in the hope of finding some of the spare parts they needed and Reg and Burra went to the general store to buy a few basics, after first stopping by at a house to sell their gold to a local agent.

Reg handed Burra a hundred dollars after leaving the buyer's house, apologising for the meagre wages as he did. But it didn't bother his young offsider; it was more than he had earned in a long time. He had nothing to spend it on anyway, coming out of the general store later with only some snack food and a few cans of soft drink. He didn't even bother buying the insect repellent he would have killed for a week and a half ago.

After putting their supplies in the back of the ute, Reg walked to the phone box on the opposite side of the road.

"I'm gunna give ya mother a bell. I want ya ta 'ave a word with 'er too."

Burra followed unenthusiastically. He had been slowly moving into a different world over the last few days and this felt like an imposition to him. He knew all he would be getting was the same old nagging lectures about behaving himself, and snippets of news that he really wasn't interested in hearing, especially if it was about his over-achieving sister.

He stood a little distance from the phone box; hardly listening to the muted conversation his grandfather was having with his mother as he vacantly surveyed the comings and goings in the wide main street. Occasionally men in khaki drove past in dusty four-wheel drives, stopped at the general store, post office or the mines department, before heading back out to the tailing-heap horizons they and their fellows had built at both ends of town. A couple of young women pushing prams stopped to speak outside the general store, their conversation punctuated by bursts of laughter as they peered at each other's recent contributions to the population. Not far away a group of Wongai children were playfully pushing each other around, until it got a bit serious and the smallest of them was left standing miserably behind as the others ran off.

Burra smiled at the familiar childhood scene, then his gaze drifted a little further along the street to fall upon someone sitting at the back of a small, grassed park on the other side of the road. The old man was almost hidden by the shade thrown from a healthy salmon gum and it was only the whiteness of his hair contrasting against his dark skin that brought him to Burra's attention.

The man sat cross-legged with his head bowed, as though sleeping, but as Burra stared at him he slowly raised his head to stare directly back, his eyes shining clearly from the shadows, and slowly, the activity on the street dissolved between their locked gaze. Suddenly, Burra felt drawn to go over and speak with him.

"G'day," Burra said to the old man as he walked up to him. But the old man neither spoke nor even looked at him now. Then, as though in response to some unspoken command for respect, Burra sat down next to him and stared directly ahead.

On the ground beside the man lay some artefacts, spread out as though they were for sale; a couple of boomerangs, a didgeridoo, clap sticks and a carved emu egg. But what took Burra's attention was the slender spear sitting in the cleft of an oval-shaped thrower.

Burra looked out onto the street, waiting for the old man to speak, and when he did it was like the rough, rustling sound of wind blowing through the peeling bark of the tree under which they sat.

The words came first in an Aboriginal tongue, of which Burra understood not one syllable, until near the end, when he was shocked to hear the word 'Burra' sounding out loud and clear.

"Eh! 'Ow did ya know me name was Burra?" came the stunned response, as he turned to look at the man.

The old man's eyes remained fixed firmly ahead and there was no answer for Burra until the look-away respect returned; then words that he could finally understand drifted to him in the man's rough, nasal whisper.

"Take the spear back ta yer country."

"Eh! What country?"

"Yer on the edge of it."

There was a longer silence and Burra understood that the old man would not be offering any more. He then rose and picked up the spear and thrower. It felt perfectly weighted in his hand, as if it were made for him. But he couldn't just take it. He pulled out a fifty-dollar note from his pocket and slipped it under one of the boomerangs.

"Thanks... see ya," Burra said as he walked away.

There was no reply.

He put the spear in the ute and walked over the road towards his beckoning grandfather.

"Don't worry, luv... 'e's doin' okay... fer a teenager. An' we're 'opin' ta get 'im eatin' with a knife an' fork soon," Reg concluded, a loud, cackling laughter coming through the receiver as he handed it to Burra.

The conversation with his mother didn't last long. He was totally distracted by the meeting with the old man, and just nodded and uttered the occasional 'yeah, Mum' and 'no Mum', surprising his mother with his lack of argument as she re-laid the ground rules of behaviour for someone called Kenny. He rang off with a muted "See ya, Mum."

As the two of them headed back to the car, Burra glanced towards the small park where he had been seated a few minutes before. The old man was no longer there, nor anywhere else to be seen in the street.

As they neared the ute, Reg spotted the end of the spear resting on the tailgate. "Where'd ya get that?" he asked casually.

"Oh, I bought it from an old bloke back there," Burra vaguely replied.

Reg picked it up and felt the balance of the thin pointed weapon. "Looks like good work. What'd ya pay fer it?"

"Fifty bucks."

"Jesus, mate! We 'aven't found the gold yet! Ya shouldna paid any more than twenty."

Burra just shrugged as he hopped in the back with Smiler, the sleeper now rising sluggishly from his midday nap and sniffing the spear and thrower suspiciously.

They drove along the street and picked Charlie up from the garage, and then headed back out of town just as a small ostracised Wongai boy was sprinting down the street towards his mates, shouting with glee as he held up the fifty-dollar note he had found flapping along the footpath.

Sixteen

"I'll 'ave another middy thanks luv," came a voice from the end of the bar.

Cassie sauntered along the line of chatting, smoking, laughing heads, took another clean glass out of the washer and poured the man his beer, about his twelfth as she recalled, which meant that anytime now she would be getting the marriage proposal.

It had only been a couple of days since she had returned from Jimblebar, but Cassie was doing it tough. Could she take another three and a half weeks of this? She had already begun crossing off the days; eight-hour shifts on her feet dispensing the pretend good humour, constantly parrying the remarks about the more prominent parts of her anatomy, when all the while her mind was out in the desert somewhere picking up pieces of gold. She poured another beer, wishing right at this moment that she could just turn the beer taps around and fire-hose the lot of them, extinguish all the smoke and drown all the smart-arsed comments, but she knew they would probably only open their mouths and scream for more. She sighed inwardly. Right now the only thing she could feel happy about was that she wasn't suffering the hangover of the vicious migraine she had experienced yesterday. She glanced up at the ceiling as she recalled the strange incident the afternoon before, when her thoughts were suddenly interrupted by another request.

"C'n I 'ave a pack o' those pork scratchin's, darlin'?"

Cassie sighed again as she strained to reach up and take a packet off the top of the snack tree.

"D'ya want me ta come around an' give ya a lift up, luv?" came an offer from another head, causing a burst of loud laughter to ripple along the bar.

She turned around after retrieving the packet and, without glancing at the old man who had delivered the comment, fired off her reply, "I don't think you'd be capable of liftin' anything now, would ya mate? You probably wouldn't be able to find it any more."

"Just you try me, luv, there's many a woman who's come back askin' fer a repeat," the old man drivelled.

"Yeah? Probably wonderin' what it was they had in the first place," came the instant response, delivered without a smile but bringing another ripple of laughter from the other side of the bar.

More empty glasses were pushed towards her and Cassie poured more beers. She was only two hours into her shift and the irritation level was rapidly rising. Right now she couldn't see how she could make it through even one day more and when the request for a lemon squash came right in the middle of her working the beer tap, she turned to snap at the person who had requested it.

Standing behind the row of drinkers and smiling brightly was a reasonably attractive middle-aged man dressed in an expensive business suit. Cassie held back the words she was about to deliver and looked at him a little confusedly. The voice had sounded familiar and she thought she had seen him before, but couldn't quite place him.

"G'day, Cassie," he said and, smiling at her confusion, added, "Alan Prescott. Jimblebar pub about a week ago."

"Oh, yeah. You look a bit different now," Cassie replied, as she slid the beer across the bar and poured a lemon squash from the gun next to the beer tap.

Alan Prescott settled on an empty stool at the end of the bar.

"What brings you in here? You're liable to get assaulted lookin' like that," Cassie continued.

"Oh, these are my Perth clothes. I've just flown back from some business meetings down there. I'll be getting rid of them as soon as I get back to my unit. I was just driving past, saw the pub and remembered that you said you worked here." Prescott took a mouthful of his drink and then smiled smoothly as he added, "The fact of the matter is I've been feeling a little guilty over my come-on to you at the pub that night, and the behaviour of the two roughnecks with me. I wondered if you might like to go out and have a meal sometime and help me ease my guilt."

"No need to feel guilty. You didn't say anything I haven't heard nearly every day of my workin' life... bit milder than most, actually. As for the other two, I see their kind of behaviour all the time. Hang around here for a while and you'll probably see a whole lot worse," Cassie replied, not totally averse to his suggestion, but quick to destroy any false reasoning for it.

"Okay. I'll start again. Would you like to come out for a fine meal at a good restaurant?"

"Yeah... I would," came the slurred acceptance from the man seated next to Prescott.

Prescott chuckled at the comment and Cassie smiled for the first time that morning, any resistance to the invitation instantly broken. A bit of civilised entertainment might be just the diversion she needed to break up this rotten period of waiting and she agreed to a dinner date for the coming Saturday night.

Alan Prescott left the hotel feeling pretty pleased that the first part of his plan had been put into place, but his mind was still very much occupied with the meeting he'd had with his bank manager the day before, and still mystified by what had happened later at his home. As he reached his car on the opposite side of the street, a flash of déjà vu, a feeling of some sort of connection with that incident, caused him to turn and look back at the upper floor of the old two-storey pub. He stared at the façade for a while, vacantly studying it, before the sense of familiarity faded. He stepped into his car and drove to his small townhouse out in one of the newer suburbs, throwing himself on the bed soon after walking in the door; tired, but still thinking.

Twenty-four hours before, he had been sitting on the end of a bed in the master bedroom of his City Beach mansion, staring into a mirrored wall of built-in wardrobes. He couldn't escape himself in the room; thanks to his wife's obsession about her appearance there were bloody mirrors everywhere, but this afternoon they reflected a sombre image. He was looking closely at his face, searching there for whatever had terrified her and his children so much. His behaviour had frightened him too. He knew that he was a bit of a mongrel, a user of people, a womaniser, a gambler, a drinker, and a proud exponent of the art of lying, but he had never belted a woman before. There was a gap in his memory that could've lasted no more than a minute and during it what he had said and done had cowed his wife and sent his children running terrified to their rooms, and nothing he could say later would bring them out.

'You looked like a monster, daddy!' his six-year-old daughter, Kate, had simpered from behind her locked bedroom door, and his eight-year-old son, David, hadn't answered him at all.

Earlier in the day he had flown down from Kalgoorlie for another of his unhappy meetings with his bank manager, a glum accountant in tow. He knew it had been called to see how the bank could most easily deconstruct his millionaire's lifestyle for their benefit and he had nothing he could bring to the table to stop the demolition. He half-considered trying to delay the wrecking crew by presenting them with the story of riches in the desert. But he had no claim pegged, no drilling results, no assay figures on paper. All he had was what he had overheard in the backyard of an old pub, and he knew he would look like a desperate fool if he brought that up.

Prescott kept his mouth shut and listened unhappily as the vultures began to pick over his body of assets. The three-storey City Beach mansion would be going, his beach shack down at Dunsborough, which would not have been out of place next to the City Beach property, and his investment in an inner-city office development. But what kicked him in the gut most of all was the priority placed on off-loading his state-of-the-art cruising launch; a twenty-five-metre party vessel designed specifically for entertaining and impressing clients and the money-hugging friends he had gathered when his wealth was in the ascendant. While most of those had dropped away as his financial status waned, the posing effect of the vessel still remained. For any female prey he came across on his late-night gambling trips it was a sleek white lure to a floating boudoir, and a place of escape from the increasingly aggressive nagging of his wife. But it was far from a financial asset. Built at the cost of over a million dollars, it was a depreciating item that was only out on open water for a couple of weeks a year and cost a great deal to maintain, even when tied to the dock. He had been hoping that the sale of his other assets would delay the need to get rid of it, but it was glaringly obvious to anybody with a brain for finance that it would have to be the first tick on the list.

He had come home from the depressing meeting in the early afternoon, and when he called his wife in to explain the gravity of the day's events she had bawled him out again, but more ferociously than before.

'And where do you expect me and the children to live now... rented accommodation in Balga?' she had screamed hysterically, as Prescott itemised the things that would soon be missing from her very comfortable life. All the privileges of wealth were tumbling before her eyes. All the respect that money could buy would now be converted into disdain. No more morning sessions at the designer gym. No more lazy three-hour lunches at the best restaurants. No more overseas jaunts at the drop of a hat, to go shopping in Hong Kong or Singapore. She might even have to get a job! The kids would have to go to a public school! She just couldn't bear to think about any of it.

'Daddy told me when he first met you that he thought you were a loser. He warned me not to get involved with you. You are not going to do this to me! You are not going to take it all away just like that! I've had enough of your losing ways. I want a divorce and I'm going to make sure you pay dearly for the years I've had to spend with you!' she had railed, striding back and forth in front of him, as though she was back on the catwalk from where he had plucked her.

Prescott sat quietly taking her words in, head down with his eyes fixed hypnotically on the carpet, a hooded expression slowly forming on his face. He had been drinking with his accountant for an hour or so after the meeting and had made several trips to the drinks cabinet since coming home, and with each sip his mood was darkening, each word of the haranguing session taking him closer to the edge.

Unaware of what was brewing, Dianne carried on with her attack at close quarters, standing before him now, hands on hips, until she was suddenly stopped mid-sentence when she saw his body jerk and shudder as though given an electric shock. She stared in confusion as he slowly raised his head, and then in horror at the look of total menace on his face, his features so contorted with rage that they were almost unrecognisable to her. And with his terrifying countenance came a sickening stench.

Prescott slowly unfurled his body and stood up before his trans-fixed wife, closed his fist and brought it down on the side of her head, as though he was clubbing her with something. '*Stand away, bitch! I've 'ad enough of thy bloody mouth!*' he yelled, the words flying from his lips in a rough and rumbling way and carried to his wife on a rush of unearthly foul breath.

Dianne fell to the floor then desperately backed away. Prescott closed on her, body bent over; arms curled out and around like a beast preventing the escape of its prey. A fiendish smile formed on his face as her short dress revealed a glimpse of her shapely tanned thighs and the white satin-covered mound that crowned their apex. He began to hurriedly loosen his trousers and release the swelling within, when he heard his two children cry out in defence of their mother. He turned to glare evilly at them. Then their screaming retreat finally brought him back.

Prescott looked confusedly at his wife as she climbed to her feet and rushed in terror out of the room, holding a hand to her red and swollen face. He glanced down at his right hand and wrung it against the shooting pain then vacantly zipped his fly and fastened his belt before moving to the drinks cabinet. Scotch in hand, he then stum-bled upstairs, knocking fruitlessly on his children's bedroom doors before staggering up to the main bedroom in the drunken hope of retrieving the situation. All he found was an opened door to one of the wardrobes and some of his wife's clothes missing. He slumped down on the edge of the bed and stared at the mirrored door, studying his face and only vaguely registering the sound of a Mercedes starting up and reversing out of the driveway. That was it. Number two marriage gone. It wasn't unexpected, but he did feel bad about the way it had ended. He couldn't remember doing it but he knew he must have hit her. It wasn't the first time that booze had wiped out parts of his memory, but it had never made him violent before. It seemed the kids had seen it all too. He was sad about that, and their going, even though in his constant absence he had hardly developed a proper relationship with them.

The look of fear and loathing on Dianne's face had drifted in and out of his mind all the way back on the short flight to Kalgoorlie, intermingling with the desperation over his financial crisis as he shuffled the numbers that would not add up to anything but the colour red. Now there would be another maintenance order and, knowing his second wife's expensive tastes and her lawyer father's dislike of him, it all added up to a poverty-stricken future. But whatever he was, he wasn't a quitter. He still had one faint hope of financial resurrection and as he lay in the bedroom of his Kalgoorlie unit, contemplating the job he had before him, he began to get a little excited at the prospect. Bedding the attractive barmaid and getting the information required from her was a challenge he was looking forward to. His one big weakness had decimated his fortune but he still had the manipulating skills that had built it in the first place and he would bring them all to bear on this project.

Apart from his serious gambling habit, Alan Prescott was no fool. He was a smooth operator, with a likeable, bush-style demeanour that belied the devious man beneath and the vicious approach he had to business. He had managed to become a millionaire not only by the income earned through his geologist consultancy firm, but also by insider trading on the stock market. Using his knowledge of assay results on projects, he bought into share issues cheaply before any public announcements brought the stampede of investors, camouflaging the purchases in the name of bogus trusts and any shady associates he could lure with the promise of easy money. But, despite the recent pegging rush, there hadn't been a lot around to excite the market of late, certainly not the way it had been in the late 'sixties, when he had begun his insider career on the tidal wave of the nickel boom. Now his pot of gold lay somewhere out in the desert, and even though his practical knowledge was constantly throwing up doubt that it could exist in that country's geology, he would pursue the thing ruthlessly until it was proven one way or another.

He took Cassie out for their fine meal at a good restaurant, and twice more over the following week. The first time, apart from answering a few questions about his work, Prescott ventured nowhere near what he knew lay in the mind of his female companion, and in a diary she possessed. On their second meeting however, whilst drinking coffee after taking Cassie home to the cabin she had now moved into in the caravan park, he introduced the subject. He mentioned that he had been given a contract to do some work northeast of Kalgoorlie, specifically mentioning the Great Victoria Desert. It was a double-pronged approach, probing for a response now but also setting up an excuse for being in the region if he was later spotted tracking her party, a last resort he hoped he wouldn't have to take.

"I don't envy your lifestyle, havin' to go out into that sort of country to make a livin'. I thought mine was bad enough," came the innocent reply. The goldfields area was huge and what Prescott had said hadn't moved beyond coincidental in Cassie's mind. On their third date, though, her antennae began to rise when he again casually mentioned the subject of searching for gold in the desert, this time telling her that he was expecting to take off into the country east of Jimblebar in a few weeks.

It was a deliberate attempt by Prescott to finally elicit some response. He knew she had the smarts of the barmaid, but maybe he could get her to give in to that part of the gold seeker that wanted to blab about a find. Then he could offer his expertise in pegging and valuing it, get his foot in the door so he could eventually push her out and slam it in her face. His second hope was that, even if she didn't talk, she might panic and leave sooner than had been originally planned, and he had that option covered also.

But Cassie didn't show any signs of panicking, not even after what happened later that night.

It was a still and sultry evening, with the promise of a thunderstorm flashing in the western sky when, not long after he had brought her back to her cabin, Prescott finally made the night moves. And after a long drought of men in her bed, Cassie readily complied, the two of them threshing about for a couple of hours before lying back satisfied, resting after a successful expedition into the unknown and pleasantly surprised with what they had both found. After a few minutes lying in the heat and the perspiration, Cassie got up to take a shower. She stood under the cold water for several minutes, letting it wash the heat temporarily away, then dried herself slowly before putting on a light robe. When she came out she found her guest also getting dressed, explaining that he had to drive out to a prospect early in the morning, and if he hung around there he knew he would be getting little sleep.

To Cassie it seemed to be the classic departure after dessert, but she didn't mind; she needed her sleep as well. It was only later that she saw he had been doing more than dressing while she was in the shower.

Prescott had waited until he heard the shower turned on and the plastic shower curtain being pulled across, before quickly moving to the small built-in wardrobe in one corner of the cabin. He had already checked through the drawers of the bedside cabinets and looked under the mattress for what he hoped to find, although he suspected all along that the streetwise female would be too smart to leave such a valuable document lying about. He was proved right, even though he had found the diaries easily enough, stacked under some other papers in the bottom drawer of the wardrobe. But when he quickly flipped through them to find the last one, he could see that the relevant pages had been torn out. Soon after, he heard the shower turn off and swiftly closed the drawer.

After saying goodnight to her guest, Cassie had gone to the wardrobe to get a pair of briefs and a T-shirt to sleep in, when she noticed the corner of paper sticking out of the top of the lower drawer. She was not an overly neat person, except where her papers were concerned, and when she pulled the drawer out she instantly noted that the last diary was now on top. The suspicion that had begun to grow earlier that evening was confirmed; she could only guess how Prescott had found out. He must have been within earshot when she had spoken to Reg that night at the pub. But it didn't matter now. Somehow she would have to shake him off the trail. He often went to Perth. She would find out when his next trip would be and then get in touch with Reg about starting their journey while Prescott was away. She was sure that her prospecting partner wouldn't argue about going sooner when he heard about the new development.

For peace of mind, Cassie went back into the bathroom, opened the small cupboard under the vanity basin and checked the narrow gap between the bowl and the back edge of the unit. The small map and torn out pages of the diary were still there, securely jammed up next to the large red-back spider, which had set up house where no cleaner would ever go, and spared by Cassie to remain as a sort of guardian of the treasure map. Satisfied, she went back to bed and lay on the uncomfortable heat of the foam mattress, before slowly falling asleep to the sound of far-off rumbling in the sky.

Cassie awoke at about two o'clock in the morning, with the desert wind breathing softly through her open window and stroking her face. The thunderstorm had not arrived. In the fickle way of early autumn, it had threatened and then drifted away, carrying its cooling moisture off to the south somewhere. But inside her head another storm raged, the blinding headache causing her to stumble to the bathroom and bring up everything of the fine meal she had earlier consumed at Prescott's expense. With shaking hands she quickly took the powerful painkillers prescribed by a local doctor after an incapacitating migraine attack the week before. She had had a history of them, and usually a couple of strong codeine-based pills, if taken in time, were effective enough to escape the worst of the headache's wrath. This night, however, the much stronger ones she had been prescribed had no effect, and she lay in bed travelling the terrible road of pain for over three hours, with no letup in the intensity that caused her to vomit every half hour and sob constantly from her misery. Then, as the sun's first colours tinted the horizon and the desert wind died away, the headache faded with it. She quickly fell asleep, taking the miserly three hours she had left before having to get up and go to work. She hoped it would be without the hangover of the migraine, the demon that remained thumping its last malicious beat whenever she coughed or bent down, or even spoke beyond a whisper. But when she awoke again, there was not the slightest hint of the evil presence, no residue of the misery of the night before, as if she hadn't suffered it at all. Strangely, it matched the experience she'd had a week ago.

On that day, Cassie had started her shift at mid-morning, bustling around in the usual pre-lunch and early-afternoon rush, before it eventually slowed and she had time to have a coffee. She was taking her break away from the bar, sitting in a little alcove near the steps that ran up to the upper floor of the old building, when she heard that sound again.

Upstairs, there were half a dozen small guest rooms, and at the front of the building a larger one with a balcony. The front room had been used briefly as living quarters by the husband and wife who now ran the establishment until, only a day after moving in, the wife insisted that they shift to a couple of rooms on the ground floor. She didn't explain why to her husband, but for some reason she just didn't feel comfortable in the room, and since they had moved out it had only been used as a storage area.

Cassie had never ventured up the steps of the building. Her job was down below and when her shift finished she didn't hang around. But, ever since she had started work in the front bar, she had been hearing the occasional loud bump, or what sounded like someone moving around up there. She asked the owner about it, but he had said that he thought it was just the expansion and contraction of the old floorboards and roof timber. The first few times he had heard them he had gone to investigate, but could find nothing.

The sounds came again. Bump! Thump! Scra-a-a-ape! Then Cassie heard what she could have sworn was a woman talking, mumbling something incoherently, like some of the drunks she had been listening to for years. She looked into the bar. There were only two male customers there with the owner, and they were all going about their business quietly. She put her coffee cup back in the kitchen and walked up the stairs, the creaking of old timber following her every step.

The door to the front room was not locked and she opened it slowly. The interior was quite bright, the sun shining through the western aspect of the French doors and sending shafts of dust-specked light across the room. Piled up around the walls was the stock-in-trade of the hotel business; old chairs, tables, crates of jugs and glasses, advertising placards and wire racks that once held this or that brand of potato chips and other snack foods.

It seemed like a nice room to her, and she felt strangely comfortable there as she stared out through the dusty, yellowed net curtains onto the street below. She tried to open the handles of the French doors but they wouldn't budge, their internal parts welded by many years of non-use. But while she was standing there, peering at the badly weathered timber of the landing and lost in her thoughts, she felt a light breath of wind blowing on her back and a man's voice speaking from somewhere behind her. The words came faintly at first, and she thought it was just some conversation from below drifting up the steps, so she didn't turn around. But then the wind suddenly gusted, blowing down the hallway from an open window at the other end. A stench of something very foul suddenly came to her and then a voice hissed against her ear. She turned around with fright. Then the flash came and she collapsed.

She came to twenty minutes later in a spare bed downstairs, where she had been placed with the help of two of the hotel patrons after the owner's wife had noticed the door to the store room was ajar and then found Cassie lying before the wide-open French doors. When she awoke it was to a blinding headache accompanied by a violent bout of nausea. A doctor had been called, but the injection he gave her only partially reduced her suffering. Yet, a short time after the owner had driven her home to the caravan park, the symptoms disappeared, turned off as if someone had flipped a switch in her brain. She was greatly relieved and glad to be getting off the remaining few hours of her shift, but the mystery remained.

Back at the hotel, the owner's wife was mystified too. The strange-ness she had experienced in the front room soon after they had taken ownership of the pub now seemed to have manifested itself in an even stranger way. When her husband got back from dropping Cassie off, she let fly at him for earlier dismissing her suspicions.

"What'd I tell you about that bloody room? You explain to me how those French doors got to be open after being rusted shut. And how come they were closed tight again straight after? You said you didn't shut them and I certainly didn't. You won't get me going in there again. As a matter of fact, the sooner we can sell this dump the better. And if it's not very soon, I'm getting out anyway!"

Her husband could offer neither explanation nor argument. He had dragged his wife to the goldfields against her wishes in the first place and ever since arriving she had wanted to get out. Now, the spookiness of this business with the French doors had provided her with a reason and, after laughing off all her earlier concerns, right now he couldn't blame her for wanting to leave.

Back at the Gateway caravan park that afternoon, Cassie had lain on her bed trying to connect the voice that had hissed from behind her ear before she collapsed with someone she knew, or once knew. Now, as she walked to work on the morning of her second similar migraine attack, she recalled it again, the words '*Stand away, bitch! I've 'ad enough of thy bloody mouth!*' still clearly fixed in her brain, the voice that delivered them seeming even more familiar than before.

Seventeen

"Naaah… I told ya, Grandad! Don't 'url the thrower as well!" Burra laughed, as the spear went slewing forty-five degrees to the side and the thrower hurtled on further than the weapon. "Look, I'll show ya again."

Burra retrieved the spear and the thrower then stood back about thirty paces from the plastic bag he had stuck on a small bush. Taking one step forward with his left leg he then let the missile go, the narrow shaft whipping and flexing as it went, but deadly accurate, once more piercing the centre of the plastic bag.

Reg continued to be amazed. The boy had taken such a short time to master the weapon, even allowing that he had been practising with it at nearly every opportunity since he bought it, over a week before. The metal detector had been totally ignored as he honed his skill with the spear and constantly sharpened its point with a piece of quartz, and his attention to it soon brought a more practical result than spearing plastic bags. Just a couple of days ago he had come back to camp with a medium-sized kangaroo draped over his shoulders, his face beaming as he explained how Smiler had herded the small mob right across in front of him. He had speared the roo mid-flight and excitedly showed where it had entered the animal's side and pierced its heart. At the time, Reg had privately considered it a fluke shot, but now he could clearly see that it wasn't.

As impressed as Reg was with Burra's newly acquired skill, Charlie was disconcerted by it, feeling less comfortable around their guest by the minute. A clearer case of someone going native he had never seen; bare feet, no shirt; he was even wearing a band of red cloth around his head like a Wongai. Any moment now he was expecting to see him painted up and doing a knee-banging dance around the camp-fire, and wouldn't be at all surprised to see his mate joining him.

"Yeah… okay, smart arse. Give us another try," Reg said, as Burra retrieved the spear.

He followed the constant stream of instructions from Burra, took a step forward and hurled the weapon. This time it flew as it should, although well to the left of the target. Burra clapped his hands slowly.

"Not a bad throw fer an ol' bugger. Took ya a while though."

Reg smiled broadly. It felt good to watch it flying with something approaching accuracy. "Give us another go," he said, as Burra walked quickly to retrieve the spear.

After two more tries, Reg finally hit the bush with the bag stuck in it, and yelled with triumph. He wanted to keep going until he hit the bag, but Burra intervened with what should have been the older man's advice.

"In case ya 'aven't noticed, Grandad, the sun's goin' down and we 'aven't packed any o' the gear away yet."

"Yeahhh… all right," Reg replied, disappointed, feeling a little like a kid who had just been told to put his toys away.

They got back from the alluvial patch just on dusk, to find Charlie building up the fire. He had been fitting new shock absorbers to the ute, but darkness had prevented him from finishing the last one, and when he greeted them it was with the sarcasm of the irritated.

"Did ya 'it the mother lode?"

"Nuh, but I 'it the bush!" Reg replied.

He and Burra chuckled, but their enjoyment of the private joke brought a sour look from Charlie.

The next morning, the dirt from the previous day was washed and they added a measly fifty bucks to the kitty.

"I told ya. I dunno why yer botherin'," was Charlie's comment when given the results. He was lying under the ute lubricating long-neglected parts with a grease gun when he spoke.

"I guess it's ta 'elp with payin' fer all the spare parts and the fuel we're gunna 'afta shell out fer," Reg responded, his mate's negativity beginning to wear.

"Mmmmm," Charlie hummed in unenthusiastic agreement, remembering that they still had spares to buy when they went down to Kalgoorlie in a few days' time, and that didn't include any parts they might need for Klaus' vehicle, which they were going to see about later in the morning.

When Charlie crawled out from under the ute about fifteen minutes later, no one was to be seen. Then he heard a couple of yells and Smiler's loud bark coming from over the hill. He walked to the top to investigate, just in time to see Reg lining up with the spear and sending it flying powerfully straight at the white object about twenty metres in front of him, then yelling with glee when it passed straight through the target.

Smiler barked and Burra yelled, but Charlie just shook his head in bemusement.

"Are we goin' ta see Klaus or not!" he yelled at the figures below.

"Yeah, okay... we're comin'," a chastened Reg replied.

An hour later they drove into Klaus' camp and the three went straight to the German's old Land Rover ute to look it over. They had seen Klaus at the pub a couple of nights before and he had responded to their request to borrow the vehicle with his usual generosity.

"*Ja*, shuur... no vorries, mate. I haf a bit of trouble mit ze steering. Sometimes it vant to go left ven I vant to go right, but ze rest running vell... for a pommy car."

They took note of the spare hoses and belts they would need to buy and checked out the steering problem, soon realising that all it needed was a bit of adjustment, which could be done after they picked it up. Then they filled a small box with some of the explosives, fuses and detonators that Klaus used in the excavation of his alluvial mine. Both felt certain that Johnno's gold had come from a source that would need to be blown, but they wouldn't mention it to Klaus.

All they said was that they needed it for a bit of promising rock they had seen, then they parted company with him before he could bring out the booze, not wanting to wipe off the rest of the day listening to 'songs for Anna'.

They had decided the night before that there was to be no work on the dryblower that day so when they got back to camp Reg went to work setting up a dripper system to irrigate his vegie patch while they were away. And he felt quite happy with his lot at that moment, quietly whistling over his task as he punched holes in an old hose he intended to connect to the water tank. Things were not moving as fast as Charlie would like but they were going as he preferred, slow and steady, with all arrangements for the trip falling neatly into place. There was no need for rushing. The time to leave would come around soon enough.

Eighteen

"Bloody told ya! A woman can't keep 'er mouth shut! Now we're gunna 'afta race some bastard out there!" Charlie wailed.

Expecting the outburst, Reg had herded his mate out onto the veranda of the Jimblebar pub before giving him the news that someone else knew about the gold. He had just spoken to Cassie, after Jim had come out to their camp with the urgent message to give her a call. Now he stood before Charlie, just as concerned as his mate was. If Prescott had overheard him and the woman talking, then he would know that the find had to be somewhere in the vicinity of a few isolated salt lakes known as the Plumridge group; the only ones remotely near to the location Cassie vaguely described when she told him about the gold. They would have to move quickly now. He was just hoping that the eavesdropper was not properly prepared and they could get a start on him.

Reg explained to Charlie that Cassie hadn't spoken to anybody, but it had little effect. His mate still felt vindicated in his belief that, if they waited, there was the danger that someone might beat them to it, and after his initial moan he quickly began issuing orders.

"Ring 'er back. Tell 'er we'll be down ta pick 'er up early tomorra mornin'. An' we'll 'afta go out an' pick up the Land Rover *now*! We've gotta get a bloody move on!" he yelled, almost at their vehicle before Reg had taken a step towards the phone.

Reg could no longer argue against the urgency. Cassie had told him that Prescott was going to be in Perth the next day, but how soon would it be before he found out she had gone? And he didn't even have to follow them. He knew the general location and the direction from which they would be heading. All he had to do was search for their tracks in the vicinity, tracks that would easily show up in the desert terrain. And he was a geologist. He knew what to look for. It was not yet clear to Reg just how specific Johnno's directions were. If it came down to a prospecting race, Prescott would have the edge. All these thoughts raced through his usually calm mind. Charlie had been proved right about the waiting. They couldn't allow the heat factor to stop them now. They had to move, and quickly.

The moment after Cassie received the call from Reg to say that they would be leaving the next morning, she went to the pub owner and informed him apologetically that she would not be coming in any more, that she was moving on. Then that night she excitedly packed for the trip she had been preparing for even before speaking with Reg at the pub, gathering together the clothing, footwear and camping equipment she had been purchasing over the previous weeks: all essential items she considered. But the next day she would meet someone who would not be pleased about some of her purchases.

Charlie had not even met the woman who was going to provide him with what he hoped would be the biggest pay cheque of his life, but even with that possibility before him he wasn't happy about her tagging along. Owner of a treasure map or not, he didn't think she would be up to the harsh conditions out there. He considered it was no place for a townie, least of all a female.

It was about nine o'clock the next morning when the two of them finally met. Charlie was still running in full organisational mode, glorying in the fact that for one of the rare moments in his relationship with Reg his judgement had been correct, and he had been letting his mate know about it at almost every turn. Then he saw the shower bag amongst the things Cassie was loading into the ute and turned his recently acquired authority on her.

"Where d'ya reckon ya gunna get the water ta 'ave a shower?" he asked almost immediately after their brief, nodding introduction.

Cassie gave him the bemused barmaid's look. Off your brain, perhaps, she thought as she studied the strange-looking creature before her. He looked as though he had just been dragged into the caravan park behind the vehicle, with his dirt-stained clothes, regulation half-beard and grubby old beanie on his head.

Charlie lost the stare-off, but when a fold-up toilet seat went in and Cassie had gone inside to bring out her last bag, he turned side-on and moaned to Reg, "Jesus, mate... she'll be bringin' out the bloody cistern next!"

"What's the matter with ya? Don't forget she's 'oldin' all the cards. If ya don't shut yer mouth, ya might find yerself left behind tendin' the vegie patch while I'm out there pickin' up nuggets. As far as I'm concerned, if she wants ta bring a TV, washin' machine and electric oven with 'er, she can... anythin' that can't be used'll be tossed anyway... law o' the bush. As fer the dunny seat, I've gotta say there's times I wished I 'ad one out there."

Charlie dropped back a couple of gears after the lecture and the trip back to the camp was mostly quiet and polite, although he weakened near the end of it and asked to see the map.

"Yeah... right," came the stare-ahead reply.

Burra crawled out from under the Rover just as the ute drove in. He had been left at the camp to attend to the steering problem and finish the packing of the vehicle. When he reported to Reg that all was ready to go, after a quick double check of their supplies they climbed into their respective vehicles.

Without any prior arrangement Reg and Cassie got into the Land Rover together and Charlie and Burra got into the ute, Burra preferring to travel in the back with Smiler rather than make small conversation with someone whom he was still not comfortable being around. But when he called Smiler to jump up into the back with him, the dog strangely slunk away, trotting around to the back of the hut. Burra jumped off and followed him, calling him back.

"Jesus Christ, that's all we need now... a bloody moody dog!"

Charlie moaned, as he climbed out of the vehicle to see what was going on.

Smiler ignored Burra's friendly urging to go to him, skipping away whenever he got close enough to be caught, and soon everyone was trying to round up the troublesome animal. Then Charlie managed to grab his tail and Smiler turned, snarled and barked at him.

"Come near me again, mate an' I'll take yer bloody 'and off! I'm not goin' back out there fer nobody!"

"What's the matter with ya, ya crazy bloody mongrel?" Charlie exclaimed, as he drew his hand back in alarm, before walking away in disgust. "Okay, stay here ya mad bastard. There's plenty o' cans in the hut and there's a can opener on the bottom shelf," he yelled back.

The words fell on pointed ears. Food *was* a priority. Smiler gave in and walked up to Burra, following his soothing voice back to the ute, before jumping onto the back.

"See! All ya gotta do is speak their language," Charlie said.

"Yeahhh… don't I bloody wish," Smiler growled then crawled into a front corner of the ute and curled his body up defensively. If it was at all possible, he intended to stay right there for the duration.

The party set off in the stewing heat of early afternoon, moving quickly across the station country until they reached the last of the graded tracks and headed off into virgin ground. Then they made their way less rapidly through the rugged environment, heading towards an even harsher one, the stunted, skeletal trees tracking their progress and fewer birds and animals now crossing their path.

Reg knew enough of the terrain to pick his way towards the edge of the desert and they reached it in the late afternoon. There they set up camp beneath a lonely black oak, the stunted tree looking like the forward scout of an expedition leading an exhausted trail of vegetation out of the brooding land ahead.

The five had made good progress but, while they were busying themselves with setting up camp, two hundred kilometres away another four travellers were still driving through the dying light of dusk, trying to make as much progress as they could before darkness fell, heading towards the desert edge from the southwest.

*

Reg had hoped that their competition would be caught unprepared, but Prescott had been preparing from the moment he first heard that golden conversation in the darkened yard of the Jimblebar pub. He had immediately enlisted the aid of the unpaid Heckle and Jeckle with the promise of five percent interest in the project. Then he included a fourth man in the person of Terry Walters, a mining equipment supplier, given a ten percent interest in the carve-up because of the extra vehicle, trail bikes and other equipment he could provide. Although the latter already held an overdue amount of some ten thousand dollars against Prescott's name, he had agreed to supply the equipment when his share in the deal was upped from five percent, then, after being told where they would be taking it, he had insisted on going along to watch over his property.

Prescott was in Perth signing papers at his accountant's office for the sale of his commercial property and his City Beach house, snapped up at fire-sale prices, when he received the call he had been waiting for. An aging ex-prostitute he knew living at the caravan park had been paid to keep an eye on Cassie's movements and the woman had alerted one of Prescott's offsiders soon after Reg and Charlie's ute drove out of the park. He had then called Prescott.

"She's on the move! Dolly said her and a couple of old blokes packed up and took off just a few minutes ago," Jeckle had yelled down the line.

The clever bitch! Prescott thought. That was why she had enquired about his next trip to Perth during the meal they'd had two nights before. No matter, what he had hoped for had eventually come about. And he was ready, one step ahead from the beginning, two Landcruisers, each with two trail bikes fastened to a trailer behind, packed up and waiting in the driveway of his Kalgoorlie unit.

"I'll be on the plane within the hour. We'll be heading out as soon as I get back. Just make doubly sure all those water containers are filled. I don't want to die of thirst sittin' on top of a pile of gold." He hung up not feeling so bad about the fire sale he had just attended, believing that now he had a real chance to put out the flames before they consumed everything.

*

Prescott's group had headed inland from Kalgoorlie, following a gravel road northeast through the back country and cutting off nearly two hundred kilometres of unnecessary travel up the main highway and through Jimblebar. They eventually stopped about eight o'clock that night, their camp a roughly built fire, their evening meal beginning with a couple of cartons of beer, their night's entertainment consisting of firing off shotguns at any object around them. But one would not join in. By now Terry Walters had begun to feel decidedly unhappy about the whole trip, as his acquaintance with Prescott and his two blathering offsiders went beyond the business relationship and entered an uncomfortable social one.

Heckle and Jeckle had started to behave in their usual manner once the beer was broken out, becoming almost uncontrollable after a while. At one stage a shotgun blast nearly hit one of the car tyres, and Prescott didn't seem to care. He just sat back and smiled at their behaviour, occasionally following their example, including the habit of standing up out of the chair, taking one step to the side, and proceeding to take a piss almost in the face of the person next to him. It was all boys-in-the-bush stuff and didn't impress Terry at all. Right now he wished he was back at home with his wife and kids, and was almost ready to tell Prescott that he wanted to head back in the morning, when the geologist spoke to him.

The other two were at one of the vehicles, rifling through a box looking for something to eat when Prescott looked at Terry across the fire.

"Thou'll not be goin' back in the mornin'," he coldly stated in a rough, hushed tone through the dancing flames. The shadows they cast on his face painted a look of brooding evil.

"Eh?" came the incredulous response.

"What's that?" Prescott enquired, as he leant forward to stoke the fire with a stick. His menacing voice was gone, his face just tired and haggard.

"What did you say?" Terry asked.

"Nuthin' that I can recall," Prescott replied as he leant back in the chair again. "First night out and you're already hearin' voices, eh?" he added, staring intensely at Terry as he spoke.

"Yeah... guess so," Terry replied, deeply unsettled now.

Further north a more civilised gathering had settled down after their evening meal. The map that Cassie had finally produced was laid out on a card table under the fluorescent light of a lamp and Charlie was studying the worm-like markings on it while Reg read the last pages of the diary.

"Look 'ow far 'e went, will ya? 'Ang on! The trail stops in the middle of a bloody lake!" Charlie moaned. "This can't be bloody right! What does the diary say?"

"Seems ta think 'e saw someone crossin' the lake and then bogged his vehicle tryin' ta follow. Got 'eat stroke diggin' it out. Then 'e camped on an island in the middle of the lake. The last entry says 'Found gold today. Looking forward to tomorrow'."

"Whaaat? Saw someone out there? Sounds like 'e coulda been off 'is head when 'e wrote all that down. 'Eat stroke c'n do that to a man. The bugger coulda been pedallin' 'is bike without a chain fer days. We might be chasin' a four-legged emu 'ere!"

"Johnno found gold out there somewhere. We both saw it. All we need ta do is find 'is tracks ta lead us to it. If 'e travelled across a dry lake the tyre marks'll stay there fer a very long time. We'll be right. We'll find out where 'e went."

Later, as the two of them were packing things away ready for an early start, Reg quietly reprimanded his mate. "Just show a bit o' respect around the woman, will ya. Don't forget it's 'er dead brother we're talkin' about."

"Eh? Mmmm... yeah, okay," was the offhand response.

While the two men had been puzzling over the map, Burra had been doing the same over Smiler's behaviour. The dog refused to leave the back of the ute, where he had remained all afternoon. Burra placed a bowl of dog biscuits before him, looked in his eyes and gave him a quick pat on the head.

Smiler's tail wagged limply and he sighed at the sight of the food, before beginning to slowly chomp through it, his appetite gradually fading with the thought of what lay ahead.

With a planned start before daybreak everyone retired to bed soon after the map-reading session. But about an hour later, when she thought that the others were asleep, Cassie crawled out of her small tent and walked a short way from the camp. She was carrying a jar in her hand, and when she stopped she emptied her brother's ashes onto the red dust of the country that he professed to love so much.

"See ya, Kev," she said quietly, before making her way back to her tent.

Smiler had been watching Cassie and his curiosity made him briefly leave the back of the ute and go to where she had been standing. He sniffed the ground and a sad, dark memory followed him as he quickly made his way back to his corner in the ute, where he curled up in a ball again and closed his eyes, his ears only slowly twitching their way down to the sleeping position.

The warm, still night closed around the five as they slept, the silence punctuated only by Charlie's snoring until, at about eleven o'clock, the land began to breathe.

Smiler's ears pricked up when he heard the voice whispering through the camp, and Cassie was awakened too, pulled out of sleep by the pain of another severe headache. Reg and Burra meanwhile drifted deeper into their dreaming, where they both would feel the soft touch of a hand and hear a woman's voice calling out two names.

Far off to the south, Alan Prescott was sitting alone by the fire, staring vacantly into its flames, when the wind began to blow. It didn't come to him as it usually did on a hot summer night, gently removing the warmth of the day; instead it brought an instant chill to his back and he had to wrap a tarpaulin around him for protection; but it didn't keep out the cold, or what was driving him deeper into a darkening state of mind. He was thinking again of his wife and the threats she had made about making him pay for her lost years, remembering all the luxury he had bestowed on the spoilt, ungrateful bitch. He grew increasingly angrier as he swigged from a near empty bottle of whisky. Then he suddenly stood up and let out an enraged roar, sinking a heavy boot into the tangle of half-burnt timber and coals, sending embers flying everywhere.

Heckle and Jeckle slept obliviously on, but Terry Walters awoke with a start and stared worriedly at the hulking figure now growling over what remained of the fire. The man didn't look like Prescott at all, and he dared not complain about the shower of sparks he had just taken.

Prescott growled again, gulped down the remainder of the whisky then turned and violently hurled the empty bottle as if aiming it at the wind. He crawled into his sleeping bag and pulled the hood over his head, the dulling effect of alcohol eventually silencing the voice he could hear.

Nineteen

Charlie, of the untroubled sleep, was the first to rise next morning, clattering about in his eagerness to get going. Every sound he made was like a sledgehammer blow to Cassie's head, and Reg winced too at the unsubtle attempt to wake everyone. But the noise couldn't wipe away the strong imagery of the dream he'd had, of hearing that word again, and of seeing the Aboriginal woman walk through the camp, kneel beside him for a moment and draw something in the sand. It had seemed so real that he leaned up on an elbow and peered through the half-light of dawn to see if the drawing was actually there, and was startled to see a finger moving through the red dirt, outlining the two handprints, one much smaller than the other. He stared fixedly at them for a few seconds then looked across to where the artist lay in his bedroll a few feet away. For a moment Burra stared back intensely, until he gently erased the drawing.

Reg's party moved off just before sun-up. They were about five hours ahead of their pursuers, but two staked tyres on the ute would eventually cost them half of their lead. Their progress was slowed further when they hit the dune country, where the ute had to be towed through the worst of the low, scrub-covered hills. They also had a casualty to contend with.

Cassie's night of suffering only increased with the break of day. The painkillers she chewed on overnight had given her something that only slightly resembled sleep, and when the blowtorch of a sun topped the horizon and blazed straight through the windscreen of the Land Rover, the nausea rushed in again.

"Feelin' a bit crook, are ya?" Reg enquired. He had noticed Cassie's pale colour when they had started off, but now she looked almost like a corpse.

"It's nuthin'... just a bit of a headache," came the brave lie. She wasn't going to let anything get in the way of what she hoped lay before them, even a headache that had begun to take on all the qualities of a brain haemorrhage.

"Mmmmm... well keep gettin' water inta ya. Out 'ere you'll de'ydrate before ya know it. An' it's pretty 'ard catchin' up after that."

Cassie knew he was right and picked up her water bottle to drink lightly from it, but after a few sips nearly brought it all up again. Then, half an hour later, on the pretext of needing a toilet break, she asked Reg to stop and, walking quickly behind a small rocky outcrop, proceeded to throw her heart up as quietly as possible.

Charlie sat sourly waiting and when he saw Reg glance back at him in the rear vision mirror he mouthed the words, 'Bloody women!'

Cassie wiped her mouth and took a couple more of the painkillers she had in the top pocket of her shirt, chewing them quickly as she half-stumbled her way back to the car, having to take a proper drink now to get rid of the bitter taste of the bile and the medicine.

About a hundred kilometres behind, there were others who were not feeling very well either, their self-induced illness not a whole lot less miserable than the predicament Cassie was in.

"Jesus, mate... I think we might've overdone it a bit last night," Jeckle moaned, as he leaned back in the passenger seat. He took another few gulps from his water bottle then raised his head indicating at the vehicle in front of them. "And I reckon by the look on 'is face this mornin', we might've upset our revered leader too. D'ya see 'im? Wanted ta tear me 'ead off when I asked 'im which way we were goin'. Just shut yer bloody mouth and follow me! What sort of teamwork is that, I ask?"

"Yeah... 'e's turned into a real prick this time out," Heckle replied. "I dunno what's up with 'im. I just hope he knows where we're goin', because I'm stuffed if I do. All I know is we're out in the bloody desert somewhere! Give us a drink, will ya?" he asked, and then shook his head at the offer of the water bottle. "Naaah... hair o' the dog, mate. That other bloody stuff'll kill ya." He wrestled with the steering wheel, struggling to keep up with the Landcruiser and trailer bouncing across the rocky terrain about a hundred metres ahead of them.

Terry Walters rocked around inside the leading vehicle, grimly hanging on to the rough-ride handle, feeling greatly worried now about his decision to come along. He had tried to summon up the courage again this morning to tell Prescott he wanted to head back, but the foulness of the man's mood made him think better of it. He glanced at the driver, whose eyes stared fixedly on some invisible point ahead, as though a beacon were guiding him through the desert. When they had stopped last night Prescott had appeared a little uncertain about which direction to take, and had spent quite a bit of time scanning his maps. But today, apart from bellowing an order to one of his underlings, he hadn't spoken any more, or referred to any map. He just remained bent over that steering wheel, hardly bothering to go through the gear changes when the terrain made it necessary, foot flat to the floor when he could see a clear run ahead. He wasn't drinking any water either. It was unnatural. It was stinking hot and he must be dehydrated from all the booze he consumed last night. And something else stank. There was a vile body odour about the man, as if he had been out in the bush for many weeks without a wash, instead of just one day. Terry leaned towards the opened window, breathing in the hot but fresh air and tightening his grip on the handle as he saw a large rock looming up ahead. He sensed a distinct presence of evil about this man and right now he wished he were back in the other vehicle with the lesser kind.

After a slow and arduous morning's travel, during which time they had stopped for another flat tyre and two more of Cassie's toilet breaks, the party of five pulled up at the edge of a dry lake. It wasn't the one they were looking for. It was smaller and, according to their directions, about ten kilometres before the larger one that was supposed to have an island in the middle of it. But it was midday now and

Reg decided to call a halt for lunch. There was a small marble gum nearby and he set up a chair for Cassie beneath it. Then he gave her a saucepan half-full of water to cool herself with. It was an extravagant use of their lifeblood, but he knew she needed some relief.

Cassie stumbled over and slumped down on the chair. She trickled the water slowly over her head and sighed with the soothing luxury as it ran through her hair.

Charlie wasn't happy with them stopping so close to their goal, and he looked on with total disgust at the waste of precious water, immediately commenting on it when Reg came back to the Land Rover to get something to eat.

"I 'ope that's *your* water yer givin' 'er," he snarled.

"The woman's sufferin'" Reg stated, without looking at Charlie.

"Yeah… an' we'll all be sufferin' from 'er if ya keep 'andin' it out like that. Next thing you'll be settin' up 'er shower. Maybe even expectin' ta join 'er."

"Another crack like that an' you'll 'afta take *your* next drink o' water through yer ear'ole," came the quiet reply.

Charlie knew enough not to continue and ambled off sullenly, resentful of the woman and the delays she had brought with her, her presence lifting the level of the deeper resentment that had been simmering away ever since Burra had turned up. He felt like he had become an outsider, pushed down the order after a lifetime's friendship, and his partner's pampering of the woman served only to remind him of it. So too had the distant mood Reg had displayed since they had woken that morning. There was hardly anything said at breakfast or after; he and the boy were even quieter than usual, seeming to communicate with each other without talking as they packed the gear. It was disconcerting and just added to the feeling growing in him, that all he expected or wanted out of their relationship now was gold.

The two men sat apart as they ate their lunch, Reg pointedly joining Cassie. Burra wandered off around the lake's edge with Smiler at heel: the dog had finally decided to stretch his legs but with his antennae on full alert, and when he saw the sign he barked out loudly in recognition.

Everyone looked up as the sharp sound shattered the silence of the bush. Then Burra called out.

"There's some tyre tracks 'ere, Grandad!"

Reg got up and ambled across, while Charlie almost ran the fifty metres to the spot where a vehicle had marked the dry bed of the lake.

"These 'afta be Johnno's!" Charlie called out.

Reg caught up with his excited mate and stared at the wheel ruts for a moment before his gaze lifted to the horizon. He was right about the tracks showing up on the dry lake surface, but he didn't need them any more to find his destination and, as Charlie moved quickly back to the ute, he briefly stood gazing wistfully towards where it lay. Then the sound of a motor revving up broke through his contemplation.

Soon both vehicles were driving out onto the lake bed, following the tyre tracks across it until they reached the other side about a kilometre further on. Half an hour later, after picking their way through more dune country, they came to a halt on a rise overlooking the pink surface of another dry lake. There, the evidence of Johnno's coming and going could be clearly seen, pointing like an arrow towards a dark rocky outcrop in the middle.

"This is it, mate!" Charlie yelled from the window of the ute, as he pulled up alongside the Land Rover.

Cassie peered towards the centre of the pink and shimmering landscape and the memory of a dream suddenly rushed in with the hot breath that blew into her face, snaking its way under the surface of her mind until her aching head began to erase all thoughts again.

Smiler stood up on the back of the ute and sniffed the same air, the scent of menace drifting to his nose once more. He barked out a warning that no one heard.

Reg and Burra were now both out of their vehicles and standing silently together, neither intimidated or excited about what they could see ahead, just calmly aware of something else that was being carried to them on the wind, its voice soothing and welcoming.

"C'mon! Let's get goin'!" Charlie cried impatiently, as he revved the ute and drove out onto the smooth, sandy surface, not waiting for Burra to hop on.

Reg and Burra got into the Land Rover and followed.

Like Johnno, Charlie quickly gave in to the urge to put the foot down after the hours of laboriously slow driving, determined to be first across and madly closing on the place where Johnno had been bogged, a very worried passenger curled up even more tightly in the back. The bull was charging at the gate and, even though he could clearly see the disturbed area of ground up ahead, Charlie figured speed would get him through. But the ute gave in at the first sign of softness and soon slowed to a halt.

About a minute later, Reg pulled the Land Rover up some twenty metres behind, got out, took a pick from the back and walked up to a shamefaced Charlie.

"We'll get the Rover to the island and set up camp, then come back fer this when it's cooler."

Reg's calm words unsettled Charlie. He had been expecting a colourful resume of what he had just done, but he didn't even get the stare.

Burra grabbed his spear and began testing the ground on one side of the bogged vehicle while Reg checked the other. As they both probed, Charlie started transferring some camping gear into the back of the Land Rover and, after a brief, fearful glance at the island, Smiler jumped in too, quickly claiming a new hiding-place.

While the others went about their tasks, Cassie slipped briefly into a state of drug-induced dozing, but a few minutes later the sound of Burra's voice pulled her out of it.

"This looks okay."

Reg walked over and began to double-check the ground where Burra had indicated and the thumping of the pick sounded out like an echo of the pounding inside Cassie's head. But it was another sound that made her slowly open her eyes and peer through the white-hot glare. It was a faint drumming sound, drifting to her ears from the south end of the lake. As she squinted towards the liquid horizon, four images came into view, like riders mounted upon on waves of heat. But as quickly as they appeared they melted away and Cassie closed her aching eyes in dismissal of what she figured was just another mirage. She quietly sighed. Right now the front bar of the Royal Hotel didn't seem such a bad place to be.

The Rover made it through easily, but silence reigned inside the vehicle as they followed the tracks around to the point where Johnno had driven up onto the dark island. Then they came across the shaded place where the ash of his campfire blackened the ground and his dust-covered bedroll and battered metal detector lay.

Charlie quickly got out and picked up the wrecked machine, studying it with puzzlement, before handing it to Reg.

"It looks like 'e ran over 'is bloody detector!" came the astonished observation, his renewed excitement shattering the silence, his thoughts stampeding again. If Johnno was in such a panic to get back and peg the claim that he would leave behind his swag and an expensive detector, then the find had to be huge. He became frantic with anticipation now, not noticing or caring that Reg had put the detector down without a word or even a glance. Nor was he bothered with the setting up of camp; his prospecting instincts were sweeping him away as he hurriedly traced the quartz wash towards the ridge.

Smiler stayed where he was, curled up and head down again amidst the jumble of gear in the back of the vehicle, not even looking up when he felt a bedroll taken from under him.

Cassie weakly laid the bedroll out on the ground of the shaded grove, collapsed onto the soft bedding and slowly drifted into a miserable kind of sleep.

Reg and Burra moved off in the same direction as the man who had now disappeared over the ridge, but moving over the ground in a slower, fluid way, not a word passing between them as they went. In his hand, Burra carried the ever-present spear, but now he also had the thrower with him. Reaching the top of the ridge they stopped briefly and looked down towards the bottom of the slope, their eyes immediately drawn to the place of the dancing.

Charlie saw the two standing on the ridge. "There's water 'ere!" he shouted excitedly, his words echoing around the island as he splashed the cooling liquid all over his body.

For a moment Reg and Burra remained where they were, eyes fixed on where the ash of the old fires lay. Then Charlie's voice intruded once more.

"Are you two bloody deaf, or what? Whaddya *doin'* standin' there? C'mon! There's a quartz blow up 'ere... I'm gunna check it out," he yelled, as he made his way up the slope.

Reg and Burra turned to watch the man clambering up towards the cave, and then they headed towards it, reaching the foot of the slope just as Charlie spotted the entrance.

"There's a bloody cave 'ere!" Charlie called out, before quickly disappearing inside. A great echoing yell immediately followed and he came racing out just a few seconds later.

"Jeeesuuuus bloody Christ! Ya won't believe what's in there, mate! There's a bloody great seam o' gold runnin' through the ceilin', and bits of specimen layin' all over the ground!" He held up a piece of the stone. "We've cracked it, mate!" he screamed, and then ran back in.

Reg and Burra approached the entrance then stopped. A sound began to drift to their ears and Burra placed the spear and thrower, gently, almost ceremoniously, on the ground outside the cave.

The sound grew louder, the clinking of clapsticks followed by the plaintive cry of a woman slowly building in volume. Down in the circle of fires, a thin spiral of dust lifted from the centre, spun and eddied, before being carried away on the soft breeze now whispering across the island.

The desert's voice spoke to Cassie as it went, causing her to shift in her sleep, before it drifted on towards the cave, breathing up the slope and swirling around the two standing at the entrance. Then it alerted those who rested inside, telling them that others were approaching.

Charlie looked up when he heard the Aboriginal words and stared at Reg for a couple of seconds, before snorting with amusement.

"Yeah... good one, mate." he said, and then went on with his frantic ore collecting.

The sound of the clapsticks grew even louder and the man and the boy entered the cave, oblivious to the other presence scrabbling around on its floor as they walked towards a back corner. They stared at the two skeletons for a moment and then turned to the handprints sprayed upon the wall. Reaching out together they laid their hands against them. A warm sensation flowed into their palms and soon the darkness fell away. Now they were outside the cave, where a woman waited, a boy child upon her hip and a small girl clinging to her leg. The rhythmic clinking of the clapsticks abruptly halted and another sound came rumbling to the man's ears. He leant down and picked up the spear and thrower that lay at the woman's feet, turned and fitted the weapon to the thrower then balanced himself ready to let it fly.

The sound had come like the far off rumbling of thunder before it began to break up, its separate parts condensing, its tone sharpening and forming into words, and when the voice finally broke through, Reg and Burra's hands dropped from the wall.

"C'mon you two. What's the matter with ya? Forget about the bloody rock art. Get stuck in! We've got a bank account ta open!" Charlie shouted, as he filled his pockets with his booty and then began to gather another armful.

Reg looked at Charlie with puzzlement. "Whaddya doin'?" he asked, as he stepped towards him.

Charlie continued with his frantic collecting, discarding some of the rocks he had picked up for others that looked richer. "Whaddya mean, what am I doin'? What's it bloody look like? I'm collectin' our future, that's what." He stood up and pointed to the serpent painting on the roof. "Look at this jewel shop, mate!" he said, as he reached up to touch it. "This is where Johnno took that chunk out. I reckon I could put a charge in 'ere and open the whole thing up without bringin' the roof down."

A voice yelled at him.

Charlie's hand came away instantly. He looked at Reg, once again unable to understand a word of the language cast at him, but not laughing this time, fear now rushing in at the sound of the threatening tone.

"I think ya could do with a cuppa, a Bex an' a good lie down, mate. I reckon the 'eat's got ta ya," Charlie said, as he backed nervously away.

Then Burra began to yell too in the language of the Nangatadjara as he stepped forward menacingly.

Charlie's fear now suddenly turned to anger.

"Right, ya fuckin' young bastard! Let's have ya!" He rushed at Burra, but just as he was about to lay into the boy, Reg stepped in and stopped him with a savage right cross to the side of the head.

Charlie hit the dirt then sat up and shook his head. "Ya king 'it me, ya prick! 'Ow low c'n a man get?" He scrambled to his feet, let out a roar and ran at Reg.

Reg flattened him again.

"Carn't you see what yer doin'? Carn't ya see where ya are?" he asked, totally confused now by his partner's behaviour.

But Charlie believed he could see everything. That's what all the silence and the strange moods were about. They were planning to keep it all for themselves, and from that thought came the words he could no longer hold back, lancing a sore that had been festering for a lifetime.

"Fuckin' typical! Ya all stick together in the end, don't ya... no matter 'ow much white ya've got in ya! The moment the kid turned up, it's been nuthin' but you an' 'im! So much fer sixty fuckin' years, *mate!*" he yelled, tears forming in his eyes as he delivered the shattering words, hating himself for saying them, but unable to stop the tide of poison rushing out. Then his voice began to rise, sounding female in pitch as he finally screamed out, *"Yer all thievin' bloody niggers! Yer all fuckin' savages!"*

As Charlie yelled out those last words, back down the hill, Cassie silently mouthed them from her miserable dreaming sleep.

"Ya've gone mad, ya bastard! Just get outta here!" Reg yelled.

"I'm not leavin' the gold! It's mine as much as yours!" Charlie shrieked back, his voice bouncing off the walls, until a rumbling tone suddenly sounded out from the entrance.

"Nay laddie... it be ours."

The riders had arrived, the approaching noise of their trail bikes unheard because of the loud argument going on within the cave, and the leader stood there now with a rifle fixed on the three inside.

Heckle and Jeckle stood smiling either side of Prescott, but Terry was lagging behind him, aghast at his threatening manner.

"C'mon, leave 'em alone. They got here first. Let's just get out of it!"

Prescott turned and without warning rammed the butt of his weapon savagely into Terry's face, smashing his nose and teeth and sending him crashing to the ground.

"That'll shut thy mouth! Ye've been lookin' fer that ever since we rode out!" he growled, before quickly turning his attention back to the three before him.

Terry slowly pulled himself up onto all fours. For a moment his face felt absent and he watched almost in a detached way as blood and saliva mixed with chips of teeth dripped to the ground. Then the pain set in and he began to groan, his fears that morning of the bad day ahead now terribly vindicated.

*

Prescott and company had reached the lake almost at the same time that Charlie had bogged his ute a couple of kilometres to the north, and it was there that the leader had spoken for the first time since they had broken camp.

"We'll take mounts from 'ere. An' bring yon pegs!" he barked.

Terry Walters was totally confused now, his earlier trepidation ballooning as he helped unload the bikes and then strapped a bundle of surveyors' pegs across the handlebars of his machine. Mounts? What the *fuck* was he talking about? But soon his confusion would turn into dismay when Prescott placed a high-powered hunting rifle across his lap just before they raced onto the natural speedway. The man seemed to have sunk deeper into a hypnotic state, his dark mood reflected in a twisted and sour countenance, and there was that strange pommy accent. His offsiders appeared to be under some sort of influence too, obeying orders without a hint of their usual smart-arsed responses, and Terry knew that somehow he had to try and get away from them. He didn't care any more about the gold or the equipment he would be leaving behind, he had spare keys to his vehicle and he figured if he could get a big enough break he could beat them back and drive off.

As they rode into the waves of heat rising above the lake, Terry hung back waiting to take his chance, finally making his move halfway across, but Prescott seemed to have prior knowledge of the plan and turned in unison with him. The other two immediately joined in, and although Terry was able to lead the three of them on a wild chase for a couple of minutes, Prescott eventually drew up next to him with the rifle pointing across a forearm.

"Thou wanted to come, and thou'll play thy part!" Prescott roared above the din of the idling trail bikes. Then he rammed the rifle barrel hard into Terry's side. "Now move off beside me where I can watch thee!"

Terry winced with pain and then obeyed, a reluctant hand upon the throttle now as they started to move once more across the lake, Prescott riding close to him, waving the rifle at him whenever he slowed.

The riders eventually climbed up onto the island from the other side, halting on the rocky edge of the basin, before clambering down and then up to the cave, drawn there by the loud argument going on within.

*

"Well, if it isn't the spear-chuckers from the pub! Why don't ya 'avago at me now, *boong*!" Heckle snarled at Burra.

"Better watch out, mate! 'E might point the bone at ya," Jeckle chipped in. Then both of them broke into loud laughter.

"Shut up you two! We've got work te do. I'll deal with yon friends 'ere. Go and get pegs and start bangin' 'em in. I want 'ole island covered. By look of what be 'ere, this be the big one."

Heckle and Jeckle obeyed and quickly moved off down the hill and back to the trail bikes, while Prescott kept the gun steadily trained on the three before him, his eyes swiftly glancing back and forth to the ceiling as he edged slowly closer to inspect the glint he had seen coming from it. Halfway there, his foot caught on a pile of bones, causing him to briefly look down before bad-temperedly kicking them away.

Reg saw his chance and lunged, but Prescott was quicker, pulling the trigger and sending a high calibre slug tearing through the upper part of Reg's body. He fell heavily to the ground and Prescott quickly ejected the spent cartridge and slammed another live one into the firing chamber. His eyes glazed over as he placed the barrel against Reg's forehead. *"Damn thee t' hell, thou heathen nigger!"* he yelled. His finger began to pull on the trigger, but suddenly, as if something had slammed into him, he staggered to the side, almost falling over. The gun discharged past Reg's head and clattered to the ground. Prescott grabbed at his throat and stumbled out of the cave and down the slope, wheezing and groaning as he clawed desperately at his neck, his eyes staring with a look of terror, his legs slowly sagging under him as he went. Then he tripped over a rock and toppled face first into a boulder, the sound of his snapping neck reverberating loudly through the amphitheatre.

The report of the gunshots had boomed out of the cave's entrance like cannon fire, causing Smiler to sit up and bark loudly, both noises rapidly pulling Cassie out of a familiar bad dream before the loud cracking sound of a spine ended it. But, just before she emerged, the woman's voice came to her once more, this time the broken sentence concise and complete, *"It's time ta rest now, Rosie,"* it whispered.

Cassie sat up, clear headed now, no headache or nausea and no memory of the dream. She climbed to her feet and looked around. Seeing no one about, she walked quickly over the ridge, with a cautious dog following her. The loud wailing of a voice led her to the cave and as she neared it she was shocked to see Prescott's face staring grotesquely from behind a boulder, and a stranger on his knees with his hands held against a bloodied face. She stepped inside and saw Charlie sitting on the ground cradling Reg's head and sobbing loudly.

"Don't ya die on me, ya black bastard! Don't ya dare die on me!" he cried out, feeling utterly helpless to do anything about what appeared to be a fatal wound in his mate's chest. Then he saw one of Reg's hands move and heard his voice utter some faint words.

"Stop yer blubberin' ya ol' bastard. I'm not dead yet. But I think I might be needin' that Bex."

Reg had banged his head on a rock when he fell, knocking him unconscious, and the effect of that injury was now pounding away along with the pain of his bullet wound.

"Ya mongrel! Ya bloody prick!" Charlie cried out in jubilation.

Cassie now moved quickly: she pushed Charlie firmly to one side then tore Reg's shirt open to examine the wound. It was serious enough, but his ribs had deflected the slug up and away from the lungs to exit out the top of his shoulder. As long as the flow was stemmed and they got to a doctor quickly enough, it wasn't going to kill him.

"Give me your shirt, Charlie. Go and get the first-aid box, Burra!"

At first Burra didn't move. He was still grappling with what he had seen. There was a gap in his memory, too. He couldn't remember entering the cave. The last thing he could recall before seeing Charlie flattened was approaching the entrance with his grandfather. His memory of the whole morning, in fact, was blurred, veiled, almost as if he had been tripping out.

"Burra! Get the bloody first-aid kit!"

The sharper command finally shook Burra into action and he raced out of the cave and down the slope just as Heckle and Jeckle were coming up it.

The gun reports and the cracking sound that quickly followed had instantly snapped the two out of their drink-induced stupor. Now they were simply confused, scrambling hurriedly out of the way of the fierce-looking youth who sprinted towards them, his fists raised and ready for resistance. After he passed they moved tentatively on, soon coming across their employer's body, They stared dumbfounded at him for a moment, then a voice hissed at them from near the entrance.

Although Terry was as mystified as anyone about what had happened, the pain of his damaged mouth overruled all. Right now he didn't want to know anything. He just wanted out. His words came slurred by blood and saliva, but the emphasis was clear.

"You two... get on those fuckin' bikes! Get over to the vehicles and bring 'em across *now*!"

The puzzled pair meekly complied. They quickly headed back to the trail bikes, kicked them into life and rode off.

Burra soon returned with the first-aid box and Cassie bandaged Reg well enough to put a stop to the heavy bleeding, then cleaned up the cuts on Terry's mouth and nose and bandaged his face against the assault of flies. There was not much else that she could do for the two men, but she still had half a packet of her strong painkillers left, which would provide some relief for them on the journey back.

Charlie got up from where he had been supporting Reg, and took the sharp, uncomfortable objects out of his pockets. He stared briefly at them, shook his head in disbelief and threw the worthless pieces of granite back onto the floor of the cave. Then he took a last glance at the ceiling, where he saw nothing but the faded yellow ochre of a serpent painting, with no sign that anyone had ever chopped into it; maybe the heat had gotten to him, too. As for the dead person, he didn't have a clue, and more to the point, didn't really care. It looked as though the man had had a heart attack, or a stroke, and it couldn't have happened at a better time or to a nicer bloke. He took his mate's good side and lifted him up, the practical tasks ahead quickly dismissing all of his unanswerable questions.

The humans left the cave, but there was a certain canine member of the expedition who was still seeking an answer to one of his questions, remaining behind to briefly sniff around and confirm that all the menace had disappeared from his radar. Finally satisfied with the reading, Smiler then turned to follow the others, but just as he reached the entrance something made him stop. Ears at attention, he turned around to peer into the shadows at the rear of the cave. Where the water flowed from a hole in the wall, two blazing red orbs glowed in the darkness.

"That'd be bloody right! Get outta me way... I'm comin' through!"

"Crazy bloody mutt," Charlie complained, as the yelping form flew past, spraying dirt and pebbles on the people slowly making their way down the slope.

The ambulance party got their patient to the Rover just as the two Landcruisers rumbled up onto the island. Cassie then quickly turned the rear of one of them into a hospital bed, while Charlie and Prescott's two now very subdued assistants went to retrieve his body, using his swag to carry it back. Then Charlie quickly tied it down on one of the trailers as Heckle and Jeckle went to get the remaining trail bikes.

While he was waiting for them to return, Burra poked his head in the back door of the Landcruiser to check out how his grandfather was. The old man appeared to be asleep and Burra stared at him for a while, the vision of what he had seen in the cave quickly returning. The whole incident couldn't have lasted for more than a few seconds, but it remained vividly fixed in his mind. He was staring in shock at his grandfather lying on the ground with a rifle barrel pushed against his head when, just as Prescott screamed out those words, something came whipping and whistling through the entrance of the cave. The spear's impact nearly knocked Prescott off his feet as it penetrated his neck, a third of it protruding out the other side, blood spurting from the wound. For a moment Burra stared incredulous at the grisly sight and at the wounded form lying on the cave floor, then his gaze shot to the entrance. There, he saw his grandfather frozen in the stance of a hunter who had just let a spear fly, and then the image disappeared. He turned back to see Prescott stumbling towards the entrance, clawing at his neck, the spear no longer sticking through it and no sign of blood, the image of the naked Aboriginal man lying on the cave floor replaced by his grandfather's form.

At first, Burra could only surmise that the heat had got to him, but there was something that hallucinations couldn't account for. He remembered having the spear and thrower with him as they walked up to the cave, but his quick search around before helping his grandfather down the slope turned up nothing. There was no answer for it, and now he no longer wanted one. Instead, he placed the incident with all the other inexplicable happenings of the last couple of weeks, feeling a strange sense of being privileged at having experienced them.

A smile began to slowly form on Burra's face in recollection of his grandfather's first clumsy attempts at throwing the spear. It wasn't a bad throw fer an' ol' bugger, he thought. Starting to close the door of the Landcruiser he glanced again at his grandfather. The old man's eyes were open now and staring at him, a secret smile upon his face, then his eyelids dropped and the smile faded.

Burra closed the door and walked towards the Rover, but before getting in he stood gazing out onto the lake bed and the desert beyond. There was a calm look in his eyes and after a few moments he turned his gaze to the red soil at his feet. He held one hand out, palm facing the ground, his fingers stretched wide and straight over his country. Then he curled them up in a triumphant grasping motion.

The gold hunters left the island a few minutes later, stopping only briefly to pull the bogged ute out, where Burra took over the wheel and his furry partner became a navigator once more. Then the convoy moved off across the lake bed, soon reaching its edge and entering the rugged expanse beyond, following the sun and the wheel ruts back towards the west.

The desert watched them go, silent and still in the afternoon, then its voice began to whisper again in the night, drifting out of the east like a song, gathering the footprints and carrying them away, into the future, into the past...

Author's Note

The incident involving the raiding of the prospectors' camp by Aborigines and the subsequent murder of the Aboriginal family group has been constructed from two sources; the chapter 'The Golden Mountain' from the book *Battling for Gold* – by John Marshall, and parts of *A Gold Seeker's Odyssey* – by L.R. Menzies.

Apart from historical figures, all characters within this book are fictional and the town of Jimblebar does not exist.

ISBN 141209284-1